THE
KING-
MAKERS
OF
PROVIDENCE

THE KING-MAKERS OF PROVIDENCE

JOHN HOULE

BookPress®
publishing

Published in Des Moines, Iowa, by:

Bookpress Publishing
P.O. Box 71532
Des Moines, IA 50325
www.BookpressPublishing.com

Publisher's Cataloging-in-Publication Data

Names: Houle, John C., author.
Title: The King-Makers of Providence / John Houle.
Description: Des Moines, IA: Bookpress Publishing, 2023.
Identifiers: LCCN: 2021921229 | ISBN: 9781947305373 Hardback | 9781947305830 Paperback
Subjects: LCSH Providence (R.I.)--Fiction. | Politics--Fiction. | Politicians--Fiction. | Political campaigns--Fiction. | Thriller fiction. | BISAC FICTION / Thrillers / Political
Classification: LCC PS3608.O85543 K56 2022 | DDC 813.6--dc23

First Edition
Printed in the United States of America
10 9 8 7 6 5 4 3 2 1

To my father, Carl A. Houle,
for teaching me how to persevere.

1

Four Years Ago

"I'm not burdened by personal conviction," Henry Mercucio admitted. With the top down and AC/DC blaring from the stereo, cell phone pressed against his ear, he slid his black convertible up to the curb in front of a crowd of gawkers in their Sunday best. "If you're telling me we gain five points, then Congressman McNally supports a $1,000 tax credit for working families." On the other end of the line was a pollster tracking the gubernatorial race. The sight of a political operative in a heated conversation was not unusual in the middle of an election season, but the mourners' glares told Henry he might be overdoing it. He pressed the button to redeploy the drop top and attempted to speak in lower tones. "I know, I know. He voted against it last session, but if it comes up now, we'll just say we're for it. Do you really think people remember what he voted for last year, and do you think they care? That would mean they're actually paying attention to what's going on, and you and I both know the truth."

As he stepped out of the car, he returned his phone to his suit jacket pocket. This was the last place he wanted to be two weeks before the election—a funeral in an Italian enclave of Providence, Rhode Island, a place where Machiavelli would have been at home, not only for the cuisine, but also for the city's approach to politics. In New England's second-most-important city, politics was a blood sport. It was not uncommon for nomination papers to mysteriously disappear from the Board of Elections or for political yard signs to be defaced with profanities. The destruction of political enemies by any means necessary was as alive in twenty-first-century Providence as it had been in fourteenth-century Florence.

But this was a somber time. One of the city's beloved political bosses had succumbed to a life of hard living. Antonio Campagna had been a heavyset man with a calm temperament and vivacious personality, whose years of service to the people of his district had drawn more than 2,000 people to pay their respects. Senators, congressmen, councilmen, business leaders, carpenters, teachers, and firefighters all filed through the receiving line. Campagna had worked thirty years in the Providence Public Works Department as a laborer, a foreman, and eventually as its director, earning the admiration and respect of his community. But his evenings had been spent on the front lines of the local Democratic Party as a ward committee member and ultimately the influential ward committee chairman. There was no election for a political boss; it was something earned through respect, loyalty, and influence. He never had a problem delivering bodies for political events since putting labels on mailers or making get-out-the-vote phone calls earned volunteers Maria Campagna's lasagna and stuffed shells. It was old-time politics, where loyalty was purchased through favors, but a man's word was ironclad.

With the highest voter turnout of any area in the state, the district had always been a key opportunity for Democratic politicians to pay homage to the man who could guarantee a bloc of 15,000 votes, and those who challenged the natural order sealed their political fates. When an ambitious political upstart refused to wait his turn and instead challenged a candidate in a primary supported by the Campagnas, the young man not only lost the election, but also his city job, the very same one that had been procured for him in the first place. It was unwise to challenge the political reality in this part of town. With Campagna's two sons serving as councilman and state representative, the family still retained its hold on the district even now, after the patriarch's death.

Congressman Ray McNally was from the old school, and he religiously made the election year pilgrimage to the Campagna district. This time, however, he was honoring an old friend. At the moment, McNally was in the political battle of his life. Reasoning that it was better to be one of fifty governors than a member of Congress from the minority party of a minor state, he gambled his future as a tenured-for-life congressman for a chance at becoming the state's chief executive. The lifelong Democrat, the son of a carpenter who had risen to political stardom with the backing of the state's powerful union machine, was facing a formidable challenge from the patrician Republican attorney general, whose family represented some of the state's oldest money. With the family name and an unlimited war chest, Jeremiah "Jay" Whitfield was on his way to purchasing the election and maintaining the Republicans' national majority of governors.

Leading Congressman McNally's campaign was Henry Mercucio, a thirty-year-old graduate of Boston College and Georgetown Law School who had traded a promising law career for his passionate first love—politics. He'd caught the political bug while in college, interning during a hotly contested senatorial campaign.

After taking a year off to work for the president's re-election, he'd met the congressman, then the president's regional campaign chairman. Throughout law school and during his first years as a young lawyer in Washington, D.C., Henry remained close to Congressman McNally as his political adviser. He had counseled him to wait for an open senate seat, but the governor's office was a post McNally had always coveted. Even though he disregarded Henry's advice, the congressman had ultimately tapped him to run the campaign.

Henry now found himself seven points down with two weeks to close the gap. That was the only thing on his mind as he walked through the brass doors of Saint Bartholomew's Church. He needed McNally to focus on the last televised debate, where he hoped to use debate footage in a series of television ads to contrast his candidate's knowledge and experience with his opponent's inexperience and ineptitude. Standing stoically in the church, he began calculating in his head the general voter turnout along with the union numbers and the political base needed to deliver victory. Like any true believer in politics, Henry held on to the hope that his candidate could still win even though the polls predicted defeat. He argued that the polling numbers were unreliable, since they did not factor in McNally's enthusiastic union support. If union members and their households came out in droves as promised, Henry rationalized that McNally could close the growing gap with his Republican opponent.

Amid the grievers, however, only Henry was preoccupied with the election. Congressman McNally, standing with one of the bereaved sons, motioned to him. Henry dreaded the congressman's introductions, which reminded him of his father's insistence that he kiss one of his old aunts.

"Henry, come over and say hello to Councilman John Campagna."

Henry said the things expected in such situations. "I'm very sorry for your loss. Your father was very well-respected."

"Thank you for coming, Mr. Mercucio."

Councilman Campagna appeared unimpressive—short and overweight with a receding hairline—but he carried himself with the grace of a man aware of his power. Unlike many other politicians who felt the need to remind their followers how important they were, Campagna did not need to project his power. Humility governed him, but when challenged, he emulated the tiger. Ask the fellow council-man who had broken ranks with leadership and had voted against the council's budget at the request of the mayor. In the next election, Campagna had recruited and financed the councilman's successor, defeating him by a wide margin. Campagna did not crave war, but when attacked, especially when it involved his selfless plans for his city, he showed little restraint in taking out his enemies.

After obliging the congressman, Henry approached him with a careful eye trained on the people he was greeting, ready to move him along to the next potential voter. He motioned the congressman toward the door, but the congressman brushed off the gesture. After a few more minutes of Henry's silent entreaties, McNally turned to him with an uncompromising look.

"You're supposed to be at the senior center in half an hour," Henry told him.

"Forget the seniors. I'm going to John Campagna's house," he said. "Call Kerry and tell her to reschedule the senior center."

"You can't," Henry whispered. "They're expecting you. We've got coffee and a vanload of ice cream. They're a vote we need."

McNally put his hand on Henry's shoulder. "Listen. I don't expect you to understand. I owe it to the Campagnas. It would be disrespectful if I didn't go to John's house."

As his boss turned to greet another supporter, Henry faded back into the crowd of mourners. Never before had he seen so many people in a church. In fact, St. Bartholomew's had to open its basement to accommodate the overwhelming turnout, who had to watch the funeral on close-captioned TVs provided by a local electronics store. No longer was it about honoring a life well-lived. Antonio Campagna's funeral had become a showcase for the who's-who of Providence's political and social elite. The funeral procession was so grand that four additional stretch limousines had been ordered to accompany the hearse and two family cars. The mayor and city council, along with the leadership of the state senate and state house of representatives, had each commandeered their own limousines. This had forced the governor to add his black Suburban to the caravan and the other general officers of the state to follow suit with their vehicles. The city and state police had no choice but to shut down city streets and five miles of highway along the interstate to accommodate the convoy.

They had all come to honor a man who had dedicated his life to public service, who had taken care of the people who needed a helping hand in life. There was plenty of proof of that in the crowd. Walking down the aisle was the widow who had recouped her husband's survivor benefits after Campagna had talked to the union bosses. At a pew near the casket was the young man whom he had helped find a city job. And there was the United States congressman who had never forgotten that the first endorsement he had won in his first race for state senate had been from Campagna's ward committee.

But there was also the city councilman hoping to win support for the council presidency. Hovering near the door was the attorney general, who did not want to concede Campagna's base to McNally. And of course, never to miss a political event, was Mayor Jack Donovan. Though he had battled Councilman Campagna over budgets and city contracts, he would not miss an opportunity to touch the flesh of nearly 700 potential voters. He made his grand entrance with little regard for protocol or ceremony, forcing the bishop to delay the mass so the mayor could meet and greet his flock.

The hypocrisy and self-serving behavior of the politicians faking their remorse betrayed the ideals of public service that Campagna had embodied. This cruel sense of irony struck Henry. He had graduated from college and law school with youthful idealism. But after this emotional roller coaster and the lessons it had imparted, he was uncertain he wanted to ride again. The tumultuous campaign had broken Henry's altruistic spirit. The unscrupulous tactics and arbitrary morality had forced him to question his role in a system that seemed to care more about maintaining power than representing the people's will. As a political consultant, Henry understood that campaigns were not unlike high school elections. The most popular kid always won, not the person who put forth the best ideas.

Henry was nostalgic for the politics of Antonio Campagna's time, a kinder era epitomized by what a politician could deliver to his community, not by what he could take for himself. He knew what had changed politics. It had been in his hands only two hours before the funeral—a $100,000 check to the television station for commercial time. The injection of money into the system had created a dependency; without cash from wealthy donors, corporations, and unions alike, campaign staffs could not be hired, professional ads could not be broadcast, and victory could not be attained. Today's politicians had traded walking door-to-door and hearing the problems and issues of their neighbors for neatly packaged sound bites and carefully crafted thirty-second clips. Gone were the days of neighborhood rallies and volunteer-packed halls, only to be replaced by high-end fundraisers and professional phone banks. It was the cold, unattached politics of the present Henry didn't like. Politics had become a business, one in which he no longer wanted to ply his trade.

A breed of disciples who aggressively pursued their own self-interest was the by-product of this form of public service, no longer regarded as Plato's highest calling, but instead Machiavelli's means to an end. Henry expected to have to duel with this new strain of young politicos from the opposition campaign, but he never expected that his greatest challenge would come from within his own campaign. Gordon Beako, Congressman McNally's district director, had been passed over as campaign manager in the gubernatorial bid and had used this self-perceived betrayal by McNally to punish the campaign. His principal target was Henry, and taking down McNally's golden boy had become his obsession.

The truth only suited Beako when it matched his objectives. Lies were spun, intended to undermine Henry's authority. Even though a ploy he'd devised had cost them the support of the Providence Teachers Union, Beako felt little remorse in sabotaging the campaign. He'd told the union president that McNally, under Henry's advice, planned to cross the picket line in front of a fundraiser in Providence for a prominent United States Senator, an early favorite to be president. The mayor, an independent who did not have a particular problem jibing his sails with the prevailing winds, planned to attend the Democratic fundraiser. The teachers' union, which was engaged in a prolonged contract battle with Mayor Donovan, sought to embarrass him in front of the state and national media by picketing the event and forcing politicians to perform their own version of a perp walk.

That was what bothered Henry the most. There was no honor in this game. People changed their positions, even their convictions and personalities, to suit whatever served them at the moment. The naive belief that he could effectuate change had attracted him to this business. The excitement of being part of something bigger than himself had enthralled him. He had spent his entire adult life in the political trenches.

In college, while other students were at frat parties, he had been working spaghetti dinners with the local city council. When his law school classmates were jockeying for internships and jobs, he was writing speeches and position papers for Congressman McNally. Now, instead of practicing law and earning more than six figures, he was running a political campaign for a man whose positions were determined by what bought the most votes. And although he had fallen in love with a woman he had searched for his whole life, he spent more of his time with politicians than with her. Henry desperately needed to get out of this game before he was entirely lost.

*If he is properly organized and lives as I have
said and does not lose control of himself, he will
always be able to withstand every attack.*

—Niccolò Machiavelli

Present Day

Frank Petrozella had surprised the US Attorney with his willingness to go undercover and wear a wire to provide aid to the ongoing investigation into Mayor Jack Donovan's administration. In doing so, he felt he was infusing honesty back into Providence, and he had little to lose. A month ago, the five-foot-four, balding building developer had approached his cousin, Gordie Beako, the senior vice-president and general manager of CampCo Development, for advice on leasing his commercial real estate on the waterfront. The old shipyard was slated for the new down-city project, heralded by the mayor as the next major commercial and retail development in the city, but one rejected bid after another had denied Petrozella his piece of the Providence Renaissance. He was outraged when lines were drawn around his property that excluded his warehouse from special tax incentives for redevelopment, losing out on the opportunity to unload his property for three times its value. Corrupt bureaucracy had gotten in the way.

Petrozella would make his stand at a meeting with Terry Silberman, who was notoriously linked to the Providence under-world. The FBI had offered Petrozella protection and relocation, but he refused to run. He would not let a bunch of corrupt politicians drive him out of his city. It was something a man had to do, for himself, for his family, for all decent folks who played by the rules. An honest man was the natural antidote to the public malaise.

FBI Special Agent Michael Carbonerri had been assigned to Petrozella. He walked him through each step of their plan. This was as much a coronation for Carbonerri as it was for Petrozella. A Providence native himself, Carbonerri had spent two years building a case against Donovan, only to come up short each time he thought he had a solid lead. No one wanted to talk when it came to the mayor or his chief of staff, and when the occasional city tax assessor caved under the intense pressure of the FBI, he would be swayed back into submission when a brother was fired from his city job or a son was picked up for a DWI. But the mayor could not get to Petrozella; in fact, he didn't even know who he was—a volunteer who'd walked right into the FBI's Providence office with an unwavering determi-nation to do his part to end corruption in his city.

Petrozella fought the urge to feel like a crusader as he walked up the stone steps of City Hall for his 9:30 a.m. appointment with Silberman. He opened the brass door to the mayor's office and stepped in. He waited, reviewed his calendar, drank a second and third cup of coffee, and waited longer. At least twice, Silberman poked his head out of his office and politely told Petrozella that it would just be a few more minutes. After forty-five minutes, he finally received his appointment. For a man who allegedly was the under-boss of the largest organized extortion and bribery ring in America, his office was rather unimpressive. It was a standard ten-by-ten space with the usual wall hangings depicting politicians and local celebrities. The furniture was a holdover from the previous adminis-tration, and that had been twenty years ago. What mattered about Silberman's office was its location right next to the mayor's, separated only by a private doorway.

"Sorry to keep you waiting," Silberman explained. "That was the mayor on the phone. He's in Ireland. Cultural exchange." The man was as unimposing as his office. He was average height, thirty to forty pounds overweight, and almost completely bald. He wore thick, black-rimmed glasses and looked more like an accountant than a major conspirator. He was sixty-two and had over twenty years of service to the city, or so it was called. In addition to his comfortable pension, he had socked away at least two million dollars in bank accounts in the Caymans and Switzerland, his take of the twenty-year side business he had run with the mayor.

"So you're Gordie's cousin. He's a good guy. Done a lot of business with him. We don't do business with everyone." He patted Petrozella on the back to subtly search for a wire. The FBI had warned him of this.

"I understand, Mr. Silberman," Petrozella replied, hoping his nerves wouldn't betray his mission.

"Tell me a little bit about yourself," Silberman said. "What do you do?"

"I own some property around the city. I pretty much manage it. It's commercial and residential, so between renting, selling, and doing improvements, it keeps me pretty busy."

"You've got some property over on the waterfront. The mayor's plan calls for marinas, hotels, and parks down there. It's too bad your property doesn't fall into the redevelopment zone," Silberman said as he opened his top-right drawer. That was Petrozella's cue to drop the $5,000 into Silberman's desk. "No, no. That's not necessary," he added, throwing a wink at Petrozella. While he didn't suspect Beako's cousin to be working for the FBI—otherwise, they wouldn't even be having this meeting—he was being careful not to directly implicate himself in a bribe in case someone was listening. He'd been satisfied with the absence of a wire, but there was no indication he had any idea about the video.

"I would be very grateful, Mr. Silberman, if the city could find a way to include my property in the redevelopment zone."

"Let me make a phone call for you," Silberman added, dialing a phone number he knew by heart. It rang only once before a voice answered. "Hey, Johnny, you know that old warehouse down on the waterfront, the one right outside the zone? Yeah, that one. I think you should re-work the drawings to include that property." Without another word exchanged, he hung up. The conversation lasted less than a minute. He turned back to Petrozella and boasted, "See? I don't even have to ask. I just suggested it. That's all I do."

"I see. I hope we can do a lot of business together, Mr. Silberman."

"That depends on you," Silberman said as he stood up from his desk. "That property just tripled in value." He put his arm around Petrozella and walked him out of the office. "The mayor will be back next week. He's having a little party at his house. Why don't you and some of your friends come by?"

"Thank you, Mr. Silberman. I appreciate that."

"And Frank, it's a five-hundred-dollar donation each to Friends of Mayor Donovan."

"Oh, sure."

"Ya know, Frankie, there's a lot we can do together."

"I think there is, Mr. Silberman," Petrozella said, as he headed for the door.

Petrozella walked out of Silberman's office and back down the steps, heading for the doorway. It was as if he was running a marathon and the end was in reach, the exit from City Hall his finish line. Even though he was participating in a setup, miring himself in the corruption made him feel dirty. If he had any doubt about what he was doing, it disappeared the moment he had dropped the FBI's money into Silberman's desk. He climbed into his Volvo and pulled away from City Hall, never looking back.

***

Petrozella met his FBI contact at a coffee shop a few blocks from City Hall. He almost barreled over a couple of college students on his way to Carbonerri's table.

"Sit down. Relax," Carbonerri said to him. "Before you hurt somebody."

"Easy for you to say. I thought I was gonna piss my pants in there," Petrozella admitted.

"Did you do it? Did you drop the money like we told you?" the agent asked.

"Yeah, he took it. Said 'no, no' just like I told you he would, but then looked the other way when I pulled out the cash. Then he had the balls to invite me to a fundraiser at the mayor's house."

"You did the right thing, Frankie. You should be proud of yourself. Why don't you give me the tie clip? I'll run it over to our tech guys, and if it's clear, you might not even have to testify. But in the meantime, I want you to get your wife and kids together. I'm going to send an agent, and we're going to move you to a safe house."

"You said I had nothing to worry about."

"We're just being cautious," Carbonerri assured him. What he wasn't telling him was that they wanted to ensure that Silberman and his cronies did not get to him.

"How long? I mean, my wife doesn't even know. And the kids—what about school?"

"We'll make it as easy as possible. You'd be surprised how good the kids adjust. How long?" He shrugged. "Maybe a couple of weeks. After we've got Silberman and Donovan in custody, we'll need to evaluate the threat against you. I wouldn't worry though. They're crooks, not killers."

"Oh, that makes me feel so much better," Petrozella replied.

On the north side of Cork, Ireland, in a seedy section of town known as Knocknaheeny, far removed from the plush hotel where the American delegation was staying, Mayor Jack Donovan was supposed to be staying close to the action of his hometown. Word was he was on a cultural exchange, but the only thing cultural on his mind was the pretty little bar maid with the strawberry blonde hair and crooked teeth. Donovan was a man who enjoyed his vices—booze, women, cocaine—and such a lifestyle of sin was costly, even with a six-figure salary, chauffeured town car, and million-dollar campaign account. The alcohol and cocaine weren't cheap—between the two, he spent at least a grand a week—but the women cost him the most. There was his twenty-eight-year-old secretary, Gini, who made dictation a particularly pleasurable experience. Although he would have loved to parade her around in public, he had enough political sense to be seen only with his thirty-eight-year-old real estate girlfriend, Kelly Anne Dimiani. And each month, he was reminded of his ex-wife, Kirsten Donovan, when he wrote that four-digit alimony check. Between his three women, his five nights a week in the finest restaurants, and his daily cocaine habit, he was out a quarter of a million a year. His mayor's salary barely covered half of his extravagant lifestyle. The money needed to come from somewhere; that's where graft and corruption came in.

It wasn't like he'd woken up one morning and decided to steal from the people he'd pledged to serve. It had been a slow, spiraling demise that had begun with campaign cash for political favors, had gradually led to payments for city contracts, and had ultimately mushroomed into a full-blown criminal enterprise. The problem was that Donovan and Silberman were so good at it, they no longer thought they were doing anything wrong. The old industrial city that a reporter had once referred to as "a pit stop on the way to Cape Cod" had transformed itself into one of the ten most desirable cities in America. Since corrupt politics were as authentic to the area as cannolis and cappuccino, people in Providence closed their eyes to their mayor's antics. But the people might not live in such willing blindness if they knew that the more the mayor snorted up his nose, the more his white albatross required him to extort building developers and property owners. After a record five terms as mayor, he had the city running on autopilot and had siphoned away millions in illegal kickbacks, extortion, and bribery.

He was more on edge while in Ireland, since he had been unable to score the kick he had needed to make it through the boring business meeting the Irish government had organized. He had not risked bringing cocaine in through customs and had gone without any powder for the past five days. It was the longest time in the past fifteen years he had gone without a hit, but he was not an addict. He could give it up at any time, he assured himself. The reason he couldn't sleep was jet lag, not withdrawal. The reason his hands shook was from the stress of being abroad. He was one of the most powerful mayors in the United States. He enjoyed celebrity status in his own state. A book was even being written about him. Addicts were strung-out junkies who wasted through life in search of their next fix. They were degenerates, not charismatic political leaders whose decisions affected thousands. Higher property taxes for the hard-working citizens of Providence no longer bothered Donovan. The pay hike the teachers were bargaining for did not even register on his mind. The unexpected increase in homicides downtown was a matter more for the police chief than for the mayor. The Irish government's consideration of opening a consulate in Providence gave him little interest. As he watched the bar maid jiggle as she shook a drink for a customer down the bar, the only thing on his mind was when he would score some blow.

He turned his trembling wrist to check his watch. He couldn't remember when he had last anticipated the arrival of anyone as much as his cousin, Billy Cavanaugh, who had assured him yesterday he could secure his relief. Cavanaugh, a third cousin on Donovan's mother's side, was a soldier in the Irish Republican Army. Ten years younger, he was equally confident and brash since his status had yet to be challenged. The IRA ran everything from guns to drugs on the island and had brought a shipment of Colombian cocaine up the Lee River for distribution in Ireland and the UK. As a lieutenant in the IRA, Cavanaugh had access to the new shipment, used primarily to fund arms shipments from Eastern Europe. Cavanaugh had told Donovan that Cork was the drug capital of Ireland and that he could procure anything his cousin wanted.

Cavanaugh finally entered through the pub's heavy wood-and-iron door and waded through the stares and cold reception of the patrons until he found his cousin seated at the bar. Donovan looked in poor shape, greasy and pale. Two days ago, Cavanaugh had claimed five kilos of the last shipment, enough for his network of peddlers throughout the island and his American cousin. Donovan might have reached the pinnacle of politics in America, but in Ireland, to Cavanaugh, he was no better than an average street thug.

"Well, how the hell are ya, Jackie Boy?" Cavanaugh chortled, slapping Donovan on the back as he came around and took the chair beside him. "This is my American cousin, Mayor Jack Donovan," Cavanaugh announced to the bartender and patrons, who gave odd looks. "He's here in Cork for a cultural exchange."

Understanding the move for legitimacy, Donovan shook the hands offered to him, hoping no one noticed his trembling, and when the interest in him waned, the mayor wasted little time with pleasantries. "You got my stuff?"

"Relax. Have a beer. I got it," his cousin assured him.

"Give it to me."

"Fine. Here," he said as he gave the mayor a small vial, three-quarters full.

"That's all you got?" Donovan said. "That'll last me a day!"

"Nah, Jackie. I told ya I'd take care of ya," Cavanaugh said as he clandestinely opened a loose duffel bag to give his cousin a peek at a neat, white brick.

"How much?"

"How much you want?"

"Well, all of it."

Cavanaugh stared. "You want the whole thing. That's a kilo. Run you at least twenty-five Gs. You planning on staying a while?"

"If it's as good as you say it is."

"I think your nose is bigger than your head. Why don't you try a taste before you make that investment?" he said, pointing to the vial he had given him and motioning toward the back of the bar.

The mayor retreated to the toilet where the stench was barely tolerable, but nothing mattered as much as getting his fix. He tapped a bump onto his fist, gave it a snort, sighed relief, and did it again. He emerged from the bathroom a new man—confident, energetic, a stark opposite. He was Jack Donovan again.

"Give me the whole fuckin' thing," he demanded before he'd returned to his seat.

"You're my cousin and all, but where you gonna get that kind of money?"

Donovan slammed $1,000 in hundreds on the counter. "How's that for a start?"

***

If not for the $5,000 bribes for building permits and tax treaties, Donovan never would have been able to feed his addiction. He and Silberman had accumulated nearly $2 million over the past twenty years through their bribery and kickback scheme. They averaged a quarter of a million a year in cash to provide behind-the-scenes access to the City Hall treasure chest of leases and jobs. Silberman was the bagman, the buffer between the mayor and the money. He had orchestrated their enterprise nearly twenty years ago, when the mayor was still wet behind the ears as a politician and relied on a savvy operative for tutelage.

Silberman's wizardry with money had turned their second-rate kickback scheme into a truly fruitful endeavor. He had created a finely tuned machine that churned out political favors for a price. Silberman handled the lucrative side business, with the mayor looking the other way except when it came to his cash-bloated campaign account. It did not matter that the mayor had not seen a serious challenge to his reelection in the last eight years. Dinners, drinks, trips, gifts, and flowers were all billed to Friends of Jack Donovan. But when the $25,000 payments for building permits and the $5,000 payments for job promotions started funneling through, Silberman could not park the money in a federally scrutinized campaign account, so he had started laundering it through his friends, who saw their personal bank accounts flourish to more than fifty grand at times and were more than happy to take five percent as a holding fee.

The mayor's cocaine habit and uncontrollable bravado often jeopardized Silberman's racket. That time the mayor had read to elementary school students while stoned on cocaine, it was Silberman who had whisked him out of the school like a secret service agent and had then explained that Donovan was having a bout with the flu. After the mayor inflicted a tongue-lashing on a state representative for failing to secure the necessary votes to bail out Providence from its budget shortfall, a deficit incurred from the city's own failure to recover certain property tax revenue that surreptitiously had been sold away, it was the politically astute Silberman who had prevented the representative from going to the press. And Silberman was still reeling from the time the mayor had bragged to his secretary, when she was conducting more than official city business, about the millions he had in the bank.

Like any politician, Donovan had an ego that needed stroking, and Silberman was the perfect partner who could both protect the mayor from self-destruction and spin him into the savior of Providence. He had worked the political circuit, sending the mayor to every charitable event, grand opening, and senior citizens' coffee hour in the city. People joked that Donovan would attend the opening of an envelope.

Donovan was the retail face of Providence, leaving the real behind-the-scenes work to the professionals. Silberman couldn't afford to have the mayor breaking into an hysterical rant during negotiations with the school committee over the budget or on contract talks with the teachers. That was the real reason Silberman had exiled the mayor off to Ireland for the so-called cultural exchange. Teachers wanted a 10 percent raise and had threatened to close the schools if they didn't get it. It was the business of politics, and the last thing he needed was an erratic mayor lashing out at the president of the teachers' union.

At the moment, Silberman was handling a delicate situation. As the mayor, Donovan had enjoyed free reign in all the city's boutique restaurants and trendy clubs, save one. Tuscany's, one of Providence's finest restaurants, was challenging him outright. Before Donovan's trip to Ireland, the proprietor of Tuscany's, Michael Garibaldi, had thought it only prudent to mail the mayor's dinner tab to City Hall, which Donovan must have mistakenly walked out on one Saturday evening, but the mayor had sent back the bill with his autograph penned on it. An infuriated Garibaldi had filed a complaint with the police, which had then been forwarded to Silberman, who had paid the bill out of the mayor's campaign account. But when Donovan saw the payment yesterday, he decided he wanted to make an example of Tuscany's.

"I hope those fucking pricks like becoming a BYOB because we're pulling their liquor license," the mayor blasted from a bar stool. This Cork pub was becoming his favorite place to do business. Though he was an ocean away, the decibel level was high enough for Silberman to need to move the phone away from his ear. The mayor's tirade was a clear indication that he had managed to find some cocaine. Figuring there was little harm the mayor could do from overseas, Silberman went into handling mode, letting him vent, agreeing with him, and waiting it out until Donovan's next new complaint. But this time, Silberman did not indulge his antics.

"You're not pulling their liquor license," Silberman said. "There are hundreds of restaurants in this city. Forget about this one."

"Fuck 'em. I'm the mayor. It's my city. If they want to fuck with me, I'll bury them."

"C'mon, Mayor. let it go. We accomplish nothing by going after them."

"Get the health inspector over there if you have to. I don't care if you have to make up a story about rats. Just get it done."

"It's not worth the headache they'll cause, and with our income, the bill doesn't matter."

"They can't fuck with me. Get that kid we made sergeant in the department. Have him tail one of their guests and bust him for DWI. We'll show those fuckers what it means to go at us."

"That's not smart, Mayor. We should maintain a low profile when it comes to this stuff. We risk too much going after these guys."

"Why can't you ever agree with me? If you won't do it, I'll fucking do it myself."

"How you gonna do anything from Ireland?" Silberman asked, baiting him.

"All I gotta do is make a few phone calls, and those guys are through."

"You're not going to do anything. I'll take care of it."

***

Handling the mayor had become Silberman's primary job responsibility, but the official duties of running the city and its departments also fell to him. While the mayor was attending his cultural exchange, his chief of staff was entertaining Irish city officials and business leaders at the city's turn-of-the-century Biltmore Hotel. As Silberman rode up the glass elevator, he peered out over the Providence skyline of skyscrapers and hotels, many of which he and the mayor had built through extortion.

The Biltmore Ballroom, with its lavish decor and grand view of the city, was already filled with political and business leaders looking to showcase their talents on a world stage. The evening was a rare occasion for seeing the leaders of both political parties as well as the AFL-CIO president and the presidents of Providence's Fortune 1,000 companies in the same room together. Silberman walked through the crowd, showering hellos and grasping hands like any seasoned pol. He was able to pry his arm away from the grasp of an octogenarian long enough to reach for his cell phone.

"Terry, it's me," his lawyer answered.

"What's up? You coming by?" Silberman asked as he retreated to the corner of the room.

"We got big problems. You know that guy you met this afternoon? He was FBI. They got you taking a bribe," he said.

Silence struck Silberman. He shrank into the corner of the room.

"You with me?" his lawyer asked.

"Yeah." Silberman knew he was finished.

"They wanted to come down tonight and arrest you, but I got them to hold off till the morning. They're gonna let you surrender yourself at my office at 9 a.m."

"Can we beat it?"

"They have you on tape. Best I can get you is probably five years. You're definitely looking at time."

"And the mayor? They got him too?"

"Well, that's trickier. Pretty much circumstantial, but I hear they got their top FBI guy on it. They're gonna bust him as soon as he steps foot on American soil."

"So what do we do now?" Silberman asked.

"Nothing we can do till tomorrow. Just enjoy yourself tonight."

So that's exactly what he did. He went to the bar and ordered a scotch, then a second and a third. He pushed through the crowd until he found his personal assistant, Danny Conroy. Conroy was six-foot-two and built more like a football player than a political operative. His $500 suit given to him by Silberman only covered his working man's background. He had worked as a bricklayer, laborer, and bartender until Silberman had plucked him away from his favorite watering hole for less honest work. He was paid from the Donovan campaign account to drive the mayor to political functions and other events that Silberman did not want the mayor's police escort to attend. He helped keep the mayor out of trouble, but he was most loyal to Silberman.

"Get me a broad," Silberman said. "I'll be in the presidential suite."

It was not the first time Silberman or Donovan had told Conroy to fetch a woman. Conroy knew what they both liked. Donovan was into busty blondes, while Silberman liked dark brunettes. He scanned the crowd, hoping he could find something in house instead of having to go out scouring for talent. It took about fifteen minutes. The woman seemed to travel with members of the Irish delegation, and the man who had his arm around her had to be at least thirty years her senior. As a bartender and frequenter to the late-night scene, Conroy could spot a professional. He walked toward the young woman, whose dark beauty was brought out by her tight, low-cut black dress. She did not have the pale skin and light hair of an Irish woman nor the look or dress of an American. He made eye contact as he descended upon her. He motioned his head toward the bar. She dropped her head, then said something to her guest as she left for the bar. Conroy ordered a beer for himself, adding, "And whatever the lady wants."

"Thank you," she said, with the hint of an accent in her voice, which came even thicker when she told the bartender, "Merlot."

"You working tonight?" he asked her.

"Always," she said. It was apparent that she, too, was working the room, not unlike the other guests seeking jobs and promotions.

"Are you booked tonight?"

"You a cop?" she asked.

"Do I look like a cop?" In his Armani suit, Conroy's uniform was a bit flashier than a policeman's street clothes.

"No. What you looking for?"

"Not for me. For a friend. A very powerful man."

"I'm with a powerful man," she said.

"I'll make it worth your time," he told her as he peeled off hundreds from the roll of cash he carried like a weapon, under the advice of Silberman.

"Let me get rid of my date, and I'll meet you down in the lobby," she told him, her eyes never leaving the bankroll.

The deal was struck, and Silberman enjoyed his last night before he was delivered to the feds. There were many loose ends to take care of before they strung him up, and he needed someone to keep an eye out for the mayor.

4

The law offices of Warner, Isikoff, Tescht, & Evans were located in downtown Providence on the eighteenth floor of an office tower. Anyone on the elevator who was well-dressed—lawyers, bankers, secretaries—was headed to the posh offices, but occasionally, someone dressed in street clothes, obviously out of place, would walk out alongside them. Most often they were sent to a different floor, but sometimes, they were escorted to Henry Mercucio's office.

Aside from cleaning up corporate clients' and their children's DWIs and other nitwit behaviors, Henry represented a handful of small-time crooks he thought the system had screwed. He made sure they had a passionate advocate in court, his favorite being Vincent. In and out of social services until he was eighteen, the only skills Vincent had learned were how to cheat and steal. He'd graduated from petty theft to armed robbery and had spent five years in prison, where he'd learned the more sophisticated arts of his trade. His latest business was selling stolen designer suits to busy professionals in the financial district.

The stunning receptionist, with a wink and smile, rang Henry's extension when Vincent stepped off the elevator. "Your suit guy's here with a large garbage bag. Want me to get rid of him?"

While Henry had little time for Vincent's antics, he couldn't just turn him away. He was a client. "I'll be right there."

The receptionist ignored Vincent until Henry arrived to escort him through the maze of cubicles and offices behind her. When they reached his office, Henry closed the door behind them.

"Henry, buddy, I've got a great Mani suit for you," Vincent said as he took the charcoal jacket from his garbage bag.

"Thanks, Vincent. I'm good."

"C'mon, Henry. A big shot like you can't be going around in something off the rack at JCPenney's, especially if you're gonna represent me," he said, smoothing the suit out on the desk. "It's on me. It's a thousand-dollar Mani suit."

"You mean Armani?"

"Same family. It's made exclusively for the fancy men's stores."

"No offense, Vincent, but I can't represent you in a suit that could be used as evidence against you."

"Henry, my boy, it's not stolen. I buy these suits on clearance down in the fashion district in New York. It's completely legit," Vincent said with a conspiratorial grin.

"Oh, like the Rolexes? You know, if I hadn't gotten you off on that illegal search, you would've gotten the max—over $500, a felony, and three strikes. We're talking real time."

"Hey, man, I know. You did good. Real good. That's why I want to take care of my boy. Look, Henry. Seriously, it'd mean a lot to me. Please take it."

Henry stuffed the suit back into the garbage bag and placed it on the floor under his desk, making a mental note to stop by The Salvation Army on his way home.

Vincent clapped his hands together and smiled. "Now, let's get down to business. I heard one of the brokers on the other floor tell his friend this stock was going through the roof."

Henry sat down. "That's just stupid. Don't always look for the quick score, Vincent. Look for a company with high earning potential that makes good products. Invest for the long-term."

"What if a girl I know who works for one of those suits told her a pharmaceutical company has a drug that removes plaque in your arteries that's gonna get FDA approval? He told her if she gets ten K, he'll put it in when it goes public."

Henry sighed. "He just wants to put it in her. Look, there's lots of crooks selling stocks. I wouldn't invest in a company unless I knew their history, who's on their board, what other products they make, and stuff like that."

"Okay, okay, but you should meet this girl. She's a real knock-out. A handsome boy like you? Oh, yeah. She'd like you," Vincent said with a wink.

"You know I have a girlfriend. And if this woman's so great, why isn't she buying suits from you?"

"She has. Besides, I don't trouble myself with long-term relationships. She's too much woman for me. I'm like a wolf; I don't waste my time chasing the strong elk. I wait for the wounded elk."

The phone interrupted Vincent's metaphor. Ray McNally's voice crackled through the speaker and summoned him to the corner office.

"That's the end of this week's session, Vincent. I believe you know your way out. And don't try to sell anything to anybody."

McNally's office lay at the convergence of two major corridors. His secretary silently waved Henry into the office that was at least twice as big as his congressional space. Hanging from the walls were pictures and memorabilia from his days as one of the most powerful men in America. A picture with the Pope, an autographed photo from the president, and what Henry appreciated most, a letter from a child congratulating McNally on his first election to Congress, all graced the walls. The McNally library, the other partners joked, was a subtle reminder of where true power lay to all who passed.

McNally was sitting in one of the mahogany chairs set in front of an artificial waterfall. Henry always found it amusing that McNally had insisted on installing a waterfall, which he made interns replenish every day. Since he pulled down more than $500,000 a year in Providence, he got what he wanted, especially since he was a former congressman with a laundry list of contacts throughout the world. McNally's guests usually seemed a bit awestruck, something McNally had intended when designing the office. He always positioned himself with the Providence skyline over his shoulder.

McNally motioned for Henry to join the group already in the room. "Hal, you remember Councilman Campagna. And say hi to Jimmy Callahan, Deputy US Attorney."

Councilman Campagna was just as Henry remembered—short, his gut protruding over his belt, and his thin, grayish hair combed over in a feeble attempt to forestall the inevitable. The last four years had not been kind. But he had a strong, confident air to him, almost kingly, simply in the way he carried himself.

In contrast, Jimmy Callahan was in the prime of his life. He had recently celebrated his fortieth birthday and spoke like a man at the top of his game. He looked the part of someone destined for success—a thick blonde pate sitting atop his six-four frame, and although he was Irish Catholic, he could have fooled any WASP that he was one of them.

Campagna turned to greet Henry and shook his hand. "You're

making quite a reputation for yourself as a defense attorney," Campagna said. He turned back to McNally. "You better watch out that Jimmy doesn't offer him honest work at the US Attorney's office."

"Hal doesn't want to work for the other side. He's too much of a crusader. And they couldn't afford him." McNally gave him a wink. "Besides, we need him for his political savvy. Wouldn't you agree, Johnny?"

Henry smiled. Only McNally could get away with calling Councilman Campagna by his first name.

"Henry was reading Sun Tzu when other kids were reading fake news on Facebook," McNally joked to Campagna. "He was planning world domination on a Risk board when kids were playing spin the bottle," he continued as he shot Henry a grin. "Henry has a copy of *The Prince* on his nightstand."

He sobered and turned back to Henry. "Jokes aside, the reason we're here, Hal, is that Mayor Donovan is in a bit of trouble. Have a seat."

After a nod from McNally, Callahan took the floor. "It's no secret that Mayor Donovan is the FBI's most wanted politician. We figure he's siphoned anywhere from two to three million out of the city. We've conducted a two-year investigation, but we've only convicted four low-level members of his administration. And nobody will talk about the mayor."

Henry glanced at McNally. The mayor was his number one political enemy.

"I'm telling you, this guy commands real loyalty. Nothing like the usual Mafioso who might sell out his friends for a job packing grocery bags in Nebraska. That's why we want to take him down.

"We closed down the Mafia in this region, but we've got the mayor of a major city running the largest extortion ring in the country."

McNally couldn't help himself, putting his own personal beliefs back in the mix. "Why does the FBI care about him anyways, and about our fucked up little state? I mean, we've got our little thing going here, but the Feds have usually left us to it. Why are they suddenly so interested in us?"

"I said the same thing to my boss. Why do we give a shit what's going on in Rhode Island?" Callahan admitted. "Look, we may be small, but we fight above our weight. As you know, Providence metro is the second largest population center—1.3 million—in New England. And everyone knows nothing happens in Rhode Island without Providence. And this fuck-tard is more powerful than the governor, and he's basically a gangster running a crime ring. We can't have it. Plus, my boss knows that if we bag a big fish like Donovan, he gets a US Attorney gig."

"So how does he do it, the mayor? How does he run the biggest crime ring in New England since the mafia?" Henry asked. He, too, had heard stories but didn't fully understand how the mayor made his discretionary income.

"It's quite an operation," Callahan said. "Donovan and Silberman line their pockets by ripping off developers." He explained how Donovan's cronies bought up old factories, warehouses, and commercial spaces in the city and turned them into trendy lofts and artist boutiques. "To do business in Providence, you have to take care of Silberman and the Mayor first. You know he's got at least a million in his campaign account. He buys suits, meals, even gifts for his girlfriends out of the campaign."

"That's a felony. Why not just bust him for that?" Henry asked.

"Because the bastard's slippery, and in front of a jury, he can charm his way out of a twenty-count indictment. We need something that'll stick, and now we've got it."

Callahan explained that the case had turned in the government's favor when a disgruntled property owner had come to them.

"Our guy met with Silberman to talk about getting his property included in the waterfront project," Callahan said. "The cost was $5,000. Silberman then goes and invites him to the mayor's house for dinner. Told him the meal cost $500. The developer was wearing a wire, and we got the whole thing on tape. Silberman's facing at least five to ten. Considering he's sixty, you'd think he'd want to avoid retirement in the pen. But we can't flip him. He won't rat out his buddy. His lawyer says we've got shit. So we're going to try the bastard, and we're going to indict the mayor. He's supposed to come back tomorrow night. As soon as he sets foot on American soil, we'll nail him."

"Does the mayor know he's getting indicted?" McNally asked.

"No. Right now we've kept it quiet, and we need to keep it that way."

"Does he have to leave office when he's indicted?" Campagna asked.

"Only if he's convicted. As you know, Councilman, there's no provision for impeachment in the city council charter, only a recall by the voters. And we're not looking to deal. To be quite honest, a trial could take a year," Callahan admitted.

"So what do we do in the meantime?" Campagna asked.

"We can't do anything," McNally said, "Right, Jimmy?"

"We got everything covered," Callahan said. "I don't care how slippery the bastard is. He's not getting out of this one. Excuse me." He reached for his cell phone and answered it at the table. "Callahan. Uh huh. Okay. The flight number? Got it." He closed the phone and slipped it back into his jacket pocket. "I gotta go. Million things to do before he comes in tomorrow night."

"Well, Jimmy, thanks for coming in and telling us."

"A pleasure, Congressman," Callahan said. "That was the special agent in charge of the investigation. I'm going to meet him, make sure we've got everything covered." He shook hands with Henry and Campagna. McNally threw a fatherly arm over his shoulder while escorting him to the door.

McNally returned and pointed to the door. "I knew Jimmy's dad really well. He was treasurer of the state AFL-CIO. Great guy. Died of cancer when the boy was in college. I got him the job at the US Attorney's office," McNally said proudly. He then turned to Henry and said, "So what do you think?"

"I think the mayor's screwed," Henry replied.

"Yeah, but we're looking at a year from now," Campagna reminded everyone.

McNally tapped Henry's knee and pointed at Campagna. "Hal, you're a smart kid. You've probably figured out Councilman Campagna wants to be mayor. What do you think?"

"A year is enough time to raise his name recognition, come out on some winning issues, and solidify his base." He turned to Campagna and told him, "You'll need a million bucks to do it right. And I suspect it will be a crowded field, so the sooner you get out there and raise the early money, the easier it'll be to scare off competitors."

"I agree," McNally said. "The faster you get out there, the better."

"So what do I do now?" Campagna asked.

"You want to come out on some hot-button issues—safe stuff, nothing controversial, like property tax relief, making the universities and colleges pay their fair share for city services—that's always popular." McNally suggested Campagna write an op-ed expounding his views on how to change the PILOT plan to include rich non-profits. "Stay away from the controversial stuff—pay raises, teachers, education. No reason to alienate voters at this point. We need to get you media savvy too. There's a great woman at Brown who specializes in media training. Stuff like how to look into the camera during interviews and not at the interviewer. She'll help you get down that ten-second sound bite when the cameras are on you. The good thing is we've got some time."

It should have been Jimmy Callahan's big day, the event catapulting him into the limelight. He would have prosecuted a big-city mayor. His name would have been on the front page of every newspaper in the country—"James Callahan, the federal prosecutor who'd brought down Mayor Jack Donovan." Callahan had rushed to Logan International Airport to personally serve the indictments to the mayor as he stepped off the flight from Dublin following his "cultural exchange"—a laughable euphemism for an all-expense-paid junket.

But the mayor had kept Callahan waiting.

When the plane arrived, Callahan waited for the passengers to depart. Then the flight attendants and the pilots. He waited and waited, anxiously hoping for his date's arrival, to catch a glimpse of his mark. At first, in his denial, he attempted to rationalize. Perhaps the mayor had met someone on the plane and was telling one of his long-winded stories. Or maybe he had fallen ill from a bumpy landing. Maybe he had taken a later flight or had missed it, or maybe—the thought occurred to him as he frantically searched the plane with three other FBI agents, all rummaging around the bathrooms, the galley, and even the baggage compartments for any trace of the missing mayor—Donovan had missed his plane. But it was apparent that he was on the run.

This evasion infuriated Callahan, who was now even more intent on prosecuting the mayor as harshly as possible, but first, he needed to find him. He had put two years into building this case against him, and he would not see it eviscerated. He felt like one of those sorry saps left holding the bag on the train platform, standing there with his guts kicked in, his mark having leveled a stiff kick to the midsection from 6,000 miles away. No, this ache would not be easily forgotten.

This was supposed to be his defining moment, that seminal event most people waited their whole careers for, his chance for stardom. But Donovan had taken that from him. How had he known? That question bothered Callahan more than any other. He knew it was his own fault. He had told too many about the Donovan investigation. It was his first invitation to the big dance; of course he wanted to talk about it. But he hadn't counted on the inevitable leaks, for what at the time had seemed like good reasons. Who, after all, would want to protect Donovan? Was there something far more sinister at work here? Who had the most to gain from the mayor's sudden disappearance?

The mayor would become Callahan's quest, and he would do whatever it took to complete it. Until the mayor's address read "Federal Penitentiary," nothing less would satisfy.

For Callahan, the foreseeable future would hinge on waiting out Donovan. He would resurface at some point, and Callahan would be there to tighten the noose.

***

His final night in Ireland, Donovan had received an anonymous phone call informing him the US government was preparing to arrest him on extortion, bribery, and racketeering. He attempted to confirm the information with Silberman, but he wasn't answering his phones —home, cell, or office. The next call Donovan made was to his cousin. He needed to get out of Ireland, and fast. Cavanaugh told him to gather a bag of belongings and wait for one of his people to come to the hotel. In less than an hour, there was a knock on his door.

"Who is it?" Donovan asked.

"A friend of Billy's. He told me to come get you."

With that, they were gone. The Irishman, who never revealed his name, delivered Donovan to his cousin, Billy Cavanaugh, who was waiting down at the docks in one of Cork's inland coves.

With no greeting, Cavanaugh told Donovan, "We're getting you out. The Garda Siochna's got the ferry and airport covered. Our guy inside told us they're gonna make sure you're on the plane back to the States. Only way to get you out is on a trawler." Cavanaugh pointed to the twenty-five-foot fishing boat.

"Where am I going?" Donovan asked.

"Wales. Little town called Fishguard. We'll get word over there to our people. They'll take you to Birmingham."

"What do I do?"

"Let me take care of it. I gotta get you new papers—Irish passport, license, birth certificate. One of my guys will meet you in Birmingham. A lot of Micks in Birmingham. You'll be fine. They'll take care of ya."

"I can't thank you enough."

"Thank me when you're in Europe drinking a pint."

Donovan's voyage to Wales was a ten-hour ordeal over the

choppy Irish Sea, where he came face-to-face with his transgressions. With the waves crashing, the small vessel tossed about like a toy, there was little solace. He had plenty of time to think about what had led him to this point, where he had gone wrong, that exact moment when he had traded what he'd known as right for what was obviously wrong.

He'd hardly thought it immoral when Silberman had suggested that he make a phone call over to the Providence Planning Board to help his cousin's friend "get in over there." And when his chief of staff, who doubled as his campaign treasurer, had told him "the guy you helped out" wanted to express his thanks by donating $2,000 cash to the campaign, he'd decided he wasn't about to turn away the money, any money. That was how things were done in politics—contributors were given preferential treatment. So when he and his cabinet had decided to privatize janitorial services in the public schools, they had placed the companies that funneled money into the mayor's campaign account at the top of the list. When a new hotel had designs to open in Providence's revitalized downtown, they'd made building permits, entertainment licenses, and liquor licenses readily available for a price.

It was a lot to take in, but Donovan came to terms with the spiraling cycle of corruption he had so willingly embraced. Now he was a fugitive who could not return to his kingdom, banished to a faraway land. Out of habit, he reached into his pocket to finger the vial of coke he'd stashed for just such a dark night of the soul and realized what had caused his transformation. He retrieved it from his pocket, rolled it between his fingers and considered the powder inside, not unlike the grains of sand in a dwindling hourglass, and tossed it into the Irish Sea before he could change his mind. He returned to his hidey hole down in the small cabin and wrapped himself in a woolen blanket to keep away the chill.

At 3 p.m., the door to the cabin slammed open and the Irish captain shouted down to Donovan. "Welsh coast ahead. I see a light. Must be the lads." Donovan emerged to dreary conditions. A fog had settled in, but he saw the headlights of a car off in the distance.

The captain cut the trawler's engines as it slipped into the docks at Fishguard. He handled his cargo like he would any other package of guns or drugs smuggled between England and Ireland—he tossed it onto the docks for the waiting longshoreman and motored out of the cove.

Donovan was hustled out of the small fishing town for the three-hour drive to Birmingham. The cramped Fiat Punta hardly offered the amenities of the mayor's usual chauffeured Lincoln. The second leg of the journey went without a word spoken, and after a lonely drive through the gray mist of Wales, the mayor made his rendezvous.

"Well, hello, Jackie boy! How was your trip?" a burly Irishman asked as he opened the car door for him.

"And who are you?"

"Friend of your cousin's. I got your papers—Irish passport, driver's license. Your name's now Sean Murphy, from Dublin."

"Where did you—"

"Don't worry about it. We have people at the Motor Tax Office. They get us papers when we need them."

"How much do I owe you?"

"Nothing. You got enough to worry about. You missed the Garda Soichna by about five minutes. They had the airports and train station all covered. Our contact there told me they were honoring a request from the American government to make sure you made your flight back home. The Brits will be looking for you all over England, so we've got to get you to the continent. You're taking the Chunnel to Paris."

"I can't thank you enough."

"Don't thank me yet."

***

With little more than a fistful of Euros, Callahan's men safely deposited the mayor on the train to Paris that traveled beneath the English Channel. He wasted no time in Paris, realizing it was important to keep moving. Most people vacationed in England or France for about a week or ten days; Donovan did it in less than twenty-four hours. There was no time to climb the Eiffel Tower, visit the Louvre, or cruise the Seine. For a man who was conditioned to having his aides plan his entire day, the simple task of scheduling a train was alien to him. A polite French businessman rescued him from the impatient train clerk who had little sympathy for what he perceived as an old man's lack of knowledge. Donovan hopped a train to Frankfurt and traveled incognito among thousands of other Europeans. As new passengers boarded the train, he wondered whether each new face would be the policeman who would arrest him. At every stop, he thought this might be the place where the cops would storm the train and capture him.

His paranoia began to amplify as the train continued over the French border into Belgium. He felt like he was being followed. It was either the product of his psychosis, or a very real threat. In any case, he became so terrified that he hid for an hour in the bathroom. There was nothing exciting or adventurous about being on the lam. His heart pounded and his hands shook uncontrollably. He was petrified someone would report him—the trembling man in the back of the train.

His survival instinct took over, and he began to think rationally. The sprawling European cities were the most likely places for him to disappear. The authorities would look first in London, Paris, Geneva, and Rome, the rationale being that he would be more comfortable in a big city where more people spoke English. He needed to step away from himself.

***

Terry Silberman had plenty of time to think about where he had gone astray as he sat in his ten-by-ten cell in the federal penitentiary in Danbury, Connecticut. Of course, there were places better suited for his retirement, Palm Beach or Naples to name a couple. He had been offered immunity from prosecution and had been guaranteed a comfortable retirement in exchange for his testimony against Donovan. But that was a request he was incapable of satisfying. There was still such a thing as honor among thieves.

When the mayor had extended his little trip abroad, the government had raged for a suitable consolation prize. It was either a testament to his loyalty or his misguided sense of friendship that had prevented Silberman from incriminating the mayor. While many praised him for his refusal to betray his boss, some questioned his motives to protect the man who'd left him holding the bag. Some figured Silberman was simply waiting for the day he was released to collect on the millions he'd hidden in bank accounts around the world. Whatever his motives, Silberman's steadfast loyalty to the mayor had created a gaping hole in the government's indictment. Without Silberman's testimony, the multi-count case was entirely circumstantial—no witness directly tied the mayor to racketeering and bribery.

That had all changed when the mayor had disappeared. That was the irony in his decision to slip the FBI. The presumption of innocence had fled with him.

The entire City of Providence was on trial now, ravaged by indictments that touched at the very heart of its business and political establishments. The air of change was stifled, and any prospective politician who chose to ignore the public's seething disgust faced the wrath of the masses at the ballot box. And Terry Silberman was the symbol of the public's disdain for the entire system.

His much-anticipated trial lasted eight weeks, with the government parading over a hundred witnesses. The who's-who of Providence came out in all their splendor. There was the police captain who testified that much to his objection, he had promoted a candidate to sergeant upon the urging of the mayor's chief of staff. The administrative secretary of the tax board, who had erased certain back taxes from the books, broke down in tears retelling her personal account of corruption. The jury saw their government in action, petty criminals referring to cash bribes for services as "coffee and donuts." There were even a few chuckles among the jurors when a witness told the court that when Silberman had told him, "Bring plenty of coffee and donuts if they want that lease," the witness had responded, "With what we're paying you, you'll be able to build your own donut shop."

Perhaps most damaging was the government's videotape showing Silberman taking a bribe from the government's witness, a little-known developer named Frank Petrozella. Although Silberman's lawyer had attempted every conceivable legal maneuver to disallow the instructional video on how to take a bribe, the judge had ruled it admissible. For the jury's viewing pleasure, Silberman boasted how he could simply make a phone call to change a zoning ordinance, but only after a cash bribe. The jury had its smoking gun with Silberman explaining on tape to the government's witness how his money had purchased him a city contract.

There was little Silberman's masterful inquisitor could do about

Petrozella, a man who had never missed a tax payment or even received a traffic ticket. Petrozella had nothing to gain and everything to fear. But he did not waver, standing in court while recounting his bribe to Silberman. His testimony was beyond reproach. The American dream may have passed by Petrozella, but he didn't seem to mind. He was a man secure in himself and in his standing in the world. He needed no false god to bring him happiness. Maybe that kind of freedom was the American dream after all.

Silberman took the stand in a last-ditch attempt to sway the jury. He spoke at length about his faithful service to the people of the city. Arguing that he had only taken the money so he could turn in Petrozella, he attempted to portray himself as the hero, the one who fought against graft and corruption. But the jury didn't buy it, and they needed someone to punish. Since they couldn't have the mayor, they settled on Silberman. It took less than three hours for a verdict—guilty on ten counts. Silberman was forced to pay back $250,000 to the city and was handed down a seven-year sentence.

Twenty years of service to the city he loved, and for what? A prison sentence and the pleasure of sharing a cell with a bloated New Orleans city planner who had taken kickbacks from a casino operator. His cellmate's gastrointestinal problems were a form of cruel and unusual punishment. His insufferable rants of innocence were just as torturous. More than his cellmate, more than his confinement, the endless hours of boredom were the most difficult to bear. He was part of the action, if not the action itself, of a vibrant city. He was a player among players who could walk into any room in Providence and command instant respect. Restaurateurs would bring over a plate of their best veal and a glass of their most expensive Chianti before he even sat down at a table. As for the check, it never seemed to make it over, and on the rare occasions that it did, he simply pocketed it to remind himself of who dared challenge his standing in the hierarchy of Providence. Now the thrill of his life would be the bland version of tomato sauce on solidified noodles that the cafeteria served.

His only comfort was the realization that his grandchildren's lives would be taken care of, from college to little Sarah's wedding someday. He might never witness it—for all he knew, he might die in this hellhole, but at least they would be provided for. By whom, their parents would never know, but they would be afforded every opportunity he never had in life. And that was what helped him through those monotonous days—the knowledge that his grandchildren would never have to sell their souls to get ahead in life. Lord knows he already had.

Why had he done it? Why had he chosen the easy route? These were the questions that echoed in his head. The answer was greed, the reason was money. Slaving ten hours a day for twenty years to earn as much as a kid out of college was his justification. He had created the mayor and built his shining Camelot. The cash that flowed beneath his mythical city had paid for her beautiful mystique. Silberman was her architect, the man with the vision to transform her into the shining City on the Mount. He deserved proper compensation for his creation.

Like most things in life, his decision to defraud taxpayers hadn't been a carefully hatched plan but the culmination of a series of immoral decisions. He couldn't even remember the exact time when he'd accepted that first bribe, that moment when he'd traded what he'd known was wrong for what he'd always wanted—the type of respect that only money could buy. He racked his memory for that first step that had led him to the penitentiary in Connecticut, but he didn't necessarily want to recall the moment he'd sold out his integrity.

6

Donovan needed to figure out how plentiful his retirement funds were. He knew that Frankfurt, Germany, was one of the financial capitals of Europe, so he decided to take care of some business to ensure his survival. He had insisted that Silberman provide all the account numbers of the money he'd stashed in Europe and the Caymans. About $1.5 million was spread out between five Swiss banks with the remainder divided among banks in Luxembourg, the Bahamas, and Grand Cayman.

Donovan took a cab from the train station, and not knowing any German, simply said "Marriott." He paid €250 for a room that looked out over the modern Frankfurt skyline. He seemed to have been transported into a futuristic city, a virtual Oz with spiraling skyscrapers and beaming bright lights. After the best night's sleep he'd had since disappearing, he awoke refreshed and ready to accomplish the essential transaction of his new mission.

He walked through the Frankfurt financial district until he found the First Suisse Bank. He was surprised with the level of security. After walking through the entrance, he needed to be buzzed in through the second door. A manicured Swiss banker greeted him with a polite hello.

"You speak English?" Donovan asked.

"Of course! What can I do for you?"

"I want to withdraw some money. This is my account number," he said, handing the banker a piece of paper.

"Could I see your passport?" the banker asked. Donovan handed him an old passport he had stashed for times just like these, and in less than a minute, the banker asked, "Will you want Euros?"

"Euros will be fine. Give me twenty-five thousand."

"Not a problem, sir. Have a seat. It will just take me a few minutes. Can I get you some coffee?"

"No, thank you."

It took the banker fifteen minutes to return with a thick envelope filled with Donovan's money, but it seemed like an eternity. As he waited, Donovan wondered whether this would be the moment he would finally be apprehended. The banker smiled as he handed over his money, and a new sense of freedom replaced his fear.

There was nothing left for him in Frankfurt. He didn't care to see the ruins of Charlemagne's empire or visit the gardens that lined the walls of the ancient city. He was a man without an empire, in self-exile, who needed to escape beyond his own barriers. He was in search of a place to retreat, where no one would expect him to hide, yet a city where an American, or an Irishman, could blend in with the locals. Prague. It was perfect. He had been told Prague was an expatriate haven, a place for young Americans to find themselves far from the constraints of America. Prague was the perfect place for an American to lose himself.

***

After another eight hours on a train, this time a sleeper train that he did not partake in, he arrived in Prague. What could he say about Prague? It was beautiful, almost majestic. Aside from the smog that blanketed the city, he felt as if he had been transported back to a gentler age where art and architecture were beautifully merged to form a city more suitable for a canvas than a map. He hailed a taxi and asked to be taken to the Hilton. Knowing from first glance that the man was American, the driver said to him in broken English, "No Hilton. Floods ruin."

Donovan remembered hearing that floods had ravaged this country. He then turned to the next best hotel he could think of and told the driver "Marriott." The drive took about thirty minutes through congested streets more suitable for horse-drawn carriages than automobiles. The cost was €40, which he paid without hesitation. Days later, he realized that the train station was right around the corner from the Marriott, and that he had been taken. He checked into the hotel without a problem, then sacked out for a few hours. He awoke refreshed and excited to tour his new surroundings. Donovan, who was accustomed to being chauffeured the three blocks from his plush penthouse apartment to City Hall, chose a less assuming mode of transportation—he walked. He walked through the old town on the cobblestone streets lined by 16th-century buildings and churches. He made his way through the tight streets and covered alleys, by street performers and artisans, and across the Charles Bridge that had connected the two halves of Prague since the Middle Ages. He was overwhelmed by the sense of history. Providence was considered one of the older American cities, first settled back in 1636. In Providence, they were tearing down factory buildings deemed too old. In Prague, they were preserving buildings and churches that were considered old in the eighteenth century. Donovan, raised a Catholic, was most moved by the old Jewish quarter. He overheard a tour guide say in

English to a bunch of camera-clad tourists that Hitler, having burned most of the homes and buildings occupied by Jews, had preserved this part of the Jewish center of Prague as a living history for what he claimed was an extinct race.

Donovan perused his way to Old Square and dined at an outdoor café. He ate a traditional Czech dinner of roasted duck, smoked pork, sweet and sour cabbage, and sauerkraut. He drank two pints of Pivo beer to take the edge off, and the Czech beers with their double alcohol content helped quell his shaking hands from the lingering effects of his coke withdrawal. As night fell on Golden Prague, he was ready to attack the nightlife. A frequent player on the streets of Providence, he knew how to work the ladies. Of course, as the mayor, he'd practiced discretion somewhat. But three days on the run had taken its toll, and now more than ever he needed some female companionship. He spoke to the waiter who told him to try a bar called Chapeau, only a few blocks from the restaurant.

Chapeau felt no different from any American bar littered with drunken twenty-somethings looking to make a score. In an attempt to fit in, he ordered a shot of absinthe, the poison of choice in these parts. He slugged back the shot, not quite realizing its potency. After getting back on his feet, he reviewed the territory. He saw a couple so enthralled with one another, he figured they couldn't be married, and were likely having an affair. He watched some young Ivy League girls who thought backpacking through Europe was an entitlement rather than a privilege. And then there was the woman in the back corner. She was tall and thin with a tight body, a total runway model, wearing a miniskirt with black leather boots up to her knees.

He pushed out the stool next to him and winked in her direction. It did not take long for her to make her way to the bar. She could not have been more than twenty-five, but behind the pale hue of her makeup, she appeared more experienced than the young women he'd seduced back home. She took the bar stool next to him and gave him the signal that his advances were welcomed. She would glance over, look him up and down, and throw her hair back.

He struck first. "Hello. My name is Sean," he said in an imitation Irish brogue.

"Jana," she said as she took his hand.

"You speak English?" he asked.

"Of course," she said, like she was almost insulted. "And you? Is that Irish?"

"You're very perceptive. I'm here on vacation. I'm thinking of staying a while. How about you? What's your story?"

"My story? I don't have a story."

"You're Russian."

"Absolutely not!" she said sharply. "I'm Lithuanian. Calling a Lithuanian a Russian is like me calling you a Brit. We hate the Russians."

"I'm sorry. I didn't mean to insult you. Let me buy you a drink. What's your poison?" he asked in an attempt to recover.

"I'll have what you just had. Absinthe."

"I gotta tell you, it's pretty strong stuff," he told her. He ordered two shots for them.

"Let me show you how it's done," she said. "Take a spoon of sugar and light it on fire, then drop it into the absinth. *Na zdravi*," she said as she threw back the shot. "That's 'cheers' in Czech." Donovan was surprised how easily she took the shot. It took him two sips to down the absinthe, which was far stronger than anything he had consumed before this evening, and he was no stranger to illicit substances.

"Why don't I get us some beers? What do you recommend?" he asked, realizing that she was far more experienced than he.

"Get the Pilsner. It's the best beer in the Czech Republic."

He ordered a couple of Pilsners from the bartender, who seemed to be enjoying the show. "So you were about to tell me your story," Donovan said to Jana. "How long you been here?"

She took a moment to calculate in her head and said, "Seven years. I got my degree in, what you say, social work, and then I try to get a job."

"You're a social worker?"

"No, not quite. No jobs, at least not for Lithuanians. I'm a dancer. But what about you? What's your story?" she asked, diverting attention to him. She did not want to have to explain what type of dancer she was.

"I'm retired," he replied.

"You're a little young to retire, no?"

"You flatter me. Let's just say it was in my best interest to retire early."

"So what do you want to do now?" she asked.

"I think you know what I wanna do," he told her. The effects of the alcohol had loosened his tongue. "Jana, let's cut the bullshit. There's too much talking, not enough action. I'm a man of action."

"You're very sure of yourself. What makes you think I want a man of action?"

"Because, sweetheart, you came out looking like that with your six-inch boots and short skirt, if you want to call it that, so don't tell me you're not looking for the same thing."

"Then let's go," she said with a smile. "I live around the corner."

They stood, and Donovan gave her body a quick once-over. She was about five-six, but her heels put her above him. She went to the bathroom, and Donovan motioned to the bartender for his bill.

"She's not free, you know," the bartender told Donovan, feeling it was his obligation to warn him.

"All women cost money," Donovan said as he counted out the bills to pay the tab. So what if the woman was a whore? He was no longer a mayor; he was a fugitive. He looked at himself in the mirror across the bar and laughed. He suddenly felt very good, liberated, and full of ideas. He saw her reflection and turned. "Are you ready, my dear?"

***

Back at her flat, her hooks in Donovan, they had reached the most uncomfortable part for her—the proposition, the actual sale. Jana Strakova was a professional, and before making a man too excited, she always defined the rules: €500 for an hour her client would never forget. Just no kissing.

Donovan made the first attempt to break the uncomfortable air between them. "I get the drill, honey. This is a business deal."

"You Americans and your business," she said.

Donovan was taken aback. "American? I told you I'm Irish. Hear the accent?"

"I hear it, and I'm afraid it never fooled me."

He shook his head and dropped the act. "Doesn't matter. Listen, I want you, and I'll pay, but what would it cost me if I wanted a little more?"

"What do you mean?" she replied with a coy smile.

"No, no. I don't mean anything physical. What if I wanted you exclusively? What would that cost me, say for a few weeks, here in Prague? Maybe we travel a bit."

"Why don't you go back to the bar and meet some nice girl, maybe a little older?"

"Because I want a pro who understands discretion."

"So, you pay me cash, American money, for three weeks, and

I stay with you... Call it $25,000?"

"You sure you want it in dollars, or would you prefer Euros?"

"Uncle Sam's good enough for me, G.I. Joe," she joked.

"Then it's a deal?"

"Shall we, as you say, consummate our deal?"

"I thought you'd never ask."

She actually liked this one. It was business, but there was something about this character. She had enough experience to know this man was hiding something. But then, everyone had something to hide.

"He's running."

"Who's running?"

"John Campagna's running for mayor," McNally told Henry.

"How can he be running? They don't even know where Donovan is."

"The city council's declaring the office vacant. Dolan will serve as interim mayor until the special election."

"Dolan isn't running?"

"No, he's happy just being council president. He's sixty-eight and has no ambition of getting involved in another race. It's a young man's game."

"So Campagna's going to run."

"And he wants you to manage his campaign."

"C'mon, Ray. I'm done with politics."

"Listen, your firm wants John Campagna. We haven't had a friend in City Hall in twenty years. Do you realize the money this firm makes if Campagna's mayor? Our developers, insurance companies, unions—all our clients get a piece of the action. And you, Henry, the king-maker, the guy who delivered the mayor's office..."

"Or the guy who lost the mayor's race. After losing the governor's race. Yeah, they'll call me shit-maker, not king-maker. Enticing, Ray, but—"

"Listen, Hal. Bottom line, you win this one, you make partner. You'll be the youngest partner at Warner Isikoff. I know you want to marry Lyndsay, and I know you've got something to prove. Well, Gatsby, you'll have your Daisy. You become partner at one of the most prestigious firms. Her daddy will see his little girl marrying the hottest political operative around. Her dad's old money, but he respects the Henry Mercucios of the world who go out and take it."

"I told her I was out of politics."

"Henry, my boy, you're never out of politics. Everything's politics. I don't care if you're a lawyer, a doctor, or a garbage man. You have to play the game if you want to make it. And you play it better than anyone I know."

***

McNally was not the only one who recognized Henry's talents. His future father-in-law, Reginald "Reggie" Sinclair, could see that the young man his daughter had brought home from medical school was a major leaguer, but not the type he was concerned would take advantage of his firstborn. The titan of a family fortune, Sinclair equally respected the self-made man, and he could see in Henry the spirit of a fighter grounded in humility. And he made his admiration known. The night before Henry's first bench trial, a night when Lyndsay had tried to distract him from his nerves with her attempt at homemade pasta, her father had even taken the time to put in a call to Lyndsay's apartment, not to speak with her, but to wish Henry good luck. Henry had never forgotten that kindness.

Out of respect for formality, but more for the man, a week after Donovan's offer, Henry flew down to Charlotte to see Reggie Sinclair and ask him for permission to marry his daughter. He arrived at their sprawling horse farm, where he was met at the door by Mary Sinclair, Lyndsay's mother, who immediately embraced him. She knew the reason for the visit, not that it took a sleuth to figure out— Lyndsay's boyfriend of five years was here to make the honorable request. She quickly ushered him into their formal living room where Reggie Sinclair sat with Lyndsay's ninety-something grandmother. Reggie quickly stood as Henry entered the room and embraced the young man to put him at ease.

"How's the boy?" Reggie asked, revealing the name he always used to refer to Henry.

"I'm good. Thank you, Mr. Sinclair."

"We're practically family, Henry. You can call me Reggie."

"Well, that's what I wanted to talk to you about. I'd like to call you Dad. I mean, I'd like to ask you and Mrs. Sinclair if I could have the honor of Lyndsay's hand in marriage."

Mary hugged her future son-in-law again. "Mom, Henry just asked if he could marry Lyndsay," she shouted across the room.

"I can hear you just fine," the matriarch grumbled. "You don't need to yell. Give him the ring."

Mary pulled a little velvet box from her purse. "It would mean so much to us if you could give Lyndsay this. It belonged to my mother's sister, who was very close to Lyndsay. She never had children and wanted her to have it."

"Of course! I understand its significance," Henry said, not wanting them to know he was already worried about having to scramble for a ring and was planning to ask his brother to front him the money. And he knew he could never afford anything as nice as this ring, at least three karats, he figured. A ring this nice, he knew, deserved an auspicious presentation.

***

It was Lyndsay's very same unconditional love and devotion for Henry that had consoled him in his most trying moments. Lyndsay's love had helped him through the difficult time of losing his father to lung cancer. She'd been there through the self-doubt after the McNally election. While she wasn't the first girl Henry had loved, she was definitely the first who'd loved him unconditionally.

Henry equally inspired her with his grand thoughts and grander dreams. He had a charisma about him that motivated her and brought out her best. As much as he was a dreamer, he was also a thoughtful, strategic planner. He was very much what she imagined her own father must have been like when he was Henry's age, the type of man who seizes on opportunity. Her father had built his family's sizable fortune into a sprawling empire by going after business like a Roman Legion general, carefully plotting his next move, then overwhelming his opponent with brute strength and force. He also had the finesse and skill to charm his way into any corporate boardroom or pretentious country club. Henry had the same fervent attitude, that optimistic outlook and enigmatic personality that people wanted to be around, the type of person with whom men wanted to play golf and women wanted to dance.

Lyndsay had been attracted to Henry's radiant personality from the moment he had called on her as a teaching assistant in her constitutional law class at Georgetown. He had forgotten her name, calling her Linda, but had covered his mistake so skillfully that she'd known he was a player. The player he portrayed, however, was far from the man he actually was. Lyndsay could see through his bravado and hardened exterior to his true self. He passionately believed in what he said, had strength in his convictions, and pursued goals like a marathon runner, cautiously pacing yet relentlessly persevering. Many of her friends in the class, who also painfully sat through Henry's long-winded lectures about how man had traded his rights for order, viewed Henry as an obnoxious law student who merely gave his diatribes so he could hear the melody of his own voice. But not Lyndsay; she had fallen for Henry like a schoolgirl. The fact that he was her instructor had never mattered, and before long, the budding romance had grown into a courtship. And for five years, she waited for Henry to pop the question she had been prepared to answer from the moment they met.

In that five years, she had spent much of their time together arranging her life around his. When Henry had decided to move to Providence to run some congressman's campaign for governor, she had followed him. She had looked at Dartmouth, NYU, and UNC, but listed the med-peds program at Rhode Island Hospital as her top match so she could stay with Henry. Not much of a sacrifice to attend the highly rated medical program in Providence, but she'd chosen to live in a city she did not know, away from her family and friends, and with a man who at times seemed more in love with politics than with her.

At first, her parents, especially her mother, couldn't understand why she was chasing some boy to Providence. Her family had made a fortune in the North Carolina tobacco industry that had afforded her every luxury and opportunity a young woman could want. Before Lyndsay had made her final choice on medical school, her mother had offered her input. She'd asked why her daughter would pass up home and the University of North Carolina for a boy, a Yankee, to boot. What was so special about this Henry? Lyndsay's answer, quite unequivocally, was love. This was no lie or flight of fancy, Mrs.

Sinclair had realized, for what else could explain it? Henry wasn't nearly as handsome as some of the fine Southern gentlemen her daughter had dated. While Lyndsay had met many worthy admirers from the South's elite families, none of their overly inflated egos could match the authenticity of the man Henry was.

Even though the Sinclairs certainly wouldn't hold it against him, the boy was poor by their standards. He had no trust fund and had worked his way through law school by moonlighting for some congressman they'd never heard of. Henry couldn't provide the life they felt their daughter was entitled to, or so Mrs. Sinclair feared. But it was Lyndsay's father who seemed to most appreciate his daughter's future husband. To him, Henry was his type of man—a go-getter who wouldn't watch life pass him by, but would seize on opportunities, like he had once. And Sinclair understood Henry's past, knew the type of man he was from what he had already done. Henry had earned his respect.

The Sinclair family was an institution in the South, with its roots reaching back to Scottish nobility. This was no surprise to those who knew the patriarch since he carried himself with the chivalry of an ancient knight. As a young man, Sinclair had inherited a controlling interest in one of the largest tobacco companies in North Carolina. He could have sat back, remaining content to manage his family's fortune, but that wasn't his style. He had the foresight to understand that tobacco's free reign wouldn't last forever. He diversified the family company into other enterprises from dairy to coffee to textiles to real estate. So when the government regulations set in and the class-action lawsuits ravaged the industry, the Sinclair family fortune wasn't only preserved, it was thriving. He saw in Henry the same determination and perseverance that had driven him to overwhelming corporate success. Henry was the type of man who made things happen.

***

To compensate for what Henry perceived as his own short-comings, he constantly sought to impress Lyndsay. That's what he thought a woman like her needed. There had to be something else that would attract her to a guy like him. Success—that's what it was. If she believed he was successful or that he had the elements of success, that would attract her. But Lyndsay Sinclair was not an achievement, not another victory, nor a million-dollar deal; she was a person with feelings who wanted more than anything to understand the man she hoped to marry. She had never wanted pomp and ceremony. She just needed him, all of him—the true Henry.

There was no better example of his need to impress her than what he'd done to woo her in the first place. From the moment he'd met Lyndsay in that first class, he'd been unable to keep his eyes off her. He hoped to impress her with the fact that he was a law student and that he served as a political consultant up on the Hill. He figured a woman like her wouldn't want to be going with beer-guzzling undergrads whose idea of romance was how quickly they could get into her pants. No, a girl like her wanted a guy like him, a dreamer who could make dreams reality. It took him until the end of the semester before he finally mustered enough nerve to ask her out. Even then, it was a veiled invitation, asking her if she wanted to get a cup of coffee to talk about her paper. The next time, it had been a political fundraiser on the Hill where he'd introduced her to what he'd thought were important people, followed by a third date at the movies to see a John Grisham film. After three dates that could be construed as "just friends," he'd asked Lyndsay out on a real date—dinner in Old Town, Alexandria.

Their first month of dating had coincided with final exams. Henry needed something big, something she could tell all her friends back home. He had heard all the stories about her being the heiress of some tobacco fortune, so to nab a girl like that, he needed a first strike weapon to eliminate all other suitors, leaving him the only man standing. It took airplane tickets, a Broadway show, and about $1,500 he'd borrowed from his older brother, a doctor, to close the deal. In something she would tell her friends and family until they were so familiar with the story they were beginning to tell it themselves, Henry had put together the date to end all dates. All he'd said to her prior to the limousine picking her up was to wear something black, something nice. A limo had taken them to Reagan Airport. The second leg of their trip had involved the Delta shuttle to New York. Another limousine had taken them to Broadway, where they'd seen *Hamilton*. After the show and dinner at Sardis, they'd flown home. The date was the closer; but it was what he hadn't done that had sealed it for Lyndsay. He'd kissed her goodnight and had not tried to sleep with her, though she'd been more than willing. She was a keeper, something he made ever so clear, someone who was worth everything he could provide. It was the seminal event in their relationship, setting the tone for their time to follow. He would do anything, use every contact, call in every favor, pursue any lead, to win the girl of his dreams. She was that girl, the focal point of all his attention and love, and he had her.

***

Now, after five years enjoying a happy relationship, tonight was the night. Henry took Lyndsay to the same place he'd taken her their first night in Providence—Camille's, the number one destination for anniversaries, proposals, and other milestones. It was a special night. Henry could never quite place it, could never explain or rationalize it, but there was something about Lyndsay Sinclair.

Maybe it was the way she greeted everyone she knew with a hug and a kiss like she had known them all her life. Or maybe it was the fact that Henry couldn't recall whether she had ever spoken ill about anyone. Certainly there were prettier women. Certainly there were smarter, nicer, thinner, taller women, but none were Lyndsay, and none of them loved Henry. Perhaps that was it—he'd fallen in love with the way she loved him.

"Remember the first time we ate here?" Henry asked Lyndsay, who was wearing a blue dress. It wasn't every day that her workaholic boyfriend asked her to have dinner at the very same place they'd had their first dinner in Providence. Henry seemed a bit more on edge, the type of anxiety he rarely wore on his sleeve. He was always a rock, but lately he had seemed preoccupied. Her brain trust consisting of her mother, sister, cousin, best friend, and maternal aunt all felt Henry was ready to ask the big question.

Lyndsay caressed Henry's hand, her gentle touch putting him at ease. "I remember all of them, Henry."

"There's so much I want to tell you. So many things I've held back for the right time. You'll be done with your residency next year. I know they have that great pediatrics fellowship at Dartmouth, and I don't want to be the one who holds you back."

"Henry, I want to be with you."

"There are some things I need to say to you. Things I've never told you about my past."

"I don't care about the past, Henry. We have a future together."

"You know I told you who I'm named after, my dad's favorite Shakespearean character, Henry V. His dad was a usurper, so he set out to conquer France to establish his legitimacy. He explains to his future wife, Catherine, the French princess, that his father was involved in civil wars when he had him, so he was born with an iron side, and when it comes to wooing ladies, he sometimes frightens them."

"Henry, this is about me and you, not our parents, not our pasts," she said.

The interruption did not sidetrack Henry from his carefully rehearsed speech. "Many sons, all their lives, try to redeem themselves. My dad was involved in his own civil war when he had me. That's why I was born with my own iron side. Because I'm so determined to make something of myself, I sometimes have the blinders on and forget about everything else. But that's who I am. You're getting me at my worst, but I'm only going to get better."

"What do you mean you're at your worst?"

"Please let me continue," he said with a tender smile. He knew this story must be torture for her. She must be sensing the impending question.

"I'm sorry. You were talking about King Henry and how he took over France."

"Thank you," Henry said. "So after he wins France, he sets his eyes on the French princess. It's the most beautiful language in all of Shakespeare. He asks Kate to take a man of plain and uncoined constancy. He goes on to explain that guys who can speak their way into women's hearts can often reason themselves out again. He tells her that a man's hair grows thin, his beard grows white, how his back will stoop, how his face will wither. He then says, 'but a good heart is like the sun and the moon, or rather the sun and not the moon, for it shines bright and never changes, but keeps his course truly.'"

"That's beautiful."

Henry could see her eyes were watering. "I'm not the most handsome guy, my hair's thinning, I'm not rich, I'm ten pounds over-weight, and I have something to prove. I don't have a lot of money. In fact, I owe more than I have. But I think—well, I know—I'm a good man and would make a good husband. The only thing I have to offer you is my heart. Will you take my heart? Will you marry me?"

What had started out as a trickle became a gush, and by the time his words were through, Lyndsay was in tears. "Yes, I'll marry you, Henry! Because you're the most beautiful man I've ever met!"

He reached across the table to kiss her.

"In the middle of the restaurant?" Lyndsay asked.

"Nice customs curtsy to great kings," he said, leaning over the table, taking her in his hands, and kissing her.

At that moment, the entire restaurant erupted in applause.

The next morning, Henry was in his office at 7 a.m., reviewing his cases when his phone rang. It was McNally, who asked him to meet for breakfast at the new Omni downtown. By 8 a.m., he was sitting across the table from Councilman Campagna as former Congressman McNally brokered the deal.

"The firm will allow Henry to take a paid leave to manage your campaign. Your campaign pays him an additional $25,000—that's paid over the three-month special election. If you win, your campaign pays Henry a win bonus of $25,000 to be paid over the following year—not exactly Kosher, but he just got engaged and could use the cash."

"I don't have a problem with that," Campagna replied.

"We want good government. The firm's interest is to see strong, new leadership in City Hall. We respectfully ask that you allow our clients to bid on city contracts."

"Your firm represents some of the best companies in the state. I don't think that'd be a problem."

"Henry runs the show. He calls the shots. He consults with you, but you're the candidate, and he's the pro. If you do what he says, you'll win. If I had listened to him, I'd still be in Congress, probably the number two or three Democrat in the House."

"Henry's reputation precedes him, Congressman. I already know he's the best there is."

"May I say something?" Henry asked. "This is a dirty business. If you simply feel the need to improve the community, it's a better idea to run a non-profit or start a charity. Before you give up three months of your life, put yourself on the line, watch your children cry when they hear their daddy called bad names, think this one through. Is this what you really want?"

"Henry," Campagna said, "my father taught his kids that the highest honor was serving your fellow man. Maybe I'm a bit naïve to think I can change things, but to just sit back and do nothing? That's worse."

"Fair enough," Henry said, offering his hand. "You have a campaign manager, Councilman."

"Mr. Mercucio, you have a candidate," Campagna said, taking it.

"We've got three months to pull this off," Henry said. "That's not a lot of time, so we have to move fast. We need to get your message down solid and get opposition research done on both you and your opponents."

"See? I told you he'd take care of everything," McNally inter-jected. "Henry's at his best when he's in the game."

"Whatever you need," Campagna told Henry.

"You're mine for the next three months. You're not a husband, you're not a father, not a lawyer, not a councilman. You're a candidate. I know that sounds brutal, but you need that type of commitment to win. Are you prepared to sacrifice your entire life for

THE KING-MAKERS OF PROVIDENCE 67

this?"

"I am. I've talked to my wife. She's surprisingly excited. And my kids, well, I told them Daddy wouldn't be around to take them to soccer and dance. They're good kids. They understand."

"Then let's get started."

***

The first task Henry gave himself was to commission a benchmark poll to test positions and voter attitudes. The sixty-five-question poll offered invaluable insights into how the campaign would be waged, as well as an understanding of the level of voter apathy toward the current political situation. Of the 500 likely voters who had completed the survey, nearly two-thirds believed "things were heading in the wrong direction." When asked who was to blame for the current crisis in Providence, three-quarters listed former Mayor Donovan, who had yet to turn up during his vacation from federal authorities. A significant majority of 62 percent listed fiscal accountability as their number one concern, followed by quality education and lower property taxes. As to what quality they looked for in a mayor, more than 80 percent reported "honesty and integrity," with "experience and vision" coming in a distant second at 10 percent. Henry also examined a general feeling he was sensing on the street. He had the pollster ask, "Would you be less likely to support a candidate who engaged in negative campaigning?" Seventy-nine percent said yes, leaving Henry with the impression that in the current climate, people wanted an honest dialogue without the mudslinging. Henry also tested the profiles of the potential candidates:

Candidate A is a city councilman who has dedicated much of

his professional life to Providence. He refuses to engage in negative campaigning and instead focuses on the issues important to Providence. He supports improving education by holding schools and teachers accountable, helping senior citizens by repealing property taxes on their automobiles, and improving public safety by hiring more police officers and firefighters.

Candidate B is a retired business executive who has never held public office but has extensive experience in the private sector in running a major corporation. He believes it is important to point out his opponent's weaknesses in television and radio ads. He supports cutting property taxes, reducing social programs, and offering school vouchers for parochial and private schools.

Would you be more likely to vote for Candidate A or Candidate B?

"Candidate A" soundly defeated "Candidate B" by a two-to-one margin. The head-to-head question that pitted Councilman John Campagna against businessman Malcolm Prescott was less decisive. Campagna held a five-point lead over Prescott, 37 percent to 32 percent, with 31 percent undecided. Henry saw from the numbers that negative campaigning would backfire in the current state of pessimism and that cutting taxes was not the answer the voters were seeking. He could see that people wanted honesty and integrity and were willing to pay a premium for that type of government.

Armed with his data, Henry began crafting the Campagna platform. He unveiled his scripted message in McNally's office. In addition to his candidate, State Representative Paul Campagna (John's brother), campaign chairman Felix Salaso, and McNally were also in attendance.

"Councilman, I'm going to speak very frankly, probably more frankly than anyone has ever spoken to you, so I just want you to know that before I start."

"I have too many people telling me what I want to hear, Mr. Mercucio, so I welcome the truth," Campagna said.

"Ninety percent of everything you know about politics is wrong. You think you have to leave here and spend every day and night greeting as many people as possible. In the next three months, you can't possibly shake hands with the sixty thousand voters you need to win this thing." Henry had deduced that 62,251 was the winning number in the special election. Providence's total population was 180,000, of which about 60 percent were registered voters. Voter turnout during a presidential election could run as high as 65 percent, but a special election only garnered about a 50 percent turnout. People simply did not bother to come out unless they were electing their president. However, the mayor's position was important, so still half the eligible voters were expected to come out.

"So what do you want him to do, hide out in this ivory tower?" Salaso asked, referring back to Henry's claim that they knew nothing about politics, something he refused to accept as a man who had been on the front lines for thirty years.

"No, Mr. Salaso, but I don't want to burn him out by going to every little event. Sure, he has to be out there. But shaking hands is not going to win this. The message we put out through TV, social media, and direct mail will."

Salaso nodded his head, realizing that when it came to running campaigns, the kid before him was supposed to be the best.

"You're not going to win this election because you're the best candidate or because you've identified the best issues," Henry lectured. "You're going to win this election because we're developing the better message, and we're spending all our resources delivering it to the people who vote. I'm here because I know how to develop and deliver the winning message. So what's your message, Councilman? Why should you be mayor?"

"It's time for a change! It's time for the little guy to have a voice! It's time to return City Hall back to the people," Campagna fired back with determination in his voice.

"Not bad. It's time for a change," Henry pondered aloud. "We have a building boom in town. Mayor Donovan could waltz back in here and win reelection even though he's one of the FBI's most wanted. But you say it's time for a change. No one wants change. Change sounds good, even exciting, but people fear it. You want to know why? They're worried they may actually have to do something. No, they don't want change. They want comfort that their kids may actually learn something in school, that they won't be robbed when they go downtown, that their trash will be picked up every Thursday like it has for the past forty years."

"Then, Mr. Mercucio, what is our message?" Campagna asked.

"I'm going to show you."

Henry began his PowerPoint presentation. The screen was divided into four categories: "Campagna on Campagna"; "Campagna on Opponents"; "Opponents on Opponents"; "Opponents on Campagna."

"This is called the Leesburg grid," Henry said. "We're going to analyze our strengths and weaknesses. So we've got 'Campagna on Campagna': What does John Campagna say about himself?" The question lingered in the air. "Well, what do we say about our candidate?"

Salaso had bought into Henry's strategy and answered first. "John Campagna is a good man, an honest man, who will restore integrity to City Hall."

"Okay, so we have honesty, integrity, and trust," Henry spoke softly to his assistant who typed words into the graphic from behind the conference table. "What else? Councilman, what have you been doing on the city council for the last ten years?"

"I sponsored legislation that created an enterprise zone in Providence. It's resulted in new jobs throughout the city."

"So you're a visionary. You've created opportunity that has translated into new jobs." He then turned back to his assistant and said, "New Vision for Providence. We've got 'Honesty, Integrity, & Trust' with a 'New Vision for Providence.' Anything else?"

"Yeah, how about the fact that John's always been there for the working guy and the unions?" Salaso offered. "His dad was a union guy all his life. That's gotta be good for something." He had no idea that Henry had already formulated the message.

"We've got a guy who has honesty, integrity, and trust. He has a new vision for Providence, and he's a working man who's working for working people. Good. Now, what do our opponents say about Campagna? And since no one has announced yet, let's go with the most likely: Malcolm Prescott, Representative Pagalini, and Senator Clark."

"Prescott's going to say I'm a dirty mafioso who wants to rip off the city. He'll try to link me to the corruption," Campagna said.

"So they'll say you're on the take," Henry shot back, then nodded to his assistant to put it on the screen.

"You've never taken a dime from Donovan! You had to work with him. He's the goddamned mayor," Salaso said.

Rather than engage, Henry attempted to keep everyone focused. "What else will they say?"

"They'll say me and my brother have a dynasty in Providence, and that we're only there because of our father," Rep. Campagna added.

"Add 'dynasty' to the list," he said to his assistant. "We've got a candidate on the take, who's only there because of his dad, and he's managed to create a dynasty with his little brother. That's what our opponents will say about us. Fair enough. So what do we say about them?"

"Prescott's a rich blue-blood who has nothing better to do, so he runs for mayor," Salaso editorialized.

"So we have a rich guy who's out of touch. Good. What else?"

"Representative Pagalini is a womanizer. That might not matter to us, but there's a lot of people out there who won't vote for a guy like that," Campagna admitted.

"And Senator Clark might be this bright liberal woman from the East Side, but that won't play out in this city. Maybe in the East Side, but not on the South Side or The Hill," Rep. Campagna said.

"I know Senator Clark," Henry said. "She's a good lady, but she's got no shot. Moderate to conservative women do okay in mayorals. But liberal women, that's another story. They get elected as legislators because they're perceived as sympathetic, but not as chief executives, because some people view them as not tough enough. That's not my opinion. I know some liberal women who would make great mayors—it's just the reality of it. So what do we say about our opponents? We've got a guy who's out of touch and two others who are not mayoral caliber. But what do our opponents say about themselves?"

"Prescott thinks he's the second coming of Christ. He believes he has some sort of mandate. I don't know where he gets it from, but he's a legend in his own mind," Salaso said.

"We can use that against him," Henry told Campagna. "Hubris is a man's greatest enemy. It blinds him, prevents him from seeing the truth. Mr. Prescott's excessive pride will be his undoing. What about Pagalini and Clark? What's their story?"

Salaso quickly responded. "Pagalini's a self-righteous prick.

He thinks because he's progressive, he's 'Mr. Sensitivity,' 'Mr. Fucking Nice Guy.' But as soon as you turn your back, he'd screw you over."

"If he's such a prick, how's he also a nice guy?"

Campagna couldn't resist explaining why a lot of the old-timers, Salaso certainly being one of them, despised Pagalini. "Henry, this guy Pagalini will sweet talk you to your face but turn on you for a better deal. Sure, that's politics, but there's also something called a man's word."

"Okay. I get it. Pagalini's a snake and can't be trusted. What about Senator Clark?"

"She's one of those limousine liberals who's never worked. Her daddy owned enough property to buy her way into politics. So she can afford to be liberal. She doesn't know what it's like to go out and earn a paycheck, you know? To decide which bills you pay this month," Campagna stated.

"But how does she define herself?"

"Oh, she thinks she's Hillary Clinton. She wants to be the first female governor and thinks her path goes right through City Hall," Salaso said.

"But she's got a lot of money," Campagna acknowledged.

"And that's her problem," Henry realized. The bright senator's wealth could also be used against her. She simply could not understand the plight of the working man.

"Here's how it works," Henry said as he drew a big circle in blue marker on the large canvas next to the PowerPoint monitor. "This is the outer circle. In here we'll put 'Donovan Crony,' 'Political Dynasty,' 'Family on the Public Dole,' and 'Voting Record' because I'm sure they'll dig up stuff. All this goes in the cold area." He then drew a red circle and said, "This is the warm area. We put in 'Dedicated Public Servant,' 'Vision for Providence,' 'Working Man,' and 'Impeccable Record.' Then we've got our core message: honesty, integrity, and trust," he said, drawing a circle around the words. "Here's how it works. When they go after you for the dynasty," he said, pointing to the word, "we counter with, 'I am proud that my family has been dedicated to public service.' When they call you a Donovan crony, you say, 'I'm proud of my record and how we've built our city.' When they say you've been on the public dole, again you say, 'I've dedicated my life to this city. For the last ten years, I've had the privilege of serving on the city council.'

"So, then, we've got our message. Honesty, Integrity, and Trust: A Worker for the Working Man. Here's why it works. Your main opponent, Prescott, is an arrogant SOB who knows little about government. At the same time, we'll build you up as the man with integrity, whom you can trust, the honest working guy who will be there for working families. We inoculate you with your integrity to ward off accusations against corruption. 'A Worker for the Working Man,' that's our slogan. 'Honesty, Integrity, and Trust' is our message. These words will be included in every press release, public statement, and TV ad."

***

In his announcement speech, Campagna spoke about wanting to restore honesty, integrity, and trust to City Hall. He referred to himself as a working man and pointed to his experience on the city council as the reason he was best positioned to effectively run the city. Campagna's announcement was backed up with an introductory television spot featuring the candidate sitting with his wife, son, and daughter on their front porch with him saying, "The reason I'm running for mayor is for John, Jr., and Gina." Henry also mailed to all registered Democrats and Independents in Providence what he called "the portrait piece"—a picture of Campagna's family with the tag line, "For working families." The timing of the announcement was also carefully calculated. Henry had received word that the university was conducting a public opinion poll in two weeks. He planned the announcement so he could spike the poll numbers. It was all a grand show produced by the shrewdest of directors.

A prince should be a fox, to know the traps and snares,
and a lion, to be able to frighten the wolves;
for those who simply hold to the nature of the lion
do not understand their business.

—Niccolò Machiavelli

"Did you hear who's running Campagna's campaign?" asked Gordie Beako, Senior Vice President of CampCo Construction.

"I saw. Henry Mercucio," said Paul Martin, CampCo's chief legal counsel.

"Remember when I worked with him at McNally's? If he hadn't blown our wad on direct mail and had put it all on TV like I'd told him, we would've won. He thinks he knows everything."

"Why do you care?" Martin asked.

"Those pricks at Warner Isikoff, and you know McNally's behind this, they think they can take what we've got. You know

McNally set that whole thing up with his boy from the FBI. The mayor's screwed, and if we don't protect our interests, we lose. We need City Hall. Whatever it takes."

"Gordie, I just don't know if this is the right time to go after McNally and his golden boy."

"If we don't stop him now, what could he become?"

"Then we have to find our own candidate, and we need to bring in a pro."

"I'll do it," Beako told him.

"You're gonna run for mayor?"

"No, shithead. Me and that guy over at D&D, Nick Dean, we know how to get to Henry."

"What have you got against this kid, anyway?" Martin questioned.

"He goes around telling everyone I fucked up McNally's campaign."

"That was four years ago, and look at McNally now. He makes four times as much as he made in Congress," Martin reminded him. "Henry's gotta make six figures plus. I just don't get it."

"Paulie, I appreciate the advice, but either follow me or get the fuck out of my way."

"I'm with you, Gordie, but I'm telling you, this isn't right."

"Right or wrong, please. You're not that naïve. We're not in the 'right' business. We're in the 'creating opportunities' business. We've got this kid, and he's a threat."

"How does he possibly threaten us?"

"If John Campagna's elected mayor, he'll come in on his high horse and take it all. But I know a thing or two about who Henry really is."

***

While Henry cherished the belief that he was some sort of born-again Terracotta warrior, he was more like a fallen angel. For Henry, his awakening had come on the streets of Las Vegas.

"You know when they say, 'What happens in Vegas stays in Vegas?' Yeah, I lived that," he had told Lyndsay a year after they'd started dating. If she was really the one, then she had to know about his darkest hour. Henry had flown out to Vegas for spring break in his last semester of law school. Through McNally, he had met lobbyists from one of the larger casino interests and had taken them up on their offer to put him up in their posh hotel. And so had begun Henry's spiral into darkness.

It had all started quite innocently with Henry catching up with some of his other law school friends who had been staying down the strip from him. In fact, if it hadn't been for his buddies Kevin and Brian, he might have still been walking the streets. His two pals had flipped a coin to see who would be going to Vegas to bring Henry back. And like many of the best Vegas stories, this one involved a mysterious woman. All of his friends who knew about Henry's Vegas transformation agreed that it had been one of the best stories on the strip.

The vivid memory of walking down the strip without a shirt or shoes, completely out of his mind, was seared into his subconscious. Henry even thought he'd heard the voice of his brother call his name, but he attributed it to some sort of hallucination. Henry's missing week had been analyzed by psychiatrists, therapists, priests, and his family. Often his own best psychotherapist, Henry deduced he'd suffered some sort of psychotic break, alcohol psychosis, or even worse, intentional self-sabotage. He faintly remembered sitting outside some fast-food restaurant on the strip, his feet blistered, his face sunburned, and some kind soul handing him a pair of socks. He didn't remember how he'd gotten in touch with his lobbyist friends, but somehow, they had tracked him down and had taken him to the hospital. But instead of improving, Henry had grown wilder, spouting out conspiracy theories. The emergency room nurse had told him to quiet down or be restrained, and finally, they'd put him into a room. Believing that his roommate was being poisoned, Henry had tried to take the intravenous lines out of his arms. When nurses and doctors had surrounded him, he'd decided to check himself out of the hospital against the recommendations of medical personnel and had returned to the street.

Somewhere in Vegas, Henry had finally succumbed to his aching feet and had thought hitting an Asian spa might be the right remedy. He'd walked in and asked for a pedicure, a logical solution for his current predicament. The ladies had endured his two-day streetwalking fragrance and had taken pity on him, allowing him to soak his feet. But when it came to payment, Henry had been penniless. They'd called the police on this vagrant, and soon, Vegas blue had arrived. They'd patted down Henry like a common thug, and after discovering he was weapon-free, the officers had asked him if he knew anyone he could call. He had implored the officer to call the government relations team of the casino where he was staying, and before long, Henry had been rescued again. They'd paid off the spa owner and had taken Henry directly to the airport, walking him to his gate like the Secret Service, so their protected asset could not escape.

The only thing Henry remembered about his plane ride was the flight attendant apologizing to the couple next to him for his odor. Upon landing, Henry had seen a kind face in the airport—his mother. He was unaware that his parents, along with Kevin and Brian, had been working with the lobbyists in Vegas to get him on a plane back home. His father had even wanted him arrested so that they could finally get ahold of him, while his mother had feared him lost for good. There had been no arrest, only unanswered questions, like who was the girl from the casino he'd been involved with before everything had gone dark?

Henry had left the confines of his high-class casino and hotel to see the other side of Vegas. He'd found himself in a carnival-like atmosphere, and like so many young men, he'd been enthralled by the pretty barmaid in a short plaid skirt and white button-down blouse. She'd offered to show him around, and he'd quickly agreed. Through blurred memories, Henry can still recall taking shots in the hotel's top club, his female escort telling him that they were in the roped-off area that required a $1,000 minimum. Out of his mind, Henry had even accused her of being a Mossad spy, since he'd figured she must somehow be involved with his lobbyist friends, whose boss was one of the greatest benefactors to the Israeli government.

"You gotta chill," the barmaid's thuggish friend had told Henry, and that's all he remembered. But the scar of Vegas would follow him. Had he been drugged as some suspected? Or had he partied his brains out, as his lobbyist friends opined? Or had it been a psychotic break, like one psychiatrist had diagnosed? It would remain one of Henry's great mysteries, but if anything good came from it, then being scared straight had ignited a new fire in him.

As a special dose of reality, when he'd returned to Washington, Henry was reminded just how unforgiving his world could be. His lobbyist friends had called to inform him that they'd received a call from someone back home.

"Henry Mercucio doesn't know what he's doing. If you want to build a casino in Providence, you've got to go through me," Beako had said.

10

Summoned first thing in the morning to McNally's corner office, Henry could only wonder what the congressman had in store. While McNally had enough work—if that was what backroom deals were called these days—he always seemed to inject himself back into Henry's life. He appreciated all McNally had done for him—the opportunities, the fatherly advice, his commitment to him. However, Henry had now earned his passage into the real world, and he needed McNally to set him free.

McNally's gregarious laugh pervaded the partners' hallway, and Henry understood from his years with the congressman that he was entertaining someone of importance. Henry stood in the doorway with a look of bewilderment.

"Come on in, Henry, and say hello to Senator Clark."

"Congressman, I know the senator. I helped her draft the legislation to protect mothers who abandon their newborns at fire stations. It's nice to see you again, Senator," Henry said as he kissed the fifty-two-year-old state senator on the cheek. She had high cheekbones and a soft complexion, but it was her compassion that attracted Henry—helping poor women and abused children. Henry was a student of *realpolitik*, and while he applauded the state senator for her compassionate liberal views, he understood she had no shot of getting elected as the chief executive of Providence.

"Henry, Senator Clark is our newest senior associate." McNally turned his attention back to her. "Since Henry is off playing politics, we really need a top-shelf senior associate to pick up his slack. You should like Henry's clients. They're the ones no one wants here. But that's our Henry, the great crusader."

"Congressman, I've followed Henry's career quite closely."

"First off, Sarah, in this office, call me Ray. There's no need for that type of formality."

"If I may say something," Henry said. "Sarah, I can bring you up to speed on all the clients. There's a few I know you'll like. And I'm really happy we'll be working together again," Henry was relieved that he wouldn't have to destroy her in the primary.

"See, Ray? Henry's a sweet prince, and I can say that to him because I'm old enough to be his mother."

"You should meet his fiancée. She's a real princess. Now, if you wouldn't mind excusing us, I need to talk to Henry."

"Can I ask you, Senator, why you had the change of heart in running for mayor?" Henry said.

"I just didn't think it was the right time for me to run. I didn't look forward to going up against you, Henry," the state senator admitted.

"I can't say I'm disappointed to hear that you've dropped out. Does that mean we can expect your support?"

"Senator Clark has assured me she'll do whatever it takes to get Councilman Campagna elected," McNally was quick to add.

"That's right," she said. "Anything." Henry wondered what

kind of deal had been struck.

"I'd really like to get a list of your supporters. Maybe we could send a letter of support to your district. A picture of you and Campagna together?"

She looked at McNally before she answered. This wasn't part of the deal. She had told McNally she'd offer tacit support, but nothing direct like a mailer. Campagna's position on abortion had alienated her and many of the liberal members of their party. She had already felt she was betraying her supporters by bowing out of the race, but it was sacrilegious to support a candidate who was against the right of a woman to choose.

"I think we can work something out," McNally interjected, throwing a reassuring look her way. "Well, you have a lot of work ahead of you. If you need anything, just give me or my secretary a call."

"Thank you, Congressman. Henry," she said as she walked out of McNally's office.

"As you can see, Henry, I've been busy. I'm sure you've already heard that the Council President has withdrawn. I think it has something to do with that unfortunate drug bust for dealing marijuana when he was nineteen. Too bad it was leaked to the papers. We can't have a destructive primary and allow the Republicans to waltz in. We've got enough to worry about. Looks like Prescott's definitely in, and your buddy Beako is running the show," McNally explained. He knew which buttons to push, and by bringing up Beako, Henry's self-described arch-nemesis, he knew he could deflect attention away from his behind-the-scenes maneuvering.

"What was that all about?" Henry asked.

"What?"

"Senator Clark. She turned white when I asked her if she'd do a letter to her constituents."

"Ah, don't worry about it. Her ego's a little bruised that she's not running. She'll come around."

"I would have appreciated being in the loop on this one. I'm running this campaign, and I can't be looking over my shoulder every minute, wondering what you're up to. I never wanted to do this in the first place."

"Okay, Henry. Listen, it's not about me or you, it's about getting Campagna elected. Keep your eye on the ball here. I've cleared the field. Now all you have to deal with is Pagalini."

"Clark's a good lady, and Pagalini's a pretty decent guy. I'm not going to fuck up their lives."

"C'mon, Henry. Clark's father called me and asked me to do him a favor. He didn't want his only daughter destroyed, or his grandsons knowing what their mother was doing in the state house parking lot when she was twenty-five and a freshman senator. Look, this is the big time, and it calls for real players. You're one of them. Politics today, it's business. Let's not forget that. A guy like Campagna, whose shit really doesn't stink, is the guy we need. He'll clean up this goddamned cesspool of a city. So get off your high horse and get back to winning this thing. Not for me, not for you, not even for Campagna, but for Providence."

The hardest thing for Henry was accepting that McNally was right, at least in this case. He knew from the polling that Clark had no chance of winning. She was formidable in a primary because her supporters came out to vote, but she would not fare well in a general election. Her candidacy ensured a Republican victory. No matter how many people answered in the polls that they would vote for a woman for mayor, in reality, when they were alone in the booth, they still were reluctant to pull the lever for a liberal woman. Henry hoped for the day when that was no longer true. He believed women were less corruptible, had not been victimized by the 2,000-year-old political conundrum that transformed honest, forthright men into conniving, maniacal beasts. Henry believed the old adage held true: power corrupts; absolute power corrupts absolutely.

What had turned Henry so cynical at such a young age? At thirty-two, he already had a bleak outlook about the political system. Perhaps it was the fact that he had been around politics for much of his adult life. It was the only thing he had grown up with, the only life he really knew. He had the law, but its pragmatism provided little enlightenment. The interminable line of one politician after another, most believing that a good position only came from what polled high each day, had jaded his outlook. He needed someone who was real, who really wanted to serve the people, not for personal gain, but for the betterment of the community. He saw that in Campagna. He was one of those true elected leaders whose idea of service wasn't based on what he could gain, but on how he could improve the lives of average people. Campagna was refreshing, someone who believed in what he said, who wasn't a product of the media-driven world of sound bites, but a dedicated public servant who fearlessly said what he really felt.

Henry saw himself as the one who could deliver Campagna to the Promised Land. Though he would never run for elected office himself, Henry had no problem spouting advice on how to acquire it. It was an interesting dichotomy, the world in which political consultants lived. While by nature they were engulfed in the political process, they operated behind the scenes. Men like Henry believed it was downright crazy to subject themselves to the public scrutiny and personal ridicule for a job that people regarded no higher than a televangelist. Not to mention that at the city level the pay was laughable and the perks weren't worth the torment. He wondered why people like Campagna gravitated toward politics. Henry liked to think that there were still a few who actually believed in the tenets of public service.

11

"What are you doing today?" Campagna asked Henry. Knowing that his political consultant would be in the office, he had called him at 7 a.m. sharp.

"Trying to win this race for you," Henry chided.

"I want you to come with me today."

"I don't do retail, Councilman. Remember what I told you. You can't possibly reach as many people shaking hands and kissing babies as I can with TV and digital. So let me concentrate on getting your message out."

"Henry, you're so cynical. Politics is more than your clever ads. Spending some time with the people will do you some good. I'll see you at the Silver Lake office at eight-thirty," Campagna said before hanging up the phone, not giving Henry the opportunity to respond.

***

Henry drove through the city to Campagna's neighborhood on

the West side of the city. Plainfield Pike was the main thoroughfare, and over the last several years, restaurants and coffee shops had sprouted up, making this former street of job-shops and vacant storefronts the latest example of the Providence revival. For the last fifteen years, the Campagna family had rented a small storefront and used it as the Ward 7 Democratic headquarters. It was an anachronism of a bygone era in which ward bosses and precinct captains had earned votes by distributing jobs and favors from City Hall. After federal, state, and local governments began providing social security and other services, the welfare system administered by the ward bosses had given way to governmental progress. But 724 Plainfield Pike still stood as a haven for the downtrodden, a gentler face of the political machine.

Campagna was holding court as his father had done years before him. Henry walked into the forty-square-foot room to find at least ten people waiting on metal chairs to see their patron, Councilman John Campagna. He was in a makeshift office, sitting at the same table his father had once used to meet people in his kitchen.

"Come on in, Henry. Have a seat. This is Mrs. McLusky. Her husband worked with my father down at Public Works." Henry shook the frail hand of the octogenarian who was dressed in her Sunday best. Campagna turned back to the widow and explained, "Your husband and my father were great friends. Before my father got sick, your husband gave him some money. Asked him to put it aside for you in case something happened to him."

"My husband didn't have an extra dime to give to nobody," the modest widow said. "You and I both know anything he had, he lost at the track."

"You underestimate your husband. He gave my father the money so he wouldn't spend it at the track. I want you to take it. It's yours," Campagna said as he handed the widow an envelope with $5,000 in cash.

"I don't believe you, but bless you," she said as she reluctantly took the money. She did not want the money, knowing full well it was charity. But her social security barely covered her food and heat. She needed it.

As she exited the office, Henry asked Campagna, "He never gave your father the money?"

Campagna revealed the truth with a wink. The councilman then walked out of the office to greet his next appointment. Campagna received a woman in her late forties accompanied by a young man who made it abundantly clear he did not want to be there. The woman was meticulously made-up, thick mascara, deep red lipstick, and fake red nails a half-inch long. She wore a gold cross around her neck and several gold bracelets on her wrists. The young man was less formal, wearing a tight white shirt revealing a barbed wire tattoo across his bicep.

"What can I do for you, Mrs. Analdo?" Campagna asked.

She took her seat on a metal folding chair and told her story. She was disappointed in a son who had lost his job, a position which had been procured by the Campagna family. It was a tale of alcohol, drugs, and other dubious behavior. The perpetrator sat in silence as his mother cried and said, "I'm just glad his father isn't alive to see this." Paul Analdo had been a precinct captain and had fallen victim to pancreatic cancer at forty-nine.

Campagna turned to the young man, whom he had sponsored at his Confirmation a decade ago, and asked him, "What's going on, Tommy?"

The young man looked away.

"You speak to Councilman Campagna when he talks to you," his mother shouted. She then began to cry.

"Mrs. Analdo, why don't you give me a few minutes with Tommy, here? You too, Henry."

Henry escorted the despondent woman out of the office and into the waiting area. A few elderly women were drinking coffee, gossiping, and putting labels on envelopes. Henry was in one of those awkward positions of not knowing what to do, so he asked Mrs. Analdo if he could get her anything. She politely refused and thanked the young man she noticed wasn't much older than her son. He appeared far more successful, a man who obviously had earned Campagna's trust. Little did she know that while Henry may have been afforded all the privileges her son had shunned—college, graduate school, and a good career—he, too, could squander his talents and follow an equally undesirable path.

After about five minutes, Campagna emerged with his arm around the young man's shoulder. He said, "So you go see Mr. Salaso. I'll talk to him, and he'll put you on my driving schedule. You'll be with me almost every night until the election's over. And if I win, well we'll just see then. Is that okay with you?"

"Yes, Councilman," the young Analdo said. "And thanks."

"Mrs. Analdo, everything's okay. Tommy and I had a little talk. He's going to come work for me on the campaign."

"Thank you, Councilman. I knew you'd straighten him out. He's a good boy. Just got on the wrong track since his father died." He kissed the woman on the cheek and walked her out the door.

"C'mon, Henry," Campagna said. "We're going."

"Where?"

"The hospital."

"Is someone sick?" Henry asked.

"Yeah, a friend."

***

The person in the hospital was the father of a local political operative from the neighborhood. Carlos Vasquez was a union pipefitter who was rushed to the hospital after he collapsed at work. His son, Andrew, on whom he had pinned all his hopes and dreams, had attended Harvard and Yale Law School. As the city's demographics shifted from Irish to Italian to now Latino, Andrew Vasquez was viewed as a future leader of this emerging power base.

As they took the elevator to the Critical Care Unit, Campagna asked Henry, "Doesn't your fiancée work here?"

"No, she works at the children's hospital. She's in pediatrics. Well med-peds, actually."

"Noble profession," Campagna said as they stepped off the elevator. They walked directly to the room without asking for directions. Inside the room, they found a man who seemed too young to be in intensive care. Vasquez was in his late fifties and had endured a life of hard labor and equally hard living.

"How you doing, Mr. Vasquez?" the councilman said to his constituent.

"Councilman Campagna," the man said, lifting the arm to which an IV was attached. Vasquez's wife, Isabella, rose from the bedside and also offered her greetings.

"I heard you were in the hospital, and I just wanted to come by and give you my best," Campagna told him.

"So nice of you to come by. I'll tell Andrew you came."

"I hear Dr. Rubenstein's doing your bypass. He's the best. He'll take good care of you."

"That's what they tell me. But they also say I won't be able to work no more." The man confided he hadn't missed a day of work in thirty years.

"You don't worry about that. Just get better. I'll come see you after the operation," Campagna said as he looked at Mrs. Vasquez, motioning for her to meet him outside the room. In the hallway, he asked. "Are you okay, Isabella?"

"He's just too young, Councilman, too young. His heart's badly damaged. They don't know if the bypass will even work." She wouldn't cry in front of her husband, but before Campagna, the tears flowed freely.

"He's the toughest guy I know, and I know a lot of them. They don't make them like that anymore. He'll make it. But if you need anything, you come see me, okay?"

"I will. Thank you for coming."

Campagna left the CCU with Henry in tow. Henry came out of his schooling session to show Campagna he knew what he was attempting, "So that's Andy Vasquez's dad. I get it."

Campagna turned sharply but waited for the elevator door to close before he responded, "Sometimes it's more about humanity than politics. I've known Carlos Vasquez for more than twenty years. He's a good man, and it means a lot to him that I came by. He's one of my constituents. I come see them when they're in the hospital."

"I didn't mean to imply it was only about politics," Henry tried to clarify.

"I know, but the reason I wanted you to come with me today was because sometimes you—and not just you, but all of us—forget why we do this. It's not the power. It's not the benefits. It's the people. Take Mrs. McLusky. Her husband left her penniless. Social security barely covers her rent and food. So me and a bunch of the guys, we take up a collection. We raise her about five grand. Now, she won't take charity, so I tell her that her husband had given it to my father to hold for him."

"And what about that kid you gave the job to?"

"Tommy Analdo. I told his father I'd look after the kid. I got him a job at Public Works. His boss knows he's a political appointee, so he gave him a hard time. But that's no excuse to show up to work high and tell your boss to go fuck himself. So I give the kid a second chance to drive me around, where I can keep my eye on him."

"So this was all a game. Remind the jaded political consultant what it's all about."

"I don't need to teach you anything, Henry. You need to just see for yourself why what we do is, in fact, important. A lot of these people don't have anyone to turn to. They come to me because I at least try to help them. You think a guy like Prescott cares if a widow's got enough money to get by or a kid can't keep a job? Oh, sure, they give to the United Way and serve on the boards of charities to convince themselves they care, but they don't do the work that's necessary."

***

Campagna was the embodiment of his neighborhood. He was the one they turned to for help, for comfort, for a chance at a better life. He never let a hand go empty. Never turned away a friend or even a stranger. He was what politics was supposed to be. It wasn't about his ambition or having something to prove. Nor was it about money and big houses. It was about service and the belief that one man could truly make a difference.

Henry wondered if Campagna was a dying breed, an old-time politician who was more comfortable shaking hands with constituents than spewing rhetoric before the cameras. Perhaps Campagna was better suited for a different era. Campagna may have represented the politics of the past, where the political machine ruled, but he understood that he was caught in the politics of the present. In order to return City Hall to the people, he needed to rely on the masters of demagoguery to secure victory. Henry might have doubted whether a truly honest man could win in today's tumultuous political climate. But in the case of Campagna, he was determined to unleash everything at his disposal to ensure that this good man was delivered to the people.

12

"Ah, shit," Henry said to himself. "Lyndsay."

He had forgotten he had a Campagna fundraiser and would miss Lyndsay's much-anticipated performance in the kitchen. He called her, hoping to catch her before she prepared dinner.

But the call came just as she was arriving home with an armload of groceries. She recognized Henry's number on the caller ID, set the groceries down, and answered. "Hey, you! What's up?"

"Hey, Lynds, I've got bad news. I have a Campagna fundraiser tonight at the University Club. It's all heavy hitters, $500 a head, so I have to go. Hey, why don't you come with me? It's open bar, good food. It'll be fun!"

"You know I hate those things. You just go. It's fine. I'll cook some other night," she said, hiding her disappointment. Then she changed her mind. "Actually, why not? It's not dinner alone with you, but it's better than nothing."

"Great! We've gotta be there at six, so I'll come by and pick you up."

***

The University Club was one of those posh private clubs built by Providence's power elite, but Lyndsay Sinclair wasn't easily impressed. She wasn't some girl from the neighborhood. She was a debutante herself who had frequented the finest clubs in the South.

The University Club was in the oldest section of Providence with some of the homes dating back to the 17th century. Across from the Rhode Island School of Design Museum, the club displayed some of its own priceless works of art. A steward welcomed Henry and Lyndsay and directed them upstairs for the Campagna reception. An attractive older woman kissed Henry on his cheek as she greeted them. "This must be your fiancée. Aren't you lucky, Henry? I need you both to sign in, even though you're not paying."

"Okay Lynds, here's the deal. Everyone here's giving big money, so they expect some face time with the guy they think's going to be mayor. It's probably no different than any other party you've been to. You've got the cool kids over there. That's Jack Bierman and Joe Donnelly. Jack's the market president of Providence's largest bank and Joe's the CEO of a drug store chain. They sponsored this reception, which probably will raise fifty grand tonight. Their table is by invitation only, so unless they call you over, just smile politely. See that table over by the food? That's for staff members looking to squeeze in a little dinner or the single guy who talks to the staff because he has nobody else to talk to. In the other corner, you've got the political tables. One for the senators, the other for the reps. They don't like to mix. Now, the key to these things is to keep moving. No one really wants to talk to you. They came here to buy some influence. It's all about polite conversation and not talking to anybody for more than five minutes—they're usually looking to upgrade to someone more important. So don't be annoyed if someone in mid-sentence just walks away. It means they see an opening."

"Got it. Don't talk to anyone for more than five minutes? That sounds rude," she said.

"Hey, I don't make the rules. I gotta schmooze, so give me half an hour to impart my wisdom on these guys. They want to make sure I'm not spending their money foolishly. Then we'll get out of here and go over to The Hill for coffee and dessert."

"Fine, just don't leave me too long. I don't know anybody."

"You'll be alright. Just smile and pretend you're interested in what they have to say. Nod to show that you're listening, and politely excuse yourself to get a drink. And do drink. It's open bar, so get the good stuff!"

***

The first to come over was McNally. Lyndsay never felt comfortable around him. He had quite the reputation as a womanizer. "Lyndsay," he said as he embraced her softly. "I'm glad to see you here."

"It's good to see you, Congressman."

"Don't be so formal. I'm not a congressman anymore. Call me Ray. So how's my boy? You know he's like a son to me."

"He thinks of you like a father."

"You've got a good man there. One of the best. But he's lucky to have you," he said as he winked. He kissed her on the cheek and moved on to the next guest. To McNally, this was just as much a political coronation for him as it was for Campagna. He was out of politics, at least the elected kind, and Campagna was his guy, his best chance for influence over City Hall.

"Hi, I'm Tammy," said a petite blonde around the same age as Lyndsay. "Are you a friend of the congressman?"

"Not exactly. I'm Lyndsay Sinclair, Henry Mercucio's fiancée." She shook the girl's hand, happy to have someone to talk to.

"You're lucky. Henry's the most brilliant political guy out there. Want to get a drink?"

"It's about that time. Glass of Riesling?"

Tammy took Lyndsay by the arm and walked her over to the bar. "We gals need to look sophisticated," she said, "so it's only red wine, I'm afraid. Do you know anybody here?"

"Just Henry, the congressman, and Councilman Campagna. And now you."

"You see that guy over there? That's Senator Brady. That girl he's with, the bleach blonde there, he's sleeping with her. He brings her around to all the functions, leaves his wife home with the kids. Nice, huh?"

"He goes out in public with her?"

"Yeah. Everybody knows. He doesn't seem to care. Brings her to all the parties. Now, see that real handsome guy over there, all dressed up? Yeah, he's gay, state representative, goes out with the other rep over there, actually. And see that kind of heavyset woman with the really bad eye make-up? She's a councilwoman."

Lyndsay took a sip of her wine. She was beginning to enjoy their little game of who's-who. "So who are those guys over in the back there?"

"You don't go over to them unless they ask. And they won't even pretend to talk to you. They'll stare right at your breasts. They're all big shots, corporate types. I've never met them. I'm sorry, Lyndsay, but I'll be right back. Senator Anderson, can I talk to you a minute?"

Lyndsay watched her new friend throw herself at the state senator. She saw Henry in the far corner, making his demonstrative hand gestures as he was talking. She was about to head in his direction when John Campagna came over to her.

"Ms. Sinclair, I'm sorry I took your fiancé away tonight."

"I've become used to sharing him with you," she said with a smile to make sure he knew she was joking.

"I'm sure he'd rather be spending his time with you, but we need him, too. I'd never be able to get through this without him. He's doing the right thing, helping to make this city a better place, hopefully for your children someday."

"I know he's out there working hard, but I'm sure Henry would tell you not to waste your time talking to me. Go talk to the people who paid their five hundred."

"That does sound like something he'd say. But you have to promise me that you and Henry will come to my home for dinner. No politics. That's my promise. I think we could all use a little break from it, don't you?"

"Sounds great to me. I just don't know if Henry could last a whole night without talking polls and strategy. It's become so ingrained in him. But I'd certainly like to try."

"You know, Lyndsay, there's a lot of talk at these things, lots of promises made. Let's keep this one, okay?"

Lyndsay did not feel like she was talking to a politician. "It's a promise," she said, sealing it with a kiss on his cheek. She walked back to the bar and ordered a second glass of wine. A young, serious-looking gentleman with a prominent jawline and unusually large head approached Lyndsay.

"Are you from Brown?" he asked.

"Sort of. I'm a resident, but that's not why I'm here. The campaign manager is my fiancé."

"Oh, you're Henry's girl. I'm Jay. Jay Needleman. Henry must have told you about me."

"He has! You're—"

"I'm president of the University Democrats."

"That's right. Henry speaks very highly of you."

"You can still join, you know, even though you're in residency."

"Sorry to tell you, but I'm not into politics."

"You're marrying Henry Mercucio. Of course you're into politics!"

"I'm *really* not interested," she said, emphasizing the word.

"Well, we have social events too. It's a good group of young people who share common interests. Tammy over there, she's a member," he said, pointing to the young woman Lyndsay had met, who was now hanging on the arm of a young state senator. Tammy kissed the senator on the cheek and did her duty to rescue her new friend from the grips of Jay Needleman.

"Run along, Jay. Don't bother the nice girl," Tammy said, shooing him off with a wave.

"I was just talking to her about joining the UDs," he said.

"She doesn't want to join your nerdy organization, okay?" she said. He saw he was losing the battle, so he retreated. Tammy waited until Jay was the proper distance away before she laid into him. "You gotta be rude to that one sometimes. He's like a tick. You've just got to yank him away, or he'll suck you dry."

Lyndsay laughed. She didn't want to be rude, but the kid had been pretty annoying. "Thanks for rescuing me," she said.

"No problem. He's not a bad guy, just a little too much."

"So what's the scoop on Campagna? Is he really as good as he seems?" Lyndsay asked.

"He's just a really nice guy. He relates to people, understands them, and doesn't bullshit. He tells it like it is. I think that's why people like him so much," Tammy explained.

"You're right. He seems genuine," Lyndsay said.

Tammy chuckled. "Hey, I don't mean to cut you off, but I have to go talk to Representative Santos. He's got a lot going for him, and I don't just mean on the Finance Committee."

"Go run him down," Lyndsay replied, disappointed to be left alone again. She made her way back through the crowd that now numbered about fifty and headed to the carving station. She was surprised to hear Henry's voice. "Can I have everyone's attention, please! Councilman Campagna would like to say a few words. Councilman?"

"Thank you. That was my campaign manager, Henry Mercucio. And where's his lovely bride-to-be, Lyndsay? Oh, there she is in the back. I think we need to thank her for letting us have so much of Henry," Campagna said. Everyone gave a polite laugh. "I want to thank you for coming out tonight. It means a lot to me, especially to my campaign. You raised over $50,000. But I want you to know that your money's being put to good use. We have a tough opponent who's not afraid to go negative, so we have to continue to get our positive message out to the voters. I'm going to stay the course and make you proud of this city again. I want a Providence where people are as happy with their neighborhoods as they are with their downtown. I want to bring hope and revitalization back to the neighborhoods. They've waited long enough. A great Providence means safe schools and sound schooling, with not only the largest school system in our state, but the best. That means safer streets and a proactive approach to law enforcement, where our police force is not only the largest, but the finest. These aren't simply dreams but plans we can turn into reality. And in order to accomplish the great work before us, I first need your help. I ask for your vote on March 15th, for a better Providence."

Lyndsay was impressed with Campagna. He had real conviction, like he actually believed in what he said. As Henry's significant other, she had been around enough politicians to distinguish between those who were full of shit and those who actually believed in working for the people. The man who slid his hand down her back as he passed through the crowd seemed to be more of the former.

His name was Rick Anderson, and he had been elected to the state senate right out of college. He was less interested in policy and more in what the title earned him. With no real skills or talents, it was the only carrot he had to impress the ladies, which remained at the top of his agenda. Since he hadn't been paying attention when Campagna had singled Lyndsay out in his speech, he had no idea she was Henry Mercucio's fiancée. To Senator Anderson, political speeches were simply fodder for his profession. He was there for the free booze, food, and any young thing he could lure out of the room.

"Why haven't I seen you here before?" he asked. He was a close talker, so close that Lyndsay could almost taste the vodka on his breath. He wasn't acting very senatorial.

She flinched away from his unwelcome touch. "Probably because I don't come to these things, but my fiancé thinks I should be at all of them."

"Who's your fiancé?" he asked. "Do I know him?"

"Everyone seems to," she said, and pointed in Henry's direction.

"Oh, you're Henry's girl. Great guy. He's helped me out a few times, done some of my pieces." He was referring to his political mailers.

"He's one of the best," she said. She saw Henry coming over to them, and felt relief wash over her.

"And here he is," the senator said. "Henry, I was just talking to your fiancée."

"Lyndsay," Henry said forcefully.

"Yes, I was just telling Lyndsay how you've done some work for me," the senator said, trying to hide from Henry that he would sell his senate seat for a chance to sleep with his future wife.

"Yes, Senator, and I need to talk to you again. We're really going to need you to make some GOTV calls in your district. Can we count on you?"

"Absolutely. Anything I can do for the Campagnas. You guys know that."

"Well, thank you, Senator. I knew we could count on you." He turned to Lyndsay and asked, "Having fun?"

"It's been really interesting," she said as Senator Anderson walked away, heading in Tammy's direction over near the bar.

"He's a walking slime ball," Henry said, giving words to Lyndsay's thoughts. "I'll only be a couple of more minutes. Then we're out of here, okay?"

"That's fine," she said as she watched Henry leave again. "Hi, how are you?" Lyndsay asked an older woman. "Nice to see you again," she said to one of the young women who worked in Henry's office. "This is a really nice event," she told an older man who talked to her in the coffee line. It was all such superficial conversation. People weren't really interested in how someone's daughter was doing in college, or whether a parent was put in a nursing home, or how difficult it had been to put the thirteen-year-old dog to sleep. They were in the room to win favor with the man they thought could be the next mayor of Providence. Everything else just did not matter.

13

In politics, everyone from public relations consultants to media salespeople jumps on the campaign they think has the best chance to win. They want to be in the loop when victory comes so they can secure their slice of the pie.

Nicholas Dean from D&D Advertising was one such parasite. Everyone knew Nick Dean in the advertising world. He ran the top creative shop in town and wanted to ensure he was in line when the contracts were handed out. The receptionist at Warner Isikoff rang Henry's phone and told him that Nick Dean was on hold.

"Put him through."

"You're harder to get ahold of than the President, Mr. Mercucio. You must be a very important man," Dean said.

"Well, Nick, you know the business. To be honest with you, I've got someone out of DC doing my TV spots right now."

"That's not why I'm calling. Yeah, I'd love a shot at the biz, and you should be using a Providence firm, but I know you hotshot political operatives think you know all the answers. When it comes to TV, especially in this market, no one understands it better than we do. But I'm not trying to sell you. Look, Henry, I know we had a run-in during the McNally campaign. I was hoping we could move past that. I've got something you want, some info I think you'll find useful."

"I'm listening."

"It's not something I can say over the phone. Can I buy you lunch?"

"Nope."

"Well, can I come down to your office?"

"Definitely not."

"Can I—"

"I'll give you fifteen minutes, around five. I'll come down, and Nick, I mean fifteen minutes."

***

If anything, Nick Dean knew how to impress a guest. As soon as Henry arrived at the refurbished jewelry factory that housed the largest advertising agency in Providence, he was greeted by a tall, slender blonde who took him the long way through the office. Henry wasn't impressed. He understood Dean's game. Dean's office was in the creative department, which in another era must have served as the foreman's stoop. It enabled him to keep a careful eye over the assembly line workers. To Henry, it didn't look like much had changed. He saw artists and writers chained to their cubicles and churning out product, and he remembered D&D had long been accused of being an advertising chop-shop. Henry sat down in the plush leather chair in Dean's office but chuckled when he saw a sticky note taped to his computer that read, "You look thin today." Dean was in his early forties, with a body builder's physique and a perpetual tan.

"It's good to see you again, Henry. I hope Heidi gave you a good view of our business. We got her out of Boston from one of their top shops. She was a poli-sci major from DC, just like you."

"Cut the shit, Dean. I don't want to be here any longer than I have to, so what do you got?"

"You hate me?"

"If I gave you any thought, I probably would."

"It was nothing personal, Henry."

"I know. Just business. It's always just business with you. Never personal. Bullshit. You and your buddy, Beako, kept going to McNally and telling him I didn't know what I was doing. You undermined my authority, and you probably cost him the race."

"C'mon, Henry. That was four years ago, and all we did was question your strategy. We hardly undermined the campaign."

"Fifteen minutes, and the clock's ticking. We can rehash old memories, or we can talk about what you think is so earth-shattering that you needed to see me. Your choice."

"You probably know that I'm good friends with Representative Pagalini?"

"I didn't, but I don't give a shit."

"Just listen for a minute. You're supposed to be reasonable, so hear me out. Pagalini always wanted to be mayor, but he's realized it's tough for a guy in his late thirties to win in this city. So he's been going around with this broad he claims is his campaign consultant. Everyone knows he's banging her."

"I've heard enough. I don't give a shit who Pags is banging. This a waste of my time."

"She's seventeen," Dean said.

"What?"

"Yeah, Henry. Not only is he paying for her, but she's

seventeen. It's one thing to pay, but seventeen, no one is ready for that. You know it, I know it."

"Why?"

"You know no one in this town will elect this guy."

"No, why are you telling me this?"

"Because the people have a right to know."

"More bullshit," Henry fired back. "You don't care about the people or about Pagalini. You really are a despicable human being. I knew it when Beako hired you." Henry began to leave.

"I'll go to the press."

"You do that, Dean. Go right ahead."

"Unless..."

"What?"

"You talk to Pagalini."

"Why would I ever do that?"

"Because he'll listen to you. You're reasonable."

"Okay, but why are you doing this? Why ruin a guy's life?"

"You know this will come out," Dean said. "I don't want to do it, but someone will."

"If this goes to the press, it would destroy him."

"So you'll do it? You'll talk to him?"

"I'll do it, but not for you. I actually like the guy."

***

Henry called Pagalini's campaign office after he left the meeting at D&D. It was after 6 p.m., and Henry caught the state representative before he made the fundraising circuit for the evening. They met in Pagalini's law office, which had been converted into a campaign headquarters. The representative was the only man left in the office, and Henry could sense from the moment they shook hands that Pagalini was uncomfortable. He barely looked Henry in the eye.

"I have to tell you I don't like meeting with my opposition's consultant. Nothing good can come from it."

"Like I said on the phone, I understand your apprehension, so let me just come right out with it."

"I'd expect nothing less."

"Nick Dean dropped a bomb. He came to me. I wasn't looking for dirt—that's not the type of race we're running—but I've got to be honest with you, if it's true, you can't do this."

"Don't forget that I was willing to take on the mayor when he was just a petty crook, not the FBI's most wanted. I put myself out there. Your guy waited until the mayor fled. Now I find myself ten points behind your guy in the polls. I'm only down by a couple in one of my polls. So you tell me you've got news on me. Let's hear it."

"It's one thing to convince the voters to elect another liberal thirty-something to the state legislature, but taking a working girl who's seventeen to the mayor's office?" Henry watched Rep. Pagalini's confidence fade.

"That fucking bastard."

"I don't care about the detail, Representative. We won't play that card, but Dean will. He wants us to use it, but I told him we wouldn't touch it. And he threatened to go to the press unless I talked to you first. That's why I'm here. Campagna doesn't know, and McNally doesn't either."

"I'm going to ruin him. I'll put that piece of shit out of business. He can't—"

"He can, and he will. It's now a matter of how you handle this."

"And you're the best handler in town, Henry, so how do I handle this?" Pagalini asked.

"What does he want? Everyone wants something."

"He figures I can't win, so he's looking to sell me out to prove to you that he's on your team. Dean's a self-absorbed egomaniac who just crossed the wrong guy."

"What are you going to do?" Henry asked him.

"I don't know. I'll have to think about it."

"Director of Administration," Henry blurted out. The position was the best solution Henry could come up with to get Pagalini out of the race and save a promising career in public service.

"What?" Pagalini asked, totally caught off guard.

"You serve as Director of Administration."

"You have the authority to offer me the job?" Pagalini asked.

"I do," Henry said, knowing it wasn't the truth. His mind was racing. How would he convince McNally and Campagna to accept it? Director of Administration was the top patronage job in the city. Was it a concession they would make to get Pagalini out of the race and shore up the liberal wing of the party? Henry knew he could sell it.

"If you can deliver it, I'd seriously consider it. But I'd want real power. I'd do what's best for the city."

"We'd expect nothing less."

"And Henry, I love her. I know it sounds crazy, but she got mixed up in this, and I saved her."

"Sure you did."

14

Henry's regular meeting with Campagna's inner circle was scheduled for the next morning. On his way there, he worked it out in his head how he would sell the idea to McNally, Campagna, and his brother Paul, who would all be there. Avoiding a costly and divisive primary was his main selling point. Dealing with Pagalini after the election was secondary to the big picture of uniting a traditionally fractured party behind one strong candidate. He also knew it was the right thing to do, and any time that was the case, selling the idea was easy for him.

"Are you fucking out of your mind, Henry?" McNally didn't wait to hear Henry's reasoning.

"Let me explain, Ray." If McNally wanted to run again and win, then Henry would gladly utilize the title of congressman. But when he sought to voice his opinion without hearing Henry's carefully laid plan, "Ray" was the only way Henry would refer to him. "Pagalini's one of the brightest stars in the party. He understands policy better than anyone at the state house. He could be a great asset, not to mention the fact that we wouldn't have to waste a cent on the primary and can focus on the general instead. The election's just twelve weeks away, and we've got a Republican opponent whose party's giving him a free ride."

"Will he do it, Henry? Pagalini and I are as far apart as Democrats can be," Campagna reminded him.

"Yeah, he'll do it. If anything, Pagalini's a pragmatist and understands that politics is the art of compromise. If he thinks you'll listen to him on policy, if he gets to help bring real change, he'll come on board."

Campagna turned and asked his brother what he thought. He served with Pagalini in the House of Representatives, after all.

"It's a shrewd move, John, and I like it. We keep Pagalini's base from going south and focus on the independents. Your boy here has earned his keep."

"The devil you know is better than the devil you don't," McNally said. "At least if Pagalini's with us, we know what we're getting. Helping us get elected is one thing. He'll be a pain in the ass as director, but he'll be your problem. And like Henry said, he's a top policy guy. It'll look like you're bringing in the best and brightest." He concluded his thoughts with the realization that Campagna had already bought into Henry's plan.

"Make the deal, Henry," Campagna instructed.

It was done. In a press conference orchestrated by Henry, Pagalini announced that for the sake of party unity, he was withdrawing from the primary and supporting John Campagna for mayor. He handled the questioning like the pro he was, staying on message even when a clever reporter cited the recent university poll that showed him closing the gap on Campagna. "The real issue here is making sure we restore a sense of integrity in Providence. We need a real public servant with a comprehensive understanding of city government and the needs of our people." Pagalini's shots were aimed at both the former mayor on the lam and the Republicans' retired executive-turned-politician who would face off against Campagna.

Henry couldn't have said it any better, but of course, he had written it. He had worked out every detail. The primary was over and his candidate had won, though it hadn't been the most democratic process. Now was the time to celebrate, to enjoy the victory while it lasted, because it never really lasted very long.

They celebrated the primary victory at Joe's Restaurant in Campagna's city council district, the heart of his political base. Joe's was once Giovanni's Florentine Grille, but Giovanni Brusetti, the long-time owner, had changed the name to reflect the area's changing demographic. Providence had become almost 50 percent minority, and to make it more appealing to his newly growing clientele, he'd made the name more American. Whether Providence residents were from Italian, Irish, German, or Latino heritage, the overriding factor they all shared was that they were American.

All the party faithfuls were present to pay homage to the man who was their best chance to recapture the mayor's office. It was also Henry's night. They all recognized that the young political consultant was the reason they once again had a chance to reclaim City Hall. Like the other professional politicians in the room, Henry made his rounds shaking hands and kissing blue-hairs. He retired to the corner of the bar, occasionally holding court for the dedicated faithful who wanted to shake hands with the man they regarded as the new king-maker of Providence. Pagalini made his way to the bar to thank Henry for sparing him an almost certain defeat and an opportunity to still serve his city.

"So this is where the king-maker sits," Pagalini joked.

"I'm glad you pols are starting to realize who really runs

things," Henry quipped. He was beginning to show the effects of the alcohol he did not often oblige.

"Listen, Henry. We really owe you our thanks. You did the right thing for all of us. It's not easy for young guys in this business. I mean, I just introduced my girl to my parents. For everyone to find out that she sold herself—God, that's not how I want my parents and the rest of my family to find out."

"You've still gotta come out. You know Nick's gonna drop a dime eventually. Beat him to it. We'll plan it all out after you talk to your family. You'll show everyone that you rescued this girl. It could be your defining moment."

"Thanks, Henry. I'll think about it. Oh, did you hear that Dean's gone over to the other side? The GOP hired him to do media for Malcolm Prescott." The scion was the recently retired chief executive of Prescott Textiles, one of the oldest companies in America, who after much prodding from Gordie Beako had agreed to come out of retirement to run for mayor of the city his family had helped build.

"It's good to see that Dean's found work. I heard his agency lost the state economic development and transportation contracts. You didn't have anything to do with that, did you, Representative?"

"You shouldn't make it a practice to screw over your friends." Pagalini was careful to downplay his involvement in influencing some state departments to reevaluate their advertising and marketing campaigns with D&D Advertising. His colleague in the State House of Representatives, Paul Campagna, had helped serve Dean a dish of revenge by calling for an audit of D&D's billing, which showed many discrepancies including state reimbursements for spas and massages.

Rep. Campagna approached the two political animals, eagerly seeking to involve himself in the pride.

"Gentlemen, this looks like a great place for a conspiracy. Pags, did you tell Henry what we did to Dean?" Pagalini glanced at Henry, alerting him that Campagna didn't fully understand the reason for the retribution.

"Yeah, he told me. You can't play for both sides in this game. Dean got what he deserves."

Pagalini excused himself as Rep. Campagna took the opportunity to share his thoughts on how his brother could win the general election. After he was finished expounding his theories, the visibly drunk Campagna threw his arms around Henry. Embarrassed by the uncomfortable embrace, Henry pulled back.

"C'mon, Henry. You're one of us." John Campagna quickly came to the aid of his political star and took his younger brother away from Henry and any constituents.

"We're all just happy you're with us, Henry," he said as he walked his brother away toward the confines of the family tables.

With the politics of the evening behind him, Henry took a minute to call his fiancée. Lyndsay had gotten a big enough dose of politics at the recent fundraiser and had decided to sit this one out. As he put away his cell phone, he caught a glimpse of an attractive brunette shooting back a shot of vodka.

"So you're the great Henry Mercucio," the young woman, who could not have been a day over twenty-one, said with a slight slur in her words. She was a pretty girl, petite like Lyndsay, but a bit more voluptuous.

"Well, I don't know how great I am."

"That's all I hear at dinner, how great this Henry guy is who's running my uncle's campaign."

"You're a Campagna?"

"I'm not, but my mom is. I'm a Keane, Jamie Keane."

"So Jamie Keane, what are you all about, then?" Henry asked as he sipped his Macallan 18. When he drank, he usually drank twelve-year-old scotch, but today was special.

"I'm not into politics, if that's what you mean. I hate politics."

"That's funny. So do I."

"Yeah right. You're like this big political guy."

"Doesn't mean I like it."

"Then why do you do it? Or are you one of those guys who just loves power?"

"Well, I happen to think your uncle is a great guy."

"Whatever. So do you want a drink, Mr. Political Guy? Hey, Freddie, give us two kamikazes. You do shots, right?" After two shots on top of the three scotches, which were generous Country Club pours, Henry was the most inebriated he had been since Vegas. People were filing out of the bar, and he knew if he didn't get out soon, he might do something he regretted. But Jamie wasn't letting go that easily. She would brush her leg up against his thigh and caress his hand after he made what he thought was one of his witty comments about the people in the bar. When Henry asked for the check, she went right for the kill and grabbed his inner thigh. He was stunned by how forward she was. He was used to women like Lyndsay who were a bit more demure.

"You can't drive, Henry. Why don't you come back to my place and sober up?" she said.

"I have a fiancée, Jamie, I don't think she would—"

"Who said anything about your fiancée, Henry?"

"You're right. I shouldn't drive home."

***

Jamie's apartment was a tenement that her family had owned for two generations. She lived on the first floor with a roommate she told Henry was at her boyfriend's place. Before he was through the door, Jamie was all over him, hungrily kissing him on the lips. Henry almost felt as though he was looking down at his life from above and watching a horror story. He came to with a snap and realized what he was doing—cheating on Lyndsay, whom he loved more than anything. He had to get out of there.

"I can't do this. I'm sorry."

"What?"

"This is wrong. I'm sorry." Henry grabbed his things and walked out of the apartment.

"You're an asshole, Henry Mercucio," she yelled. Then she grabbed two wine glasses and hurled them at his head. They missed Henry but shattered against the wall.

***

Finding her purse on the kitchen floor, she grabbed a bottle of Tylenol she had filled with Xanax she had purchased on the street—much cheaper than paying for health insurance and a co-pay. She had already taken one before her uncle's party, needing a little something to help her through the political event her mother had forced her to go to, something she saw as nothing more than a bunch of blowhard politicians pretending to support her uncle. Needing a quick release, she crunched on the pills like they were candy. Swallowing the powder with a half-empty beer from the counter, she waited for the pills to fill her emptiness.

She took a cab to a party in an old factory building across town. Feeling little discomfort or pain, though her body temperature was exceeding natural levels, she danced until six in the morning. Her new friend, Raúl, whom she had intimate knowledge of from the back seat of his retrofitted Honda Civic, took pity on her and drove her home. Even Raúl, who was barely conscious himself, knew there was something wrong with Jamie. Her body was burning and beads of sweat were streaming down her neck. And it wasn't from the intensity of the romance in the back seat. In fact, their coupling hadn't been particularly pleasurable for either of them. But, being the gentlemen, he brought Jamie back to her apartment and left her on the couch. To him, she was just another rich white girl who had partied too hard.

The prince who causes another to become
powerful thereby works his own ruin.
—Niccolò Machiavelli

Lyndsay rose before Henry and was careful not to wake him. She understood the pressure he was under and was happy to see him sleeping in. She had to be at the hospital by seven, but before leaving, she placed a cup of coffee on the nightstand along with the morning paper, which featured the headline, "Campagna takes uncontested Democratic primary, emerges as favorite to capture City Hall." She thought that perhaps this election would erase those bitter memories from Henry's failed McNally race. It wasn't anything she wanted to go through again, watching Henry belabor every bit of political minutiae and continually ask himself, "What if?" But this campaign did seem to resurrect the passion he'd lost. She was proud of him, knowing he was putting everything into the Campagna campaign.

***

Henry had been awake the whole time Lyndsay was getting ready for work. He hadn't slept much that night, a combination of the head-pounding from the heavy consumption of alcohol and the pangs of guilt he was feeling. He called the office and left a message for his assistant that he wouldn't be in until the afternoon.

Henry drove an hour outside of Providence to his alma mater, Boston College, where his old confidante, Father Bernadine, taught ethics. The Jesuits were known for their wisdom and for counseling young men and women who questioned the path they were pursuing in life. Father Bernadine had spent long hours with a young Henry who'd painfully revealed a past filled with self-doubt and anxiety over the man he wanted to be and the man he was becoming. Father Bernadine had revealed elements of his own past, of an abusive, alcoholic father jealous of his son's ceremonial role, and of the difficulties he faced in coping with his own burdens. Henry had identified most with this eighty-five-year-old priest, and he was one of the few people who understood him the best. Once again, he knew he had to visit his old friend.

Henry solemnly walked into St. Mary's Hall, one of the largest populations of Jesuits in the world, and asked the receptionist to ring Father Bernadine's room. "Just tell him it's Henry. He'll know." Refusing the seat offered to him, Henry stood in a catatonic state until the priest gently put his arm on Henry's shoulder.

"Come with me, my son. I need to walk over to the library." As they strolled through the well-manicured grounds, Henry emerged from his trance and pointed at the chained entrance just north of the library.

"You see that chain, Father? When I was a sophomore, I was cutting across campus and rode through it. It's solid, and I broke right through it. I could have been killed, or at least hurt pretty badly. But it gave way, and I just kept going. I got back home and told my girlfriend, and you know what she said? 'Henry, I want to marry you because you're blessed.'"

"Your guardian angel was with you, Henry. And she was right. He does have big plans for you, as He does for all of us."

"I need to talk, Father. I just haven't been the same since my dad died last year. I'm back into politics, I'm getting married, and I—" Henry retreated, not quite ready to reveal what he thought was the betrayal of the only woman he'd ever loved.

"Go on, Henry."

"I'm trying to come to terms with who I am. I've always wanted to be somebody, but now I just want peace in my life. And Lyndsay, she's the only peace I have, and I almost—"

"You have a lot of pain, Henry. But you're working through it. You didn't give yourself time to mourn your father. You just jumped into something else to consume you, to compensate for the emptiness you feel inside. Jesus wants passionate and dedicated people like you, Henry, but he also wants you to live. Part of living is dealing with the pain."

"This election, it means something to me. It's not just about winning for the sake of winning. I feel a sense of purpose again. By helping this guy get elected, I'm doing the right thing. By being the guy who teaches people how to spin their words and get out of trouble, I'm actually doing something good. And right when things are going well—"

"It's okay. Whatever your sin, you will be forgiven."

"I got pretty drunk after the primary, and I ended up with my client's niece. She wanted to, but I didn't do anything. I just couldn't. I stopped her."

"It was you who stopped you. We all make mistakes. It's why

He died for us," the Jesuit said as he pointed his finger toward the sky. "It's now what you do from here on in."

"Should I tell Lyndsay?"

"If the only reason to tell her is to relieve your own guilt, that's selfish. And the guilt is your penance. Suffer for a time, then forgive yourself."

Henry pondered the priest's words and felt a sense of relief. That brief feeling was interrupted by the vibrating buzz of his cell phone. It was Campagna.

"I need to see you right away." He was barely able to choke out the words, his voice quivering. "It's my niece," he said, and the phone went silent.

Henry said goodbye to Father Bernadine and promised to call in a week. With ominous thoughts swirling through his head, he raced back to Providence. *Did she tell him?* Henry wondered. *What did she say?* While she'd been in a tempestuous state when he'd left her, he figured the night had been as embarrassing for her as it had been for him. Was it his fault? He couldn't help but feel a sense of responsibility since he'd been with her during what must have been her lowest point. The guilt was overwhelming and began taking its hold on him. His unclear mind from the lack of sleep and the after-effects of an evening of consumption was turning his shame into self-loathing.

Henry arrived at his office to find a visibly distraught Campagna slouched in the leather chair across from his desk. Henry's assistant, Sara, was somewhat taken aback by Henry's motion for her to leave, but she gracefully removed herself from the situation, gently rubbing Campagna's shoulder as she turned to leave.

"I'm really sorry," Henry offered once she'd left the room.

"Henry, she's been in and out of drug rehab since she was sixteen. We just didn't know what to do with her. She had a loving family. We did everything for her."

"I know your family did all they could for Jamie."

"Apparently not enough, Henry. My sister found her body on the living room couch, left there like she was some strung-out junkie."

Henry was dumbfounded. "I hate to ask this, but what happened?"

"She overdosed. The Xanax she took was laced with Fentanyl. She bought it off the street. She smoked marijuana, did pills, but we thought she had cleaned up. She was living on her own, was back in school, was doing well for the first time in years. We just don't know what happened."

"We'll get through this. Don't worry. I'll handle everything. Right now, the best thing you can do is be with your family."

***

The office calls did not stop for Henry. The press was all over the story. It was a difficult situation for any political consultant, let alone one who had been intimately involved. But this was where Henry shined, when he was forced into a corner. He spun it into a personal tragedy, a story of a young woman as the victim of the opioid epidemic and its grave consequences. He kept the family out of it, refusing any interviews with Campagna. He did his job. However, there was someone else interested in the story.

He was shocked to hear that Gordie Beako was holding for him. "Beako, I could lie and say it's nice to hear from you, but let's skip the chit-chat. What do you want? Looking to concede already?"

"You wish, Henry. I've got your friend Nick Dean on the line with me, and we were hoping you could meet us for a drink."

"Why would I ever meet with you? I've heard everything Dean has to say."

"Henry, I think you're going to be interested in what we've got.

Looks like we caught you with your pants down."

"You know what? I could really use some amusement. Where do you want to meet?" Henry wasn't really sure what Beako meant by "pants down"—he'd never even loosened his belt—but he refused to show any signs of concern.

"I believe you know where my office is. See you in an hour."

***

Beako's office was in downtown Providence a short distance from Henry's in the financial district. CampCo Centre, the flagship of Beako's building empire, sat securely behind City Hall. The building rose nearly ten stories above the nineteenth-century dome of traditional power in the city. Yet, like Medici's Florence, a handful of powerful families controlled Providence, and Beako was intent on keeping it that way. CampCo was an integral thread in the powerful fabric that enveloped the city.

The power elite of Providence, a club Henry was earning his way into, understood that while the mafia may have been closed down by the Feds in Providence, CampCo still wielded immense power. They had taken a gamble on a young political upstart, the former Mayor Donovan, with their initial $100,000 loan to his campaign paying off ten-fold in bid after bid of city work. After two decades of the good life under the current regime, they now faced the uncertainty of a new mayor who might not look so kindly on their dedicated service to the city. That was why the board of CampCo had tapped Gordie Beako, general manager and senior vice president, to find, finance, and deliver a candidate back to City Hall. Henry understood this reality and knew Beako was playing to win, whatever the cost.

It was the typical power charade when Henry walked into the ornate foyer of CampCo. The receptionist sat and smiled as she made

Henry wait for fifteen minutes before ringing Beako, no doubt per the instructions he'd given her. She then walked Henry through the office, past the ceiling-high picture windows that overlooked City Hall, and up the iron staircase to the penthouse suite of offices where Beako and Nick Dean were already toasting their victory.

"Do you want a drink, Henry? Macallan 18, isn't it?"

"No, thanks. Let's just get this over with."

Nick Dean took out three manila envelopes and handed them to Beako. Then he sat down on the black leather sofa across from Henry with the cockiest fuck-you grin he could muster. Leaning against his mammoth mahogany desk, Beako slipped a photograph out of one envelope and tossed it onto the coffee table in front of Henry. "This is my favorite one. What you doing there?" He tossed another. "This one's great too. I'm sure your fiancée would ask why this girl's on her knees.

Henry's ashen face betrayed his attempt to bluff his way through the situation, but he nevertheless attempted to deny the reality he was so ashamed to admit. "Nobody will believe these pictures. That could be one of ten thousand guys in this city."

"Oh, and there's this head shot, Henry, taken as you left her apartment. That's the face of a guilty man." Beako threw the fourth picture onto Henry's lap.

"You're fucking sick."

"*I'm sick?* I'm not the one who banged the twenty-one-year-old niece of a mayoral candidate... The night she died," Dean was loving this—watching the otherwise self-assured Henry fall off his game.

"You guys have nothing," Henry insisted.

"Listen, you cocky little shit. You're done. We're sending copies to Campagna, the Attorney General, and your girlfriend. Unless—"

"Unless what? I come work for you assholes?"

"Not quite."

"Fuck you guys. They'll never believe you."

"I don't need them to believe me. I just need them to doubt you. And we're not talking about some nobody here. The dead girl you're directly connected to was the niece of a very prominent man. The police are gonna want answers. Why is the medical examiner saying there were signs of forcible entry? Was she raped, Henry? They're going to want someone to blame. How did she get the drugs? Maybe you gave them to her? You're a material witness, maybe even a suspect. You know how this works. It's all about packaging and delivery. You'll be a big hit in the pen. I hear they love lawyers in there, especially cute ones like you." Dean was enjoying digging the dagger deeper.

"Why don't you sit down, have a drink, and listen to what we have to say?" Beako said, getting back to business.

Realizing he had no choice, Henry took a seat in one of the leather club chairs positioned before Beako's desk. He threw up his hands when he was settled. "Well?"

"Listen, kid. We didn't fuck up. You did. So show some humility. This can go away. We'll hold the pictures and destroy them after the election. No one knows you were at her apartment except me, you, Dean, and our PI. And we all understand discretion. It can stay that way if you play ball."

"And if I don't?"

"We destroy you, and the story ultimately destroys your candidate. You have no choice. You, him, your whole pathetic party is disgraced. Or you do what we say."

"Sounds like I'm fucked either way."

"You're bleeding, but how much blood are you willing to spill? Here's how we see it. No one can say that Malcolm Prescott wouldn't do a good job. The guy's run a billion-dollar company. He can run this place. Campagna's still got another run in him. Shit, he could run for Lieutenant Governor after a respectable showing. So he gracefully loses but still has another shot, and you save your ass."

"So what do you want me to do?"

"Certain things can go our way," Beako told him." "Debate strategy can turn up on my desk."

"Direct mail pieces don't go out on time," Dean added.

"You get the drill, Henry," Beako said with a smile.

"Are you guys fucking serious?"

"Deadly."

16

Mayor Jack Donovan's life was already filled with every excess, but the time he spent with his girlfriend-for-hire, Jana, was the most rewarding. It wasn't the typical bullshit he dealt with back in the States. No more back-and-forth courtship or struggling to say the right things, all to achieve what both wanted in the first place. Jana was a professional. She knew what she wanted, understood how to get it, and then acted on her desires. She, too, was enjoying their carefree days of rousing in the afternoon, touring the streets of Prague, and drinking gallons of red Monrovian wine into the morning hours. It was truly the good life, something she was unaccustomed to as a peddler of flesh. She believed her days of selling her body would soon be behind her. She was falling for her distinguished gentlemen friend, this "Sean Murphy," whom she still couldn't quite figure out.

Jana was off shopping with the generous allowance he had provided. For Donovan, she was the perfect cover, not to mention the mere pleasure of sharing his bed with a woman half his age and twice his experience. The FBI and Interpol would be searching for a middle-aged American on the run, not a rich paramour and his sultry mistress, a common phenomenon throughout Europe. With Jana preoccupied with her shopping spree, Donovan discreetly met his visitor in the Church of Our Lady of Victoria in Old Town, Prague. It was a meeting Donovan had worked diligently to organize, ensuring that his guest followed certain precautions to avoid leading the FBI their way.

"Is this where a man comes for forgiveness?" the figure asked as he genuflected alongside the former mayor. Fully cloaked as a tourist in khaki pants, running sneakers, and a blue polo shirt with a camera hanging around his neck, he didn't appear to be a man on a secret rendezvous.

"Cute outfit," the mayor said. "You're a riot. Did you follow my instructions?"

"I did what your email instructed. I took the plane from New York to Frankfurt. Took a train to Munich, then flew to Prague. I paid for everything in cash, and my office thinks I'm at a conference in Naples—Florida, not Italy. I gotta tell you, this place is magnificent. They don't build like this anymore—too expensive."

"Cut the bullshit. Did you bring what I asked?"

"Look, I talked to our people. They want to cut you off. They know you've got over $2 million."

"I made you bastards rich. All those contracts. Do you think you would've gotten them without me? Yeah, I got some dough, but do you realize what it costs to disappear, to be on the run?"

"To stay in plush hotels, to pay for a mistress, to live like a fucking prince," his guest countered. "We stand to lose everything if Campagna gets in, while you're over here living the good life. While you're screwing around Europe, we're fighting for our piece."

"Fuck you guys," the mayor shot in a harsh whisper. "I made

you guys, and you leave me with shit, on the run, no friends, nothing? What kind of life is that?"

"Must be tough hooking up with a twenty-five-year-old, eating fine food, and living in a place that looks like it's out of a fairy tale."

"How long can I last? It's expensive. I had to buy a whole new identity. I've only got enough to last me a couple of years, then what do I do? I'm fucked."

"I don't know what you expect us to do. We're under a microscope. The FBI's been watching us, and they probably got our phones tapped."

"You can find a way. I always did. Whenever you needed something, I was there for you. Remember the parks deal? I got the Parks Department to trade you that land downtown for your hotel."

"Yeah, I remember we gave them twice the property on the West Side for your botanical garden."

"That deal made you guys millions. That one alone. What about all the others? I bet I made $20 million for your company. You never had to go out to bid. I always got you the contracts. Whenever you needed my help to get the building inspector to condemn a property you wanted, I got it done. Now all I ask is for a small cut of our business to make sure I can retire properly."

"We really sympathize with your plight, Mayor. But we're the ones in harm's way, not you. We face a new mayor who's going to destroy everything we've built."

"That boy scout Campagna?"

"Yeah, but we've got a chance to get our own guy in. It's no guarantee."

"Who's Campagna got consulting?"

"That kid, Henry Mercucio, and McNally behind the scenes."

"I never met the kid, but I've heard he's good."

"Yeah, but we got to him. Plus, we have a good team and a

decent candidate, but Prescott's a virtual unknown. We were just out in the field, polling. Prescott's got low name recognition. His favorables are decent, in the high forties, but in a head-to-head, Campagna's got a ten-point lead."

"You guys can buy him the name recognition, and he's got a good message."

"Yeah, that might do it. We put a half a million up on TV, but we really need Campagna to fuck up big. His niece overdoses, and he gets a five-point bump in the polls."

"That's because he's got pros around him, and you guys are amateurs," Donovan replied.

"Well, that just might change."

"I'd love to talk Providence politics with you, but what about my money?" the former mayor asked.

"I'll have to run it up the flagpole. You know I can't authorize it."

"Just get me the money."

"It's not that easy. We've got stockholders and regulators. I can't just make millions disappear."

"Well, I've got faith in you. I know you can make it happen. Remember who made you."

"Don't forget, Mr. Mayor, we also made you."

"You ungrateful fuck."

"Simmer down. We don't want to blow your cover. Look, I'll do what I can, but I can't promise anything."

"I don't need promises. I need results."

"Yeah, so do we, and if we don't win this election, we're all fucked."

"That's not my problem anymore, is it?"

"It's all our problem. Your reign is over, my friend. Face it, you're done. I just came here as a courtesy. My people want to get as far from you as possible."

"Let me tell you something. If I go down, I'm taking all of you down with me. I'll cut a deal with the US Attorney and fuck all you guys unless you deal."

"You're delusional, Mr. Mayor. The only deal the US Attorney will cut with you is the length of your orange jumpsuit. I hate to tell you this, but you have no power. I'll do what I can for you, but when you start making threats like going to the US Attorney, you're not helping your cause."

"I need this money," Donovan demanded like an unruly child.

"You'll get what's coming to you. Just be patient. In time, it'll all work out."

"Unfortunately, my time may be running out," Donovan said.

"You've got plenty of time. How many people wouldn't love to be here? Couple million bucks to just hang out in Prague. That can go a long way in this town."

"I can't stay here. I have to keep moving, and that's expensive."

"Like I said, I'll see what I can do," Beako assured him.

Lyndsay Sinclair was planning to return home to see her parents in North Carolina for the long weekend. Of course she wanted Henry to come, but she knew that with the special election, it wouldn't happen. It was good for her to get away. Henry had become a stranger again. She barely saw him during the week, him coming home after midnight most nights, sometimes even sleeping at the office. The Saturday nights he'd promised her had been traded for dinner with Campagna and his wife, or with McNally, or with some other politico she didn't know. She went along so she could have some time with him, but she needed more. She couldn't remember the last time they had more than a polite conversation. But she hoped Henry would be himself again soon.

For Henry, there was no time for anything but politics, especially with the first televised debate between Campagna and Prescott approaching. And now it had become about more than an election, his very own survival was at stake. He figured he was through in politics and could never return to Providence. Understanding the law, he knew he couldn't be implicated in the girl's death, but that might not stop a politically motivated prosecutor looking to make his mark. The other side of the dilemma was that he liked Campagna, believed in him, and even thought he might actually be able to clean up the mess that was Providence.

Henry struggled with the vision of the man he wanted to be and the reality of who he was becoming. The dilemma swirled in his head, dominating his every thought, and truly testing who he was. There was no avoiding the inevitable. He had lost, but it wasn't only a campaign. His moment of weakness had cost him his integrity, and now he was forced to choose between saving himself or betraying Campagna.

As he brooded over Campagna's briefing papers, a thought occurred to him. Maybe there was a way out, and just maybe he could pull it off. He remembered a passage from a historical text on strategy he had been forced to analyze in his political science class in college. He pulled out the copy of *The Art of War* that was wedged between *Constitutional Law* and *The Prince* on his office bookshelf. He turned to the section, "Planning Offenses," and reviewed the text:

If you are equal in strength to your enemy, you can engage him. If fewer, you can circumvent him. If outmatched, you can avoid him. Thus, a small enemy that acts inflexibly will become the captives of a large enemy.

Henry figured that as long as his enemy, Beako, was stronger, he held the advantage. Henry decided to employ the strategy of circumvention. He would appear to throw the election, but at the same time, do everything he knew to win. It could certainly buy him the time he needed as he searched for the winning solution. In order for his plan to work, he needed to convince Campagna to do something so outlandish that it would leave little doubt that Henry was honoring the deal to work for Beako. The answer to his dilemma was right in front of him, in the spin he had written to every conceivable question that could be hurled at Campagna in the debate. The challenge would be convincing a politician, even as honest a pol as Campagna, to abandon the art of spin, to actually answer difficult questions posed to him instead of carefully avoiding them. And it wasn't like Henry was actually doing something wrong. He would simply advise his client to tell the truth no matter what the political ramifications.

***

Henry unveiled his plan at the final debate prep session in McNally's office. McNally, the most seasoned political veteran in the room, was the first to speak up. "That's political suicide."

Campagna sat expressionless as Henry tried to sell him what on the surface sounded like insanity, but actually made perfect political sense. He couldn't hide from the fact that his niece had overdosed on drugs. There was no special way to handle what Campagna's operatives had unsympathetically labeled the "niece issue." Admitting that his niece had a drug problem and sharing how her tragic demise had ripped through his family would strengthen Campagna's image as an honest, compassionate man, Henry argued. He went a step further, encouraging Campagna to abandon the endless hours they had spent crafting his message.

"You know what, John? The era of spin is over. I say you take this crap and toss it," he said, dramatizing it by tossing the papers in his hand. "Tell them what you think, not what they want to hear. When they ask you about taxes, look right in the camera and tell the people, yes, we'll have to raise taxes. Mayor Donovan left our city on the verge of economic collapse, and while I'll explore every solution from cutbacks to curtailing spending, the reality is we'll have to raise taxes."

"Now, wait, Henry. It's one thing to admit the truth about his niece, but saying you're going to raise taxes, well, we might as well just throw in the towel. He can't win being that honest," McNally lectured.

Henry listened to McNally's argument, but quickly turned his attention back to Campagna. "You're going into one of the most impossible jobs in America. You have Donovan, who if he came back today, would still win because for God-knows-what reason, the people love him. The city's teetering on bankruptcy, and sure, you can talk about budget cuts and hiring freezes, but the reality is you'll have to raise taxes. You can either bite the bullet now and admit it, or run from it, get elected, and let it come back and bite you in the ass. So, best-case scenario, you tiptoe around the issue using some crafty language and get elected. A year later, the city's broke, the firefighters' contracts are up, the teachers want a raise, and you're forced to raise taxes. You can forget about your campaign promises —returning integrity to City Hall or investing in our schools. The tax issue isn't going away. You'll have to face it now, and the people will reward you for it. You'll look like the responsible candidate, the one who's not bullshitting them. Don't take the people for granted; they're smarter than we give them credit for."

McNally stood up and mockingly clapped his hands. "Brilliantly argued, counselor. Well done. Except John's not going to have a chance to raise our taxes because he's going to die out there. They don't want the truth," McNally countered, pointing to the Providence skyline.

"No, they don't want the truth, Congressman, but it's about time someone tells it to them straight," Campagna said, breaking his silence. "I like it, Henry. Let's do it. For too long Donovan's pulled his charade. The people are going to have to face the truth that this city's falling apart. I'm not going to be another one of those politicians that looks right at the people and lies to their faces. That's not why I got into this race, and I thank Henry for reminding us why we're all here in the first place, and that's to serve the people of Providence."

***

As instructed, Henry bundled together a copy of Campagna's debate briefing papers into a manila envelope and left them in the drop mailbox at CampCo with a note for Nick Dean: "Here's your pound of flesh." He still felt the shame of betrayal regardless of the fact that he was actually deceiving his enemies, not giving in to their demands. Even though he had overhauled Campagna's real debate strategy by simply advising his client to speak the truth, the documents he had photocopied at 2 a.m. in his law office still provided his opponent with a glimpse into the deliberations of the Campagna campaign team. Beako and his operatives now had insight into the inner workings of Campagna's campaign strategy. It didn't matter to Henry that Campagna was abandoning their carefully crafted answer to the niece issue—that she had fallen victim to another Fentanyl-laced drug—or that he was prepared to admit he would be forced to raise taxes. He still thought he was breaking the trust he had developed with his candidate, a bond so strong, Campagna would actually risk his political future on the advice of a young man in a morality crisis. Henry was playing a game of treachery where one misstep would not only lose an election but also destroy his life. His plan had its repercussions, taking its toll on Henry's emotional well-being. Food no longer appealed to him, and sleep had abandoned him.

Henry knew Beako and his people would study Campagna's briefing papers, analyzing his vulnerabilities and searching for the zinger that might turn the tide of the election. He anticipated Beako would attempt to paint Campagna as soft on crime, carefully using his niece's death to illustrate his inability to protect the city's children. If Beako fully bought into Henry's information, his next move would be to have Prescott go after Campagna on his city council record for voting for three tax increases. They would attempt to lay a trap, forcing him to admit that he would raise property taxes. At the same time, they would tout Prescott's private business experience as the right antidote for a failing city.

It was just as Henry expected as he sat in the audience during the debate the next day. His stomach churned when Prescott sympathetically offered his condolences to Campagna for the death of his niece. Prescott then looked at the television camera, as he had been coached to do, and spoke passionately about the need for more police and more arrests for people peddling drugs to kids. Then he asked Campagna, in light of his personal tragedy, if he would still vote against the establishment of a drug court as he had done previously as a city councilman.

After thanking Prescott for his sympathy, Campagna responded with a heartfelt account of his family's personal tragedy. "I lost a niece to drugs, so I know first-hand the devastating impact they've had on our city. But the drug court goes too far. Yes, I believe we need to lock up people who sell illegal drugs. But giving jail sentences to people who suffer from addiction isn't the answer. The drug court legislation would put people convicted of possession or under the influence of drugs in jail after their third conviction. These are the people we should be treating, not jailing. That's why I voted against the drug court—it does nothing to help the victims of drug abuse. Mr. Prescott, you'll understand this the more you're involved in politics. There are no perfect answers."

Prescott searched for something to say in his one-minute rebuttal. The briefing papers outlined a detailed response to the niece question, offering that his niece had fallen victim to a type of Xanax she's purchased on the street. They never expected Campagna to admit that he believed in treatment rather than incarceration for drug offenders. Prescott ruffled through his papers, looking for the right answer, and then retreated with, "Councilman Campagna, again let me say how deeply sorry I am for your family's loss."

Bill Grasnor, the veteran news anchor selected to moderate the debate, attempted to drive the conversation back to political ground. "Councilman Campagna, the Donovan administration has left the city in considerable debt, the city's bond rating has dropped, and the firemen and teachers are both up for contract renewals. What do you plan to do to bring financial stability back to the city?"

"The fact is our city is in severe financial trouble. We have a $50 million debt, our bond rating in the last five years has fallen from an A-minus to a B-minus, and both the firefighters and teachers have been working under old contracts. As the chairman of the City Council Finance Committee, I have proposed incremental tax increases that the previous administration consistently vetoed." Campagna paused, looked right at the camera and stated, "The only solution is to raise property taxes. We have a $500 million budget, and to meet the city's needs—to pay our firefighters and teachers the raises they deserve, to restore financial solvency and improve our bond rating—I'm afraid I see no alternative. And let me add, anyone who tells you he won't raise taxes is only telling you what you want to hear. I'm telling you the way it is. We're talking about the future of our city. We can either bury our problems like we've done for the past twenty years or face up to them and do what's right for our children and our children's children."

"Mr. Prescott, your response?" Grasnor asked.

"The fact is Councilman Campagna is a tax-and-spend liberal in the pocket of the unions, and his only answer is to raise taxes. The truth is, I've run a billion-dollar business, so I know how to make tough decisions. I'll have the guts to cut expenses, to cut the fat from the budget—"

"Fat, meaning new teachers, new fire trucks, a new middle school," Campagna fired back. "You businesspeople come in here and think you have all the answers, but you don't know the first thing about running a city. Your answers are always, cut expenses, tighten the budget. So what are you going to cut? Are you going to tell the firefighters they don't need a new ladder truck to keep our people safe? Are you going to tell the students in the West End that history books that don't cover 9/11 are just fine? No, Mr. Prescott, this city needs real leaders who offer real solutions, not country club Republicans who get bored after making their millions."

At least half of the audience in the community center applauded loudly, while the other half sat listlessly, not knowing whether to boo or clap. Aside from the media covering the debate, there were no independent voters in the audience, with the room equally divided between Campagna and Prescott supporters. Prescott attempted to recover, pressing Campagna on the tax issue. "Mr. Campagna has never found a tax hike he didn't like. He says there's no other solution but raising our taxes. That's because he's a politician, not a businessman like me. Don't let his political speak fool you."

"Wait a second," Campagna said, throwing his hands in the air. "It's not political speak. It's the truth."

The truth, Henry thought. How simple it was to know, but how hard it was to speak. For the first time since he could remember, a feeling overcame him. Henry felt good about himself, like he was doing the right thing. Campagna had come across as compassionate and professional, while Prescott appeared stiff and bumbling. It wasn't as if Henry had unearthed some brilliant scheme to win the election. He had simply advised his client to speak the truth. In the age of spin, the truth had been lost somewhere between political consultants and public opinion polls. But for Henry, it wasn't as easy to admit. How could he tell Campagna that he had been with his niece before she died, or that he had made a deal with Beako to throw the election? His strategy had bought him time, but it wouldn't be long before Beako and Dean figured him out. And if that happened, it could cost him everything. The stakes had risen. No longer was it just about Henry. It had become a battle for the future of Providence.

18

Henry watched the clock next to his bed as the minutes became hours and the darkness became light. The thud of the newspaper rescued him from another sleepless night. He envied Lyndsay who typically slept through with a clear conscience. How had things gotten so far out of control? He didn't have to search long for the answer. He could pinpoint the exact moment of his fall. His only solution was in everything he despised about politics and the back-stabbing, two-faced nature of the business. He was becoming the epitome of everything he detested, the ultimate politician playing both sides. Never before had he been faced with such a test in which the decisions he made not only could take him down but also everyone around him.

Henry had lost count of how many endless nights he had endured. They were never entirely sleep-free. He wandered in and out of sleep as he watched 1 a.m. turn into 2 a.m. and then 3 a.m. into 4 a.m. Somewhere in between, he had blacked out for half an hour. When 5 a.m. arrived, he was out the door, eager to be one of the first to see the *Providence Journal*. He ripped open the newspaper and began reading the top story above the fold: "Campagna to Prescott: This city needs real leaders with real answers." The story began, "In a startling admission, Democratic candidate for Mayor, John Campagna, admitted that if elected, he will raise property taxes by as much as $3 per thousand. He then lambasted his Republican opponent, businessman Jack Prescott, for his political inexperience, calling him 'a country club Republican...bored after making [his] millions.'" Further down, the story read, "A poll of 500 registered voters after the debate revealed that 68 percent believed John Campagna had won the debate. Eighty-four percent had a favorable opinion of Campagna while 51 percent had an unfavorable opinion of Prescott."

As he sat in his car, Henry realized he couldn't have hoped for a better story. His candidate had prevailed, despite the unsavory reality of the truth, and the people were rewarding him for his honesty. Henry knew the debate would be the topic of discussion in every coffee shop, office, and bar room in Providence. Only about 250 people had packed the City Hall chamber to watch the debate live, and only about 10,000 had watched it in its entirety on television. For the most part, the majority of the people's opinions of the candidates' performances were formulated by what they read in the newspaper, saw in clips on TV and online, or heard from their friends and co-workers. Debates were rarely won on stage, but rather in the news. Henry couldn't wait to watch the ten-second clip of Campagna proclaiming the city needed real leaders. Honest, sincere, and professional was how Campagna came across in the living rooms of the voters. No one, not even the candidate himself, could ever have suspected that it was all part of a plan hatched by the shrewdest of operators.

His mentor, Congressman McNally, who'd questioned the

wisdom of Henry's plan at first, now understood its brilliance. McNally called Henry on his cell phone while the paper was still in his hands. "Well, kid," he said. "You're not going to get many mornings like this in politics. Great move, Henry, getting Campagna to admit everything. You exposed Prescott for the fraud he is and made Campagna look like even more of a saint. I don't know how you pulled this one off, but my hat's off to you, kid."

"All I did was tell him to speak the truth," Henry said.

"It was a brilliant setup. You played to your candidate's strength, his sincerity, and his honesty, and you made it work. You've got eight weeks to win this, and considering Prescott just imploded, Beako and the boys are going to pull out all the stops. Just be prepared because they've got everything to lose now. They're coming after you, Henry."

"I'm one step ahead of them."

***

In the five years he had known Vincent, Henry had never seen his apartment. Vincent always seemed to show up at his office. And when he slipped up and the Providence Police Department caught up to him, Henry was usually there to bail him out. Usually, the trouble was a result of Vincent neglecting to grease the right cops.

When Henry called and asked to meet, Vincent assumed he had finally taken him up on his offer to dress him in one of his finer Mani suits. Henry walked into Vincent's one-bedroom townhome in a duplex on the south side, which was decorated with Mani, Hickey Freeman, and Ralph Lauren suits. Vincent had taken the time to display some of his finer apparel for his star attorney who had rescued him from many a legal jam. Henry couldn't help but cough in the haze of cannabis Vincent had smoked shortly before his arrival.

"Nice place. I like what you've done to it, with the suits and all," Henry joked.

"Hey, buddy, you gotta give me more advance notice when you're coming over. I could have gotten you some even better stuff."

"I'm all set. Thanks." Henry hoped he meant the clothes and not the pot, as he began to count in his head how many crimes he was a party to simply by being in Vincent's apartment.

"Then what is it, Henry? I mean, I don't want to be rude, but my place ain't exactly one of those places a guy like you is used to."

"I've got a problem I thought you might be able to help me with," Henry said, coming right out with it. With Vincent, there was no need for idle chit-chat.

"Whatever you need, you know I'm here for ya."

"I need you to talk to someone for me. A guy who's been giving me a hard time."

"Talk?"

"I thought you could maybe persuade him a little."

"Who is it?" Vincent asked without hesitation. He seemed downright eager.

"Nick Dean. He runs D&D Advertising downtown."

"I'll take care of it," Vincent said. He stood up straight, a man proud to offer his talents to a friend. "Not a problem."

"Wait a second. Don't you want to know why?"

"Don't need to, Henry."

***

Vincent, in his purple velour V-neck exposing his gold chain and hairy chest, was visibly out of place in Tribeca's, Providence's self-proclaimed hip spot. The nightclub catered to a clientele Vincent did not understand, but he was there to do a job for a friend. Although he had not expected this Dean character to be a problem, he'd come prepared with the best muscle he knew, his little cousin Joey, who worked as laborer when he wasn't breaking bones. Vincent blew by the tight-shirted bouncer at the door without even acknowledging him, while Joey gave him a quick shot to the chest instead of the cover charge. The bouncer buckled over in pain.

The bartender, hoping to avoid the fate of the bouncer, didn't hesitate to reveal the identity and whereabouts of Nick Dean. The two wiseguys pushed through the crowd with little regard for the men donned in their black t-shirts and bare-backed females showcasing their talent in their low-rise jeans. Joey found Dean attempting to reclaim his youth on the dance floor. Vincent tapped him on the shoulder, but before he had the chance to turn, he grabbed him by the ear and ripped his earring from the lobe. Although Dean worked out at the gym five days a week, he was easily tossed to the floor. He lay in the middle of the dance floor as his two attackers stomped his chest, ribs, and head. They pushed Dean's face into the floor and dragged him by the hair until his face was a bloody mess. Satisfied with their work, Vincent and Joey walked out of the night club with a confident stride, leaving Dean like roadkill—disturbing, but not important enough to do anything about.

***

There were few people who would call Henry's cell at 2 a.m. —his mother and maybe Campagna or McNally. Knowing it was someone or something important, he reached and grabbed it from his dresser.

"You little shit! You almost killed him!" It was Beako's voice shouting at him.

"What are you talking about?" Henry asked.

"Dean. Seems a couple of goombahs just walked into Tribecca's and kicked the shit out of him. You wouldn't know nothing about it, would you?"

"First of all, I don't even know what Tribecca's is. Second, do you really think I'd have Dean taken out?"

"I think you're a fucking bastard who'd do whatever it took to save his ass. But this time, you've gone too far. Dean's got two broken ribs. He's in the hospital."

"Maybe Dean pissed off the wrong guy?"

"Yeah, Henry. That's exactly why I called you first," Beako said as he slammed down the phone.

***

The stakes had risen, and Henry was playing by a new set of rules. Beako took the pictures of Henry and Campagna's niece from his locked desk drawer and sealed them in an envelope. On the package, he wrote, "Lyndsay Sinclair, 147 Oak Branch Road, Charlotte, NC," and dropped it in the mail. Beako's PI had followed Lyndsay to the airport, where she had boarded a flight to Charlotte. She had several large bags with her, and they were unsure whether she was going home for the weekend, a week, or indefinitely.

It was a chess game, and his enemy had made his move. Beako had been forced to react. He'd launched the first strike, but Henry had proved he was willing to increase the number of casualties on the other side. This was war.

19

It was unusual for Reginald Sinclair to be home in the early afternoon. But this was no ordinary day. His first-born daughter was coming home from her medical residency in Providence, and he didn't want to miss a moment of her stay. It was a rare occasion when all four daughters were home together. His second daughter, Bridget, had agreed to pass up skiing in Vail with her classmates from UNC to be home with her older sister. He knew Bridget's sacrifice would ultimately cost him—he would probably have to agree to send her to Paris next year. His two youngest daughters, Jenny, fifteen, and Julie, fourteen, were both at their private high school, pushing their teachers' buttons. Julie had announced to her English teacher that she had refused to read *Romeo and Juliet* because it sent the wrong message to young women about love. And the principal had called the house after Jenny had accused her gym teacher of being a sexist pig when he wouldn't allow her to play flag football with the boys. Raising four girls was undoubtedly a challenging endeavor, but he was grateful for every moment.

His daughters kept him young, though at times, he thought they might be the primary reason for the gray streaks in his hair. He had argued that his salt-and-pepper look made him more distinguished, but Jenny joked that he had more salt than pepper. Sinclair kept in good shape and was only ten pounds heavier than he'd been as the back-up wide out for the UNC football team his senior year. He worked out four times a week to keep his body strong and mind sharp for the grueling days he faced on the corporate battlefields.

More than his money, more than his power, Sinclair cared most about protecting his four daughters. The first pair were some seven years apart from his two little darlings, who were beginning to try his patience with their insistence that they were far more mature than their older sisters had been at their age and should be able to date. Sinclair would never be quite comfortable with his daughters dating. His wife reigned over that area of their lives and had strictly forbidden their dating until the girls were sixteen, just as she had with their older sisters. But their family circle was expanding, and there would be a new member of the Sinclair clan—this Henry Mercucio.

Sinclair's wife, Mary, had mixed feelings about Henry, but they were driven more by his social standing rather than his treatment of their daughter. Certainly she would have preferred a boy from one of the southern families, but Lyndsay was old enough to make her own decisions. Sinclair himself was more supportive of her choice and looked forward to having another man in the family with whom he could hunt and watch football. But it was more than male bonding that appealed to him. He had a strong sense that Henry wasn't one of those lazy rich kids his daughters tended to date whose idea of work was managing a trust fund, as he had done initially. He saw the burning desire in Henry, that underlying quality that breeds greatness.

One would never know by looking at him that Sinclair was

worth more than a billion. In fact, neither his daughters nor his wife knew exactly how much money they had. Sinclair wasn't the type to advertise his wealth. Sure, they lived in a 10,000-square-foot mansion in a gated community outside Charlotte, but he neither dressed with opulence nor drove an expensive car. Sinclair was a billionaire with middle-class taste. He didn't need designer suits and a flashy Mercedes to feel successful or appreciate his worth. All he had to do was look into the eyes of his daughters to understand how fortunate he was.

He worked to ensure his girls would have every opportunity, and Lyndsay's decision to pursue a career in medicine pleased him. The Sinclairs knew their daughter's decision to go to Providence had been based more on her feelings for this dynamic young lawyer than the strength of the university's family-focused atmosphere or its medical program. Mary was especially uneasy having her first daughter so far away, but she was adjusting, much to the displeasure of the younger girls whose lives she still micromanaged. Now that Mary had a wedding to obsess over, her younger daughters were granted a temporary reprieve from their mother's chokehold.

Despite his money, Sinclair was a working man who felt more comfortable in the office than on the putting green. He had taken up golf later in life, and after golf schools and private lessons he was able to score in the mid-80s. When his girls were younger, he'd been preoccupied with dance recitals, field hockey practice, and chauffeuring them. Now that hanging out with Dad wasn't cool anymore, he had a little more time to fine-tune his golf game.

He was changing into his country club attire when he heard his five-year-old Beagle viciously howl, as though someone was breaking into the house. It was just the mailman, but Sinclair was thankful that Buddy took his responsibility in guarding the home so seriously. He rummaged through the mail and opened a yellow envelope that he mistakenly thought was addressed to him. Lyndsay rarely received mail at home, and he automatically assumed it was his. He was stunned by what he saw. It was a man with a woman hanging on him, her lips against his, and the man looked like Henry. Why would Henry do this to his daughter, but equally disturbing, why would someone send these pictures to Lyndsay? His calm temperament prevailed over his immediate flash of anger and utter disappointment, and he began to analyze the situation. The careful and deliberative judgment that had helped him orchestrate complex business deals was now at work.

Even though Sinclair had little doubt that it was Henry in the pictures, and though he could easily derail the marriage, he had no desire to do so. Henry had earned his place at Sinclair's table, and now the business titan was ready to return the favor. With the photos in his hand, his mind drifted back to "the incident," as it was referred to on the rare occasions it was discussed, that had occurred five years ago, when their relationship was still new.

***

Henry and Lyndsay had been at dinner in Georgetown when they had run into a bit of bad luck. With eyes only for each other, they had been walking from the restaurant where they had been celebrating their first six months together, unaware of the danger ahead of them. Trouble had come in the form of a blunt object blindsiding Henry, knocking him to the street. Lyndsay had been thrown to the ground, but Henry quickly had made it back to his feet. What would later be diagnosed as a dislocated shoulder and a concussion had not rendered him helpless. Startled and dazed from the blow, he had been able to quickly regroup and strike back with utter ferocity. The assailants, who had assumed they had found themselves easy prey, had been unprepared for the wrath that had been unleashed upon them.

Henry had pulled Lyndsay up, had shoved her away, and had told her to run as fast as she could. "Get help," he had screamed as he struck at those who wanted to rob him of all he was. He had bashed the eyes of the smallest of the three, temporarily blinding him. He had then gone after the next man, who was at least a hundred pounds heavier than he, leveling the hardest kick he could muster to the man's stomach. Reacting with the precision and form of a warrior, Henry had picked up the steel pole that had fallen to the ground in the melee—the blunt object that had struck him in the head—and had lunged at his third attacker. He had been able to knock the man off of his feet before his two comrades, who were enraged from their injuries, had overwhelmed him. Henry had then taken a beating that would have killed most men. His ribs had been kicked in and his knee had been busted. And just as his head almost had received its final blow, the cavalry had arrived in the form of DC Metro. Lyndsay had gotten help.

It had taken four weeks for Henry to fully recover, but with no health insurance, he had been left on the floor with the rest of the indigent. Lyndsay had refused to leave his side, and it had taken the intervention of Congressman McNally and the President of Georgetown University to convince the hospital to move their boy to a room where his girlfriend would be able to watch over him.

Reggie and Mary Sinclair had rushed to DC, where they found their daughter unwilling to leave Henry. Mary Sinclair and Henry's mother, who had flown in from Cape Cod with her other son, had gone to Lyndsay's dorm room and retrieved her clothes and essentials. Mrs. Mercucio had been instructed by her son to take a brief reprieve from Henry's bedside vigil. Reggie Sinclair and Henry's brother, Paul, a well-respected cardiothoracic surgeon from Boston, had ensured that the young man received the highest level of care.

His brother insisted on a complete battery of tests from MRIs to psychological evaluations, while Reggie Sinclair had moved Henry to a private room in the hospital's new wing. Sinclair had pleaded with Henry's brother to allow him to foot the bill.

"Your brother saved my daughter's life," Sinclair had said.

"I understand, but he's my little brother."

"Do you have a daughter, Dr. Mercucio?"

"I do," the doctor had answered. "Her name's Sarah. She's five years old."

"And if some animals tried to do God-knows-what, and then some kid had the courage to protect her, wouldn't you do what I'm doing?"

"I understand, and we appreciate it, but it's a family thing."

"As far as I'm concerned, Dr. Mercucio, your brother is family. You concentrate on getting him whatever medical help he needs, and I'll take care of it. End of discussion," Sinclair had said.

Sinclair had been informed by the lead DC detective that the men who had jumped Henry, who also were in intensive care partly from Henry's assault and the DC cops' retribution, had been wanted for the rape and murder of a young college couple. Apparently they had held up two George Washington University co-eds at gunpoint, had raped both the girl and boy, and had killed them execution style on the outskirts of town. The detective had little doubt the same fate would have fallen on Henry and Lyndsay.

His wounds would heal, but the scars—physical and psychological—would always remain a part of Henry's life. It would take a two-week treatment of anti-anxiety medication and six months of weekly counseling sessions before Henry could resolve the turmoil he had lived through, and Reggie Sinclair, who had been there beside him, holding his daughter's hand through her boyfriend's recovery, would never forget it.

Sinclair knew Henry to be passionate, but stupid and disloyal were out of character. The photos went into his secure desk drawer, and Sinclair took a piece of stationery and began penning a clandestine message. He knew exactly what to do.

20

When he met Beako after hours in his CampCo office, Henry had no idea his secret was already out. Beako seemed more confident than usual as he slapped Henry's back and put his arm over his shoulder.

"How you doing, buddy?"

"Fuck you, Beako."

"We expected you'd try to pull something cute, but having someone kick the shit out of Dean? Never thought you'd go that far."

"I don't know what you're talking about."

"Sure you don't. Whatever, Henry. Tell me, was that your brilliant idea for Campagna to go off the reservation in the debate?"

"Hey, I only write it. I don't control what comes out of his mouth. Maybe you were wrong, Beako, and this guy thinks for himself and does the right thing. Imagine that."

Beako sat down in his black leather chair, lit his cigar, and gazed out his window over City Hall. Henry knew he was trying to appear intimidating and was only masking his real fear that someone as forthright as Campagna might just walk into City Hall. Henry didn't buy the act, but he wanted Beako to think he was playing his game.

"I need you to do something so we know you're with us," Beako said. "I want you to confirm something."

"Now what?"

"It seems that your guy, Campagna, sees a shrink and is on an antidepressant."

"You think people are really going to care that he's on Prozac?"

"Actually, it's Paroxetine," Beako said, looking down at his file. "Your guy's been on twenty milligrams a day for the last year and a half."

"What did you do, break into his doctor's office and steal his file? Not even you would do that, Beako."

"It's not important how we got it, Henry. It's what we do with it. Now, what we need to know is what he'll say. How he's going to play it."

"Who are you guys, the Plumbers or something?" Henry said, referring to the Nixon operatives. "Let me see if I've got this straight. You want me to tell you how Campagna's going to respond to illegally acquired information that he's on a commonly prescribed medication?"

"That's where you come in, buddy. It's not illegally acquired if he comes out and admits it, now, is it? We want you to tell Campagna to announce that he sees a shrink and is on medication. Here's a copy of his prescription."

"You're beautiful, Beako. You enjoy this, don't you? You can't win a fair fight, so you use whatever you can get to fuck over the other guy. How do you sleep at night?"

"On a pillow full of money."

"I'd expect nothing less. It's always about the bucks," Henry fired back. "Things like loyalty, honor—they're just cheap words you throw around when it's convenient but mean nothing."

"Get off your pedestal, Henry. You got yourself into this one all on your own. Now deal with it."

"I'm dealing with it every day of my life now, thanks to you."

"I feel your pain. Now get out of my office before I start to get misty. And, Henry, you try pulling that shit like you did with Dean, you're not going to know what hit you."

"That's too bad what happened to Dean," Henry said. "He's such an upstanding gentleman. I'm sure he didn't have it coming."

***

Playing fair was for boy scouts and the Jesuits, not for politicians and strategists. Beako was taking no chances. That was why he'd brought an old friend into the game. Amos Miller was an ex-cop who had grown up in the same neighborhood as Beako. He had been kicked off the Providence Police Force for drinking on the job and for beating a young black kid nearly to death with his nightstick. Beako had bailed out his friend through some contacts at City Hall and had procured a medical discharge from the force. After he'd cleaned himself up through thirty days in rehab, he'd again turned to Beako, who'd assisted him in obtaining a private investigator's license.

Most of the time, Miller spent his days and nights tailing wayward husbands. But his real money came from special assignments from Beako, who paid him $500 an hour to obtain information on his political enemies. The money he received from Beako, always in cash, was twice his usual rate for snapping pictures of cheating husbands. The pictures he had taken of the girl and Henry Mercucio had earned him an extra grand and a new assignment from Beako.

After a week of tailing Henry Mercucio and coming up with the goods on him, Miller was assigned to John Campagna. He was a pretty routine guy who took his two kids to school in the morning and arrived at his law practice by 8 a.m. He was home in the evenings by six unless he had a city council meeting or political fundraiser to attend. There were no mistresses, no questionable business deals, basically no dirt. But on one Wednesday morning, Miller discovered information so invaluable he knew Beako would pay him a couple of grand for it. Campagna's Wednesday appointment was with Dr. Robert Tomasso. Careful to avoid being seen, Campagna went in through the side door of an office building. Miller followed him, using the front entrance instead, and watched from the florist next door as Campagna walked into the doctor's office. He politely asked the florist, as he purchased a dozen roses for his girlfriend, what type of doctor Tomasso was. "Psychiatrist," the woman said. After an hour, Campagna left the office carrying a small brown bag. Miller walked into the office and picked up a business card from the receptionist's desk. The card read, "Robert Tomasso, MD, Psychiatry." Miller had what he needed and walked out of the office before the secretary had even realized he was there.

His work wasn't finished. Thursday was trash pick-up in Providence, so he camped out near Campagna's home until three in the morning. He drove by the house and took the trash bag out of the bin out front. Rummaging through someone's trash wasn't what he had envisioned doing when he was in the police academy, but the endeavor proved fruitful when he found a small orange pill cylinder with the inscription "John Campagna, 20 milligrams, Paroxetine, Dr. Robert Tomasso." It was the equivalent of finding a wedding ring in the trash. Miller figured this little pill container might be enough to buy him a week in Florida.

21

*For whoever thinks that among great
personages recent benefits will cause old injuries
to be forgotten, deceives himself greatly.*
—Niccolò Machiavelli

John Campagna wasn't the first politician who hadn't been entirely honest with the people closest to him. In fact, Henry had become accustomed to his clients deceiving him. That was the nature of criminal law. Henry knew many in politics who found it more convenient to embellish or outright lie rather than admit the truth. They simply saw the light through their own prism. Although Campagna's concealment wasn't as devious as Henry's own betrayal, his failure to disclose treatment for depression could be enough to cost him the race.

It was the lowest point Henry could remember. He had nearly cheated on his fiancée, and a young woman had been found dead.

Adding to his misery was the news that his arch nemesis had photos tying him to the deceased. How had he fallen so far, to the point where he had actually asked a criminal to rough up a political rival? Another man now lay near death because Henry had spoken. He needed to end this madness before it swallowed another unsuspecting victim.

Henry had to deal with Campagna's issue first and started to realize that the answer was tied in the truth. He would advise Campagna to tell the truth once again. It was all that could possibly free him. But it was easier to coach from the sidelines than to play in the game. He couldn't simply walk into Campagna's office, sit him down, and tell him that he had been with his niece the night she died. He couldn't tell him that Beako was blackmailing him to throw the election. In his case, the truth would bury him, and the only solution would be found further down the path of deception.

The only way to head off the damage was to release the information first. Convincing his client that this was the best course of action was the most difficult part. Henry called him and explained it was important that they meet in person for urgent business. It was almost midnight, but Henry insisted that it couldn't wait until morning.

"What brings you out this late, Henry?" Campagna asked in a tone that was neither threatening nor inviting.

"I received an anonymous letter today with a copy of a prescription for an antidepressant. It had your name on it. You want to tell me about it?" Henry asked, wasting no time with pleasantries.

"No, Henry. It's none of your business."

"You don't think it's my business, and the people of this city's business, that the candidate for mayor is being treated for depression?"

"No, I don't. It's my personal business, and that's how I want it."

"Obviously, I'm not the only one who has this information. I can assure you that the people who have this are going to use it. The damage is done. It all depends now on how you handle it."

"I don't know how you got this information, Henry, but it stinks. This thing's supposed to be between a doctor and a patient. It's not supposed to be on the front page of the papers."

"Yeah, but unfortunately it doesn't work that way. You're a public figure, and your entire life's exposed. It's the choice you made when you decided to run for office. It's not your life anymore. It's theirs now," Henry said, demonstratively pointing outside.

Campagna was upset. His usual composure had been rattled by his consultant's news. A silence followed Henry's words, an uncomfortable quiet in which both parties understood that the next words spoken often determined the course of events to follow. Campagna was the first to break the stalemate, and his words revealed that he had chosen the right path.

"Let me tell you, Henry, I wouldn't wish it on my worst enemy," he said. "You have no idea what it's like."

"Why don't you try me, John?" Henry offered. He very rarely called Campagna by his first name, though they were clearly on a first-name basis.

"It hit me when I was in my late twenties. I was a lot like you, full of piss and vinegar, thought I could change the world. I put a lot of pressure on myself. I had gone off on my own as a lawyer, I was a freshman councilman, and I had just gotten married. If you looked at me, you'd say, 'He's got it all,' but I was never satisfied and always had something to prove. At first, I couldn't sleep. I'd crash out on the couch around nine o'clock, but then I'd be up at four. I'd usually go into the office and work. Some nights, I wouldn't sleep at all. I'd be up all night worrying if I had enough money coming in."

Henry could identify with Campagna. "I know what it's like

not sleeping. It's three in the morning, and you lie there awake. You think you're the only one who can't sleep."

"Yeah, but imagine not sleeping for days at a time. That's what it was like for me. I was always on edge, constantly worrying. That's when I went to the doctor. I told him I needed something to help me sleep, but he could tell there was something more to it. He could see it wasn't me. So I started to see a shrink about once a month. He put me on an antidepressant and another medication to help me sleep. I was on both of them for a year. The medication and the therapy worked for me. I learned not to judge myself against my father. He was a great man, you know, and I felt like I never lived up to him."

"You just don't seem like the type."

"There's no type, Henry. It just happens. To guys like me, to doctors, lawyers, construction workers—it doesn't discriminate. It's something people just don't want to accept. Because if it can happen to someone like me, then it could happen to them. And for each person, it's different. For me, I couldn't sleep. Constantly anxious. It changes who you are. I've always been a good talker—I'm a politician for god's sake—but, man, I just didn't want to talk. I was self-conscious of everything that came out of my mouth. It was like this little voice in my head was constantly judging everything I said. It used to bother the hell out of me going into work, people asking me if everything was okay or if something was wrong."

"I hear you. There's nothing worse than that. I get it from Lyndsay all the time."

"Can you imagine a politician scared to be around people? I would go to council meetings feeling paranoid that someone would see there was something wrong with me. I thought I was going to lose my job, my family, everything. I thought my whole life was collapsing around me. It was a living hell."

"But you seem fine now. It doesn't seem to affect you anymore."

Henry really didn't know what to say. He knew little about depression or mental illness other than his personal encounter.

"You know what kept me going, Henry? The people. That's what got me out of bed in the morning after staring at the ceiling all night. The thing that got me out from under my covers was service to my constituents. And no matter how I felt, when I was at my lowest point, when I was really knocking myself down, it was the people who kept me going. I love being a councilman, and I'm proud of what I've done for this city. My depression has never once interfered with me serving my constituents, and I'll be damned if I let it now."

"We won't let it, John, and we won't let those bastards exploit it." Henry was in master spin mode. He could already envision it—a heartfelt interview in which Campagna told his personal battle with depression and how he had overcome it. Henry was beginning to see how Campagna's depression could further connect him with the voters. "Most people have been depressed at some point in their lives. People will identify with what you've been through, and they'll see what you've become. They'll judge you by what they see now, in this moment. But we have to be the ones who break the news."

"I don't know about this, Henry. It just doesn't feel right, spinning something like this," Campagna confided.

Henry was relieved his candidate felt that way—that he wasn't just another politician willing to exploit a personal problem. But at the same time, they had few options. If they didn't release the information first, their opponents would certainly cast Campagna's depression in the darkest light.

"Look at it this way. You don't really have a choice. If we don't talk about it, they will. We need to control the flow of information, not let it control us. It's better for us to release it first than have to respond to it. Then it doesn't seem like it's something we're hiding from. Plus, we get to frame the conversation around what we want. They'll want to portray you as someone ashamed of his illness, someone who wanted to hide it from the people, someone you can't trust. We'll display a man unafraid to admit that he had a problem. You'll talk about how you beat it, how you want to show others that there's hope, that if you can overcome depression, other people can overcome their problems too, whether it's losing their job or a loved one. You'll be their hope."

"I don't want people to say that the only reason I came forward was because it was going to come out anyway."

"Well, some may say that, but for the most part, the fact that you come out will put that argument to rest. If you're forced to respond to it, it'll look far worse. We're in damage control now, and we need to control how the information is leaked. If we allow little bits of information to come out, like that you once saw a shrink, or that you were on an antidepressant, then the questions and rumors begin swirling: were you ever hospitalized? Did you ever try to kill yourself? Instead, let's just come out with all of it—the entire thing, that you have depression, that you've been treated, that you see a doctor—so we can control the message. You've overcome it, and it has never interfered with your job as a councilman. Then it's just a one-day story about a guy who's brave enough to admit he had a problem."

"I'll do it, but I want to talk to my wife and kids first. Go ahead and make the arrangements."

22

Henry turned to a veteran reporter named Bradley Lansdown, who was known for his journalistic integrity, to break the story about Campagna and his battle with depression. He also chose Lansdown because the reporter had gone public with his own personal fight with depression. Lansdown was in his mid-seventies and had announced his affliction in a *Providence Journal* interview two decades earlier celebrating his thirtieth anniversary as a newsman. Many in the Rhode Island medical community credited Lansdown with breaking down the mental illness barriers of stigma and shame.

Lansdown anchored the top-rated local news program *Inside Providence* on Sunday mornings and was eager to interview the candidates for mayor. While Lansdown wanted Prescott and Campagna to appear together in a special debate on his program, Henry had convinced him to interview the candidates separately. The carrot Henry offered was a no-holds-barred interview in which Campagna would offer full disclosure, from his niece's tragedy with drugs to his own personal battle with depression.

"We're prepared to tell all, Mr. Lansdown, and let the people judge him for who he is. There's no one better to do it than you," Henry told him. But Lansdown hadn't survived forty years in the shrewd media world without knowing when he was being played. He told Henry he would ask tough questions, not simply give his candidate a thirty-minute infomercial.

"Don't spin me, kid. I know what you're trying to do. I'll give Campagna the interview, but he's not getting a free ride. There's already a story floating out there that he's on meds for depression."

Henry put it to him more delicately. "I would think of all people, Mr. Lansdown, you would be sympathetic to what Councilman Campagna's going through."

But Lansdown didn't take Henry's implication quite the way he'd expected. "Listen, I'll interview your guy, but don't think that because I have depression, I'm gonna give him a free pass."

"I wasn't implying that you would, just that of all people, you know what it's like. You were brave enough to go public with it first."

"Listen, kid, save your bullshit for some rookie reporter who actually believes what you guys are saying. I like Campagna, so I'll interview him. But to tell you the truth, I'll probably be tougher on him than someone who hasn't been through it. You want to know why? Because I hate people who use it as their crutch, or who only speak out because they know it's coming out anyway."

Henry saw it was pointless to argue. It was better to retreat than agitate the reporter and risk having him take it out on his client. Plus, Lansdown was onto him, and the last thing Henry wanted was for it to seem that Campagna's confession was contrived, a political move to preempt the inevitable release of damaging information. As he had explained to Campagna, there would be those who would see it that way, but there would be many more who would admire his courage for coming forward.

In prepping him for the interview, Henry intentionally asked provocative questions to bait him, but Campagna wouldn't fall for his trap. He remained composed, not once raising his voice or becoming annoyed when Henry asked the most outlandish questions. Have you ever received shock therapy? Have you ever been institutionalized? Did you ever attempt suicide? Campagna deflected Henry's barrage of questions with skill and grace. The key, Henry explained, was to remain calm no matter how offensive the question because people would judge him based on how he handled the pressure. It was essential for Campagna to prove he was mentally stable enough to deal with the challenges of the mayor's office, so he needed to appear in control. But this was just a dress rehearsal; the real test would come before an estimated audience of 20,000.

And no matter how much Henry coached him, Campagna was on his own when he appeared before Lansdown. But focusing on the camera instead of on the reporter, Campagna performed flawlessly. He paused before answering a question to safeguard himself from rushing and blurting out an answer. The tougher the question, the longer Campagna's pause. He was unflappable. In total control.

Lansdown came out of the box with a softball question. "Councilman Campagna, why do you want to be mayor of Providence?"

Campagna paused for a second, then delivered the monologue he had prepared. "My son, Paulie, asked me that very question. 'Dad, why do you want to be mayor?' You know, Bradley, kids come right out and ask you what's on their mind and expect a direct answer. So I told him, 'I want to help people.' There's no higher calling than serving your fellow man. And that's especially important today when people have lost faith in their elected officials. I want to help restore faith in government and honor at City Hall."

"And you're the one to do it, Councilman?"

"Bradley, I have a record to run on. I have served my constituents faithfully for the past ten years. I am the chairman of the finance committee, so I know our city's finances inside and out. I also believe that Mayor Donovan has accomplished a lot of great things for our city, but he made some bad decisions that I feel he should ultimately pay for. But we cannot let his indiscretions cast their shadow over our great city. I believe in the people of Providence. I see them out on the campaign trail. The waitress in the diner that serves me breakfast, how she wants to send her son to the private school because she's lost faith in our public school system. Or the city worker I ran into who said, after he was passed over for a promotion to a younger man with less experience, 'Well, that's just the way things are done here. It's not who you know, but who you pay off.' That's not right. That era needs to end."

"Councilman, do you feel a candidate should disclose to the people he represents whether he has suffered from a mental illness?" There it was: the setup question. There was no running from it now. If he said 'yes,' then he was forced to disclose his illness. If he said 'no,' he was only delaying the inevitable. Campagna handled it perfectly, pausing and then buying further time by repeating the question back to Lansdown.

"Yes, I do, Bradley. I think a candidate should disclose whether he has suffered from anything that could affect his ability to do his job. I think it's even more important today for people to know the truth about the people who represent them. But can a person serve effectively while suffering from a mental illness? Well, I'm living proof of it. I struggle with depression and have been treated professionally for recurring depression for the last eight years."

"Why did you wait until now to disclose this, Councilman? Don't you think people have the right to know?"

"Quite frankly, it never came up before. And if I had been asked, I would've answered the same way I did today. It's really never been an issue. It has never affected my job. In fact, I've never missed a vote on the city council in ten years. I've created business opportunity zones in my district, bringing hundreds of jobs to the people I represent. It didn't affect me there. I've helped balance a half-a-billion-dollar budget for the last five years, and it didn't seem to affect me there either."

"But the job of mayor is stressful. Shouldn't we be concerned that it might be too much for someone with your condition?"

Again Campagna paused, organizing his thoughts. "Yes, the job is stressful, but can I handle it? Well, I guess the best judge of that is what I've already done for the city. I'm proud of my record as a councilman. I'm sure there will be stressful moments, but I believe my experience will help guide me through the challenging times."

"Are you taking any medications?"

"I am. I take a therapeutic dosage of an antidepressant in the morning. It's no different than someone taking a pill for diabetes."

"Are you on Prozac?"

"I take twenty milligrams of Paroxetine, the generic form of Paxil."

"Then you must see a doctor," Lansdown said.

"I do. I've been seeing a psychiatrist for about eight years."

"And how often do you see your doctor?"

"It depends. Usually every couple of months. Sometimes every six months." Campagna felt as comfortable discussing his bout with depression as he did in speaking about fixing the budget or improving the schools.

"Are you depressed now?" Lansdown asked.

"No, but I think I might be depressed later about this interview," Campagna joked. "Kidding aside, I'm not really suffering from any symptoms right now, and I haven't in probably five years."

"Do you fear the symptoms could come back? That you could

become depressed again?"

"That's why I'm receiving treatment. It's to protect me from recurring symptoms."

"Do you feel your condition will be used against you?"

"I think the people of Providence are smarter than that. I don't think they care that I take a small pill in the morning to treat a condition. I believe they'll look at my credentials and my positions on the issues, then judge me on how I serve and have served them."

"Speaking of your positions, your opponent has come up with a property tax reimbursement plan for parents to send their children to private schools. Won't that hurt a city that's already in financial trouble?"

That was it. The inquisition was over, and Campagna had survived. He had not only endured Lansdown's cross-examination, but had managed to turn his weakness into a strength. Henry, of course, was nervous and anxious as he watched the interview from the green room of the television station. He felt like a concerned mother watching a child go off to school on the first day. When he walked onto the set to greet Campagna, he approached his client like a conquering prince. His plan had worked, and the keys to the kingdom were now in reach. Though he wouldn't know the full impact of the interview until the evening, when pollsters would gauge voter responses, Henry had been through the political juggernaut enough times to know when a candidate had sunk or sailed. When he saw Campagna, he threw a bear hug around him. Although they were as close as a consultant and politician could be, simply by the mere fact that Henry knew his deepest secrets, they weren't the type of men who casually displayed their affection in public.

"Home run," Henry whispered in his ear. "Home fucking run."

***

The polling numbers that evening confirmed what Henry already knew. More than two-thirds of the potential voters didn't care that Campagna suffered from depression, and he'd actually improved his favorable impression on voters by going public. Henry figured Campagna would drop about ten points, but he was surprised that his candidate had improved his image instead. He did have a nagging suspicion that people didn't want to admit to the pollsters that they wouldn't vote for a person on medication, and in the privacy of the booth, their prejudices would surface.

But for now, Henry had done it. He had turned what could have been a devastating blow into a positive development. The power was in the way Campagna conducted himself, with a kind of courage and composure that prevented voters from abandoning him. More than ever, Henry was beginning to believe in people again, people like Campagna who were brave and honest. He was even beginning to respect the voters again, who suddenly seemed willing to overlook the stereotypes of mental illness and depression to accept a man for who he was. Campagna had continually proven his trustworthiness and honesty no matter the situation or the challenge hurled at him. War had been declared. He was going to take down Beako once and for all. The battle lines had been drawn long before. The fight itself was upon them, and only one man would walk away this time.

23

Dr. Paul Martin was about to break an oath as sacred as confession—doctor-patient privilege.

Breaking his vow wasn't something he took lightly. Like many Providence residents, he had watched the Campagna interview, and was impressed with the candidate's brave admission of the truth. If this was what this election was coming to, full disclosure, then Dr. Martin felt that Malcolm Prescott should be tried in the same court of public opinion. However, Dr. Martin's motives weren't entirely altruistic. Malcolm Prescott sat on the Board of Governors of the Providence Country Club, one of the most prestigious golf courses in the state. Martin believed Prescott's vote to block his membership had been both unwarranted and hypocritical, and the highly regarded ob/gyn wanted retribution.

Dr. Martin served as the president of Planned Parenthood of Providence and was as well-renowned for his skill with his scalpel as he was for his outspoken support of a woman's right to choose. Only about ten percent of his practice involved the abortion procedure, but he was regarded by the Pro-Life community as Dr. Abortion. While no official reason was given for the denial of Dr. Martin's country club membership, his sponsors had heard that Prescott had raised the question of Martin's ethnicity. Allegedly, Prescott had said, "We don't want brown spots," a reference perceived to mean Martin's Latino heritage. Dr. Martin, who had shortened his name from Martinez shortly after he'd came over from the Dominican Republic, paid his taxes like the Prescotts, supported local charities like the Prescotts, and was just as American as the Prescotts. He resented the implication that he and his family weren't good enough to dine with them.

The knowledge hung heavy in his heart. He tried to convince himself that his actions to expose the Prescott hypocrisy would better serve the women's rights movement, but he still wasn't sure. There was always a way to justify one's actions, no matter how deceitful. The truth was this—Prescott's seventeen-year-old daughter, who was at least nineteen by now, had received an abortion, at the hands of Dr. Martin, no less. Mrs. Prescott had accompanied her, and as with many of these cases, Mr. Prescott would be the last to know.

That was typical of men like him, Martin thought. They didn't even know what was going on under their own roofs, let alone what was right for the people of Providence. Although he held sacred the Prescotts' daughter's right to privacy, Martin was beginning to believe her sacrifice would be worth it if it meant that a person like Prescott would never be in a position to influence public policy.

"Henry Mercucio, please," he said to the young woman who answered the phone. No hello; all business.

"Can I tell him who's calling?" the receptionist asked.

"Just tell him I'm someone he wants to talk to."

"Okay. Can I ask, then, what it's regarding?" she persisted.

"Malcolm Prescott," was all he said.

"Just a minute, please." She knew Henry was in his office, and surprisingly not on the phone. But she took her time transferring the call, her little way of exerting what small inkling of power she had. "Henry, there's some rude guy on the line, won't give his name, says it's about Malcolm Prescott. You want him?"

"Is he a nut, or for real?" Henry asked.

"Sounds legit. Just rude."

"Yeah, put him through."

The receptionist took another moment to transfer the call, again taking her sweet time.

After a moment, the line clicked back on. "Is this Henry Mercucio?" the voice asked.

"Yes, it is. With whom am I speaking, may I ask?"

"You may not ask. But you may listen to what I have to say."

"I answered the phone, didn't I?" Henry said.

"Ask Malcolm Prescott what his stance is on abortion."

"He's actually been quite vocal about it. He's pro-life, but so is John Campagna. And a mayor can't do anything about the issue anyway. That issue's for the General Assembly."

"Ask him again. Ask him if he would allow someone in his family to have an abortion."

"Why don't you tell me where you're going with this?" Henry said.

"Malcolm Prescott's daughter, Elizabeth, had an abortion, two years ago when she was seventeen."

"Really? Don't you need a parent with you when you're a minor?"

"Her mother signed."

"Wait a second. How do you know this?"

"That's not important. What's important is the fact that Prescott goes around all holier-than-thou while his daughter and wife are at the abortion clinic." That was it. It wasn't so much Prescott's denying him a golf membership, but the blatant hypocrisy.

"Can you prove any of this?"

"Yes, I can get you a copy of the mother's consent form."

"Then may I suggest you make a few copies of it? Send me one, and I'll be sure to drop it in the right hands."

"Look, I don't want to hurt the girl, just that hypocrite, Prescott. People deserve to know the truth about him."

"Don't worry. We'll make sure your information is used properly."

"I'm sure you will, Mr. Mercucio," he said as he hung up the phone.

***

Henry made the ten-minute drive over to Campagna's law office in Providence, which doubled as the real campaign head-quarters. The storefront in the neighborhood officially served as campaign HQ, but it was more a gathering place for the old political stalwarts and elderly women of the neighborhood for gossip.

"Is he in?" Henry asked the secretary.

"He's got someone in there. Can you wait?"

"No, I can't. Just tell him I need to talk to him, okay?"

"Fine," she replied as she walked into Campagna's office. He could hear her say to Campagna, "Your political guy's here and says it's important." She came back and told him, "You can go in."

"Henry, I thought I was meeting you at your office at 2 p.m.? What's up? Is there something wrong? Robby, can you excuse us for a minute?" Campagna said to the young politico who was sharing the most recent polling data.

"No, but there's something rotten in the house of Prescott,"

Henry said as he took the chair offered to him.

"What do you mean?"

"Seems that Prescott's daughter, when she was seventeen, had an abortion."

Campagna didn't say anything. He just sat there with the look of a disappointed father. He told Henry, "We don't do that, Henry."

"But—"

"We're better than that. We're not gonna ruin a young girl's life so we can gain five points in the polls. In ten years of politics, I've never gone negative, and I'm not starting now."

***

Do the right thing. Tell the truth, Henry thought. How had these basic tenets taught as a child become so difficult to follow as an adult? He considered the answer as he made his return from Campagna's office. All that he valued, all that he was, had been conveniently traded for the easy life, the less virtuous one. It was far more difficult to be an honest man, to live life by a set of morals, to cast aside the easy road and vehemently strive for the straight and narrow. That was Campagna. He was one of those men, true to himself, true to what he stood for, simply honest. And what was Henry? Just some slick-tongued spin-doctor whose variation of the truth was used to serve his interests in the moment? He didn't like what he had become, and he saw in Campagna's election the way to make things right for a city, for its people, and for himself. Campagna had become Henry's cause, his mission, his chance to do the right thing. All he had to do was make a phone call.

"I've got something for you, Beako," Henry said.

"You better because I'm getting sick of your bullshit," Beako replied. "I haven't seen shit from you. You find out Campagna's got depression, and the next thing we know, he's on fucking television spilling his guts. I don't know if you're really with us. Maybe I need to send the DA a little package. I'm sure he'd be interested in a nice high-profile case full of sex and drugs. It has all the makings of the type of case that careers are made from."

"What do you need me to do, whack somebody for you? You can't expect me to fully come over to the other side. It wouldn't be believable, so don't get your panties in a bunch, and listen to what I have to say."

"Alright, then. What do you got?"

"Looks like your 'holier-than-thou' candidate doesn't keep his house in order. I'd tell him to tone down the abortion rhetoric. First of all, a mayor can't do anything about it. It's state law. That little civics lesson's for free. Turns out his daughter had an abortion when she was seventeen, and his wife signed the consent form. So it either means his wife told him, and he's really a fucking hypocrite, or he has no idea what's going on under his own roof. Either way, you're fucked."

"No fucking way," Beako said. "You're full of shit."

"So ask him. It looks like your perfect little candidate's got some baggage."

"Campagna will never use it. He's too much of a boy scout."

"Won't have to. The *Journal's* already got it. Heard they're gonna set him up in the next debate. Someone in the audience is going to bring it up. Hey, it was your idea to do the town meeting format, Beako. That's what you get," Henry said. "There's only one thing you can do. It's what Campagna did. If you know it's gonna come out, then you be the one to break it. You control the flow of information."

"I don't fucking believe you, Henry."

"Don't kill the messenger. Why don't you ask your candidate, or are you afraid to?"

24

It still hurt every time Jimmy Callahan saw an article in the paper, or heard the mayor's name mentioned, or imagined the snickering behind his back. He was the one who had lost the FBI's number one suspect. Unsurprisingly, he had been pulled off the case, a lateral administrative move, he had been told, but he understood the reality of the situation. He had let the prime suspect in the country's largest extortion ring just walk out of the country. His reason for failing to block Donovan's trip abroad? He had not wanted to force the grand jury to issue a premature indictment while he was still building his case. This didn't sell with the bureaucrats in Washington who wanted to sack Donovan's empire. The Justice Department wanted results, not the mockery of an American mayor indulging his every excess from the pockets of American taxpayers.

If the mayor thought he could just thumb his nose at the American government from his comfortable confines in Europe, then he had underestimated the resolve of a man who had made it his quest to bring Donovan to justice. Like Donovan before him, Callahan had liquidated his assets, and had squirreled away almost a half a million. Since he had never taken a vacation or personal day, he found himself with an entire month to take his own trans-Atlantic excursion. Considering the lambasting he had suffered in every newspaper in New England, the US Attorney didn't think it was a bad idea for him to take a holiday. No one suspected the publicly scorned deputy was conducting his own private investigation.

His first stop was Cork, Ireland, the unknowing accomplice to Mayor Donovan's disappearance. He was bound to turn up some lead. Like Ahab, Callahan's obsession consumed him. Sleep deserted him, and food no longer satisfied him. The vision of a pride-stung prosecutor with a bewildered look, the type of grimace a man makes when he realizes his long love has left him standing alone, was the recurring vision that played mercilessly in his head. He knew that finding Donovan was the only cure.

His failure to find a lead in Cork left him in despair. Nothing more than a polite recognition of a Donovan photo from a freckled bar maid and a casual "Yeah, Yank. I saw him drink a pint here." Even the Cork mayor knew little about his counterpart's activities in his city. The last he had seen of him was at the reception he had thrown for Donovan his first night in town. Callahan doubted the mayor was still in Ireland, but where he was now was a mystery.

Callahan reasoned that if he was the mayor on the run, liquidating his assets would be one of the first things he would do. This had been done prior to his trip, which should have triggered a warning sign flashing bright red, but the tunnel-visioned prosecutor had seen the mayor's garage sale only as preparation for the impending legal costs from a federal indictment. The indictment had been the worst-kept secret in Providence, about as secretive as the extortion and bribery ring itself. *How could I have been so blind, so short-sighted as to let the mayor run?*

But drowning his desperation in beer was no way to find the mayor. Where would a man like Donovan go if he was suddenly liberated with a couple of million on hand? Think. Donovan was a different animal than most men, and while a truly grounded, rational man might disappear into a large city or hide himself in a remote village, the flamboyant, attention-starved mayor would probably use this opportunity to live large.

The mayor wasn't stupid, and he would make every attempt to conceal his identity. He probably would change the color of his hair, perhaps grow a beard or a mustache, and he wouldn't travel alone. He would need somebody. He needed to be around people. He was a politician, for god's sake. The last thing Donovan wanted was to be an average Joe, a nobody in a foreign land. There was no Silberman to pull the strings, nor any other aides to cater to his every whim. No crowds calling his name. No awe-struck young women fawning over him.

"My god, it would kill him," Callahan said aloud.

"Can I get you something, love?" the pretty Irish barmaid asked him.

"No, thank you," he said, rising. "I got it."

***

In many respects, Callahan was right. The mayor craved the action, the attention, the game itself, but drinking red wine in a sixteenth-century restaurant while smoking a Cuban cigar with a stunning twenty-five-year-old brunette, two forbidden fruits in Providence, weren't exactly torturous.

Soon a new mayor of Providence would be elected. All he had done for the city, all his work, would be gone. And for what? Because some federal prosecutor with a hard-on for him had caught him with his hand up the city's skirt. Ask anyone—he was the reason for Providence's revival. The city was alive again with glistening hotels and skyscrapers and a thriving theater and arts district. Providence was the envy of all other dilapidated factory towns. So what if he received a little extra dough from some building developers and strong-armed a few rich property owners? That was politics. The city needed strong leadership, and results were what mattered. Without Jack Donovan, there was no Providence. If he made a little cash on the side while he was working day and night for the city, then so what? Politics wasn't for the faint of heart, and anyone who said they'd entered the field to serve the people was either a fraud or simply naïve. Politics and government required tough professionals, not panty-waist do-gooders who had neither the balls to negotiate a city contract with a powerful union nor the vision to rebuild a city out of the rubble of the Industrial Age. "Go back to the comfortable world of academia," he said to those types. "Leave the act of governing to the people who know how to make things happen."

He had always believed success was open to the man who dared challenge the conventional order—the risk-taker, the maverick. His whole life, he had lived as such a man. He'd been the youngest elected mayor of a major city, and if he had survived, he would have been the longest serving. Sure, he lined his pockets with developers' gold, but that was a small pittance compared to the years of service and the sparkling revival he'd brought to the city.

Now here he was, a middle-aged man without a title, without the power he had earned from more than twenty years of service, and now without a country. It was difficult to swallow his loss in standing in the social pecking order. As he sat like a prince in ancient Prague, he realized he was a nobody. *At least I'm banging this hot broad,* he thought to himself. Though the thought soon vanished after he reminded himself he was paying for her. There was something he'd always wanted to ask her. *What the hell?* he thought, *I am paying for her.*

"Hey, how did you end up doing this?"

"I met this handsome, mysterious gentleman who offered to take me away to paradise," she said with a cute smile.

"I'm serious. What are you all about? What's your family like? What did you want to be when you were a little girl? What do you want to do now? That kind of stuff. Tell me. I wanna know."

"A lot of questions. Well, I didn't just wake up one day and say, 'I wanna be a prostitute.' I studied to be a social worker. But there was no work in Prague for Lithuanians. My friend, Ana, asked me to go to Croatia with her on a trip. There was a party, a bunch of German and Italian industrialists and politicians. I remember I made more that night than I did in a month working in Prague. So I traveled with her all across Europe, following diplomats, businessmen, and politicians. At an EU conference, I made €10,000 in a week."

"I know these parties, we have them in the US. Something about old white men and young women. We both have something each other wants."

"You know, it wasn't so bad. It was sex. The guys were rich, and we were more like courtesans. I figured I'd do this for a couple of years, make some real money, and have a nice little nest egg. Is that what you wanted to hear? That your lovely little mistress isn't a victim? That her father didn't molest her? That she actually chose to do what she's doing?"

"You're so bright. So beautiful. You can do so much with your life," he told her.

"I told you mine, now tell me yours. What did you do, run off with the church funds or something?"

"Kind of. I was an important man," he told her. "Jack Donovan. I was mayor of Providence in Rhode Island. I've been mayor for the last twenty years. I was a king, had my own little empire. Now I'm nothing. Just another schmuck, a nobody," he said as he finished his wine. He was into his second bottle of the night, and he planned on starting a third before the night was through.

"Jack, you're somebody. I knew you were a great man. What are you running from?" she asked.

"I was in Cork, Ireland, on a cultural exchange. There was a federal investigation into my administration. I guess there still is. Got word that when I came back to the states, they were going to indict me. The moment I go home, I'm arrested. I can never go back. I can never go back to who I was."

"You could look at it that way, or you could look at it like this. You're free. You can be whoever you want. It's like a whole new life for you. How many people get a second try at life?"

"But I can never be me again."

"So what? You can be whoever you want."

"The only thing I want to be is Jack Donovan," he admitted.

25

With one month before Election Day, the electorate had a second opportunity to see the two candidates express their viewpoints. Unlike the Lincoln-Douglas format of the previous debate, this time, the candidates appeared in a town hall forum at Providence College. The Green Party was having their own debate outside, protesting their candidate's denial of participation inside. The 200-seat auditorium was stocked with supporters from both sides. Not a single Independent was able to ask questions, a contradiction of the spirit of the town meeting format. It was a staged event, one with media consultants and political operatives looking to showcase their candidates in the best light. The stage was set, the actors were prepared, and the curtain was drawn.

The candidates recited their three-minute monologues of carefully woven themes. "Family values," "honest work," "impeccable record" were the ingredients tossed together for the soufflé, the consultants peeking in like chefs anxiously reviewing the faces of those devouring their creations. It was politics at its very best and its very worst. The candidates were thoroughly prepped with every conceivable issue and policy, merely mouthpieces of the issue-tested, media-savvy sound bites. Somewhere lost between political consultants and pollsters, the candidates themselves were a mere amalgam of what was salable to the voters at the moment. It was the politics of the new generation.

Campagna wouldn't sell his soul for the crown, nor was his soul for sale. His words resonated with his audience. There was a little John Campagna in everyone—the loyal parent, the dedicated spouse, and the hard worker alike. He was the common man, and common men championed his cause. It had become his election for the taking. The only man in his way—the uncommon one.

The Malcolm Prescotts were the ones who took from the common man, who strived to rise above, not mire themselves in their plight. He spoke like a man who was uncomfortable with his words. The government wasn't a safety valve for the less fortunate, but a barrier for the fortunate. Taxes didn't fund social programs but stagnated corporate wealth. The people didn't know what they wanted, and the politicians didn't understand how to deliver. There were two divergent forces at work, two conflicting principles at stake, and the new course of Providence was in the balance.

Prescott wanted to claim this prize, though he had never quite answered why. "It's time to take Providence away from the politicians and have real businesspeople in charge," he claimed. He never mentioned that his business experience involved managing money, not people. "I want to teach my children that public service is a noble pursuit," he also recited. He simply failed to recall that he had not once considered a run for public office before, had not toiled away on the city council making budget cuts or taken a phone call from an angry parent when the school committee cut funding for sports. "We need professionals, not professional politicians," he said. The fact that he was neither a professional nor a politician wasn't really the issue. Money purchased him the necessary rating points on television and the best spin-doctors to sell his words. Money made this candidate.

"There's something I need to get off my chest. Something I need to say before we go any further," Prescott said in the middle of his opening statement. It was crafted to appear with spontaneity, but he just couldn't pull it off naturally. "My opponent is planning to disclose something about my family, something he wants all of you to know about me. I know you'll see through his personal attacks. I have not made it a secret about my stance on abortion. I have said quite publicly that I would pressure the General Assembly to make it illegal in our state. I recently learned that a member of my family had an abortion. I will not let Mr. Campagna exploit what was a difficult decision and use it for political gain. I loathe this type of politics, and I refuse to play any part in it." As he had been coached, he turned to his opponent and castigated him like an unruly child. "Quite frankly, Councilman Campagna, I'm ashamed of you, in light of your family's own personal tragedy, ashamed that you would use this against me."

"I'd like to respond, if I may," Campagna said to the moderator. The debate had already gotten away from the perky news anchor who was determined to be seen as a serious reporter. The audience sat silently, unsure of how to react.

"Mr. Prescott, I respect you for coming forward with what I understand must have been difficult news. As you know, I am also pro-life. I want to assure you that neither me, nor anyone from my campaign, would ever use this against you. I have never run a negative campaign, nor do I plan to start now."

Prescott was stung by Campagna's quick retort, and he wasn't quite sure how to recover. Campagna was supposed to question his pro-life stance, question the abortion, question him. It didn't even seem like he wanted to touch the subject.

The first to speak would steer the course of events to follow. It was a defiant Campagna who fired back. "Mr. Prescott, I've often found that people who discover something troubling will deflect it by attacking someone else. With all due respect, sir, that's exactly what you're doing. It's time we end the politics of personal destruction."

"You're the one who's going around saying I'm a hypocrite," Prescott fired back.

"Whoa, wait a minute," Campagna said, throwing his arms in the air. "I have not said anything about you or the abortion issue. No, Mr. Prescott, I've been talking about affordable housing, improving our schools, and protecting our seniors—the things you can actually do something about as mayor. I'm not here to make personal attacks against you or your family. And I resent the implication."

"All I know, Councilman, is that my family's privacy has been violated. Do we have to drag our families into this? I wish this was a campaign about the issues."

"Then let's make it one, right here. Let's agree to talk about the issues. Let's both agree not to attack one another, and that goes for campaign staff too. Can I count on you, Mr. Prescott, to make this a campaign of ideas, not personal attacks?"

"I deserve an apology. My family deserves an apology."

"Mr. Prescott, right now, let's agree not to attack one another."

"But you—"

"We shake hands, and we agree to run clean campaigns," Campagna said, interrupting before he could make another accusation.

"All right, Councilman, but you have to call off your people, stop them from snooping around, digging up dirt."

"Mr. Prescott, my people aren't digging up dirt. That's not the way I campaign. I'm asking you to shake my hand, to start fresh. Let's set an example for our kids, that we can disagree and still be professionals, as you say, and not politicians. Let's show them we can be better," Campagna said as he walked from his podium and extended his hand. He remained at a safe distance, not wanting to encroach on Prescott's space. Prescott took his hand, and the crowd erupted in applause. Campagna put his other hand on Prescott's shoulder, assuring him that he meant what he said.

"Now let's get on to the people's business," he said to the moderator. The moderator took her cue, acknowledging what every-one else knew. Campagna was in total control.

"I think we've just been part of something incredible," she said. "Two candidates agreeing to refrain from attacking one another. Considering what we've been through with Mayor Donovan, I cannot think of any more exciting development. I applaud both of these men. So let's get down to the people's business. We have a question from the audience."

"My name is Walter Pavlowski, and my question goes to the councilman," the straggly-haired old man said. "The bus used to come right by where I lived, and now it don't come no more. What can you do to make the bus come by again?" Compared to the mush-rooming city deficit and the crumbling schools, it might have seemed like an insignificant question, but to this older man, it was how he saw his grandchildren, how he shopped for groceries, his very connection to life.

"I'm sorry, sir. I will call the Providence Transit Authority Director tomorrow and ask him why your bus route was taken away. Why don't you give Jenny your phone number?" he said as he looked for his aide. "Jenny, can you help this gentleman? She'll take your name and number, and we'll find out and get back to you. We'll do whatever we can do to get your bus route back, Mr. Pavlowski," he said.

Give me a tax question, a school choice question, anything but how much shit costs, Prescott thought to himself. He wasn't so lucky. The question fired at him was a variation of the political standard-bearer—the cost of a gallon of milk.

"Mr. Prescott, do you know how much you paid in property taxes, and would you advocate the roll-back of the automobile tax?" a Campagna plant asked. It was a question Henry had written, and the husky gentlemen was all too glad to attempt to trip up this rich windbag he thought had a silver spoon stuck up his ass.

"I'd have to ask my accountant how much I paid in property taxes. I'm not sure what the exact figure was, but I know I paid more than my fair share. As for the automobile tax, I'd have to look at that in more detail to see if the city could withstand losing that revenue, especially now that we're in a budget crunch. So I'm not sure we want to do that, but I'd consider all options, except for what my opponent advocates, which is raising your taxes. That's the last thing I'd do. We should be looking at controlling our spending first." He looked down at his notes, not once making eye contact with the camera or the audience. He rushed through his answer, missing the point of the question itself. He had no idea how much he paid in taxes last year. That was his accountant's job, to find loopholes and prevent him from paying unnecessarily.

But the average taxpayer in Providence didn't go to an accountant, and they damned sure knew how much the government took from them. It was just another example of how Prescott wasn't one of them.

26

Lyndsay knew there was something wrong with Henry. She could see it his eyes, in his remote look, and in his distant behavior. He was especially absent from her, more so than his usual stoic self. Henry wasn't the sort to advertise his emotions. On the contrary, he kept everything inside. That was probably why he didn't sleep much and why prior to her, he hadn't had any long-term relationships. He always called her when something happened at work or in a campaign. She was his sounding board. How many times had he practiced a closing argument on her or run a campaign commercial concept by her? But not this time. Nothing, not a "You wouldn't believe what happened to me today," or even a "Hey, what do you think of this?" Everything had become so secretive, almost like he was involved in some covert activity. She wanted to help him with whatever it was, no matter how disturbing. The only way she could receive an answer, even if it was one she didn't want to hear, was to challenge him.

She had chosen her point of confrontation wisely. She didn't want to ambush him with a line of inquiry, the type of cross-examination that would only push him farther away. Instead, she planned a quiet, tranquil setting complete with a good bottle of Californian Cabernet and chicken parmesan. She called him on his cell phone to make sure he was coming home. He promised her he would. Her entire Saturday was spent preparing for their night together. Her hair was done, her nails manicured, and her new dress purchased. This evening, she'd spent the entire $500 weekly limit on her dad's credit card. She'd bought fresh flowers and candles for the table. Everything was perfect, even Henry, who was surprisingly on time. He fully intended to keep his promise for dinner, but he hadn't expected his fiancée to go to such lengths.

Henry walked into a welcoming room of freshly cut flowers and the mixed aroma of Italian food and cinnamon candles. He didn't understand why he deserved such meticulous attention. Henry was stunned when he saw her. He was more familiar with her in hospital scrubs or jeans at best, not a black designer dress.

"Lynds, I don't know what to say."

She sat down on his lap and touched her fingers to his lips. "Don't say anything, Henry. I just wanted to do something nice for my guy."

"I don't deserve this. You're amazing," he said, still stunned.

"Why not? You work hard. You're out there fighting for what you believe in. Why wouldn't you deserve this?"

"I don't deserve you."

"Why do you say that?" she prodded.

"What?"

"That you don't deserve me. Why would you say that?"

"You wouldn't understand. Believe me."

"Why don't you try me?" she offered.

"You want to hear that I fucked up? Not just a little fuck-up.

No, the real big kind that has serious repercussions," he said, beginning to show signs of the guilt hammering inside of him. A tear trickled down his cheek, betraying the cold, calculating version of himself he wanted to project. But he could be honest with Lyndsay, be his true self, and at the moment, he could no longer hold back his feelings of betrayal.

"They've got pictures of me with Campagna's niece, and it looks bad. I didn't do anything. I just went home with her. I was drunk, but I swear to God, Lyndsay, nothing happened. These guys, they're bad guys, and they told me that if I didn't play ball with them, they'd give the pictures to the police, implicate me in her death, and tell you, ruin me, and us, and everything. What am I supposed to do? I'm running the biggest election in New England, and I'm somehow involved in a young girl's death, who just so happened to be the niece of the candidate."

"So what *did* you do, Henry?" Lyndsay asked. She tried her best to keep her composure and would later deal with the fact that there were some pictures out there that depicted her fiancé engaged in a questionable act. She forgot about that minor fact, not so minor to many people, and focused on her need to be there for Henry at this moment.

"I did the only thing I could do. I turned the tables on them. I've been playing both sides since the primary. I've convinced this guy Beako—he's running Prescott's campaign—that I'm working for them. I gave them debate briefing papers, but then I told Campagna to forget all the bullshit I wrote and just tell the people the truth about his niece's death and about having to raise taxes. You know what really sucks about all of this, Lynds? I really believe in this guy. It would've been easier to play along with those bastards if Campagna had been just another blowhard politician. But he's not. He's different. He's the most honest man I've ever met in this business."

"Wait, they've got you working for them? Like a spy?" she asked.

"Like a double agent, but I've given them precisely nothing, and so far I've managed to convince them that I'm their guy. I was the one who leaked that Campagna had the info on Prescott's daughter. They didn't know that Campagna would never use it, so I fooled them. But it's crazy. I'm trying to win an election and convince the other side I'm really throwing it. Now you know why I can't sleep."

"Can't you go to McNally or the police or something?"

"And tell them what, Lynds? That I was there the night Campagna's niece swallowed a handful of Fentanyl-laced Xanax? That she tried to hook up with me, and I actually stopped her? Who are they going to believe? The press would have a field day with this. Sex, drugs, and politics—what more could they want? They need a villain in all of this, and it'd be me."

"But you didn't do anything. Doesn't the truth matter?"

"It's all perception, Lynds. I was there. I was drunk. She's dead, and the fact that I've waited a month? Come on. Not to mention what it'd do to Campagna. The guy he trusts to run his campaign is somehow implicated in his own niece's death. It would kill the campaign, and it would kill me. The only thing I can do is what I'm doing now, and that's keep going like I'm with them."

"Henry, look at me. Did you have sex with this girl?"

"No. God, no. I told you, nothing happened." He responded like he had been accused of a heinous crime.

"I believe you, Henry. I do. We'll get through this. You don't have to do it alone anymore. I'm with you."

"Lynds, I can't bring you into this. The best thing you can do is get as far away from me as possible. I'm King Solomon, except everything I touch turns to shit."

"I'm with you, Henry. I've always been with you. Don't you realize that? Through the good and the bad, that's what commitment's all about. Let me call my dad. He'll know what to do."

"Are you fucking serious? Your father. You want to call your dad? What are you going to tell him, that your future husband, the one your parents told you not to marry, got in a little trouble? That there's a picture of him, but she's really not doing anything, and some guys are now blackmailing him to throw the election? He's got this great little scheme. He's pretending to throw the election, but he's really not. Are you kidding me? He'll have us both committed."

"My dad's not like that. He understands people. He likes you. Why would you say that?"

"You have to promise me, Lynds, that you won't tell him. No one can know. Promise me."

"I just—"

"Promise me."

"Okay."

"But you need to know that my parents like you, Henry. Especially my father."

"They wouldn't like me if they knew."

"You're wrong. They love me, and I love you. Love is unconditional," Lyndsay said.

For a moment, Henry felt like he wasn't alone, that he had someone in his corner he could trust, that they were in this together. He didn't have to face the uncertainty by himself. Lyndsay's understanding and compassion would provide the comfort he would need through his darkest chapter.

Lyndsay had offered Henry a reprieve, enabling him to slay his personal demons without fear of retribution, at least not from her. He had plenty to concern himself with, least of which was his play to throw the election. He had choreographed each movement, leaving little to chance and less to the would-be actors that could steal the show. Henry was the creator, director, and producer of his own drama and was cast in a position to determine its outcome. Only he could play out how the final scene would end. In this, he remembered his Shakespeare: *All the world's a stage, the men and women merely players. They all have their exits and entrances. In his lifetime, a man plays many roles.* Would he emerge as a heroic figure who wins the day and the girl, or would he fall to his demise in the mire of his own tragic flaw?

Before the ending could be written, Henry had a bit more treachery to commit. Beako wanted a copy of each direct mail piece the Campagna campaign had produced before it was mailed. Henry had planned for four mail pieces to hit the 60,000 households that he'd determined as likely special election voters. He'd deduced the list by selecting only those Democrats and Independents who had voted in the last three general elections for governor. He figured that Providence residents who came out to vote in gubernatorial elections were more likely to vote in a special election for Providence's chief executive. Henry decided to concentrate on delivering the Campagna message to these people. Otherwise, Henry argued, they were simply throwing darts at a board, hoping to hit the right voters. It was political science, an inexact one, and there was no guarantee.

The first piece of mail featured a family portrait of Campagna, his wife, and two children with the slogan: "For Working Families." The full-color mailer depicted Campagna as a family man, a working man, and a leader. Complete with pictures of the candidate hugging seniors and reading to children, Campagna's introductory piece set a much different tone than the mailer Henry planned to show Beako. For the special job Henry had in mind, he needed an accomplice he could trust.

"I want you do something for me, Eddy-boy, and please don't ask any questions," Henry told his graphic artist. He had known Eddy from the McNally campaign and had a great working relationship with him. Eddy didn't care about politics or money. He cared about much more important things like the start of trout season or whether he would get off work in time to meet his girlfriend for a drink. That was precisely what Henry liked about him. After spending most of his time with politicians, it was refreshing to work with someone real.

"Whatever you want, Henry, just make it quick, cause I got a hockey game tonight."

"It'll be quick, but I need you to make it look like the real thing. Can your printer there produce something that looks like it came off the press?"

"This puppy'll give you the best mark-up you've ever seen."

"Yeah, but it can't look like a mark-up. It has to look real."

"What are you thinking?"

"You know that picture we have of that bloated politician puffing on a cigar? He's a cross between Rush Limbaugh and Ted Kennedy. Make the cover really dark, grainy, and put in, 'Smoking Out Prescott.' Okay, now inside, put little non-smoking signs with these headings: 'Blowing Smoke On The Issues,' 'Blowing Smoke On His Record,' 'Blowing Smoke On You.' Now, on the right-hand side, put 'John Campagna—Real Issues, Real Solutions, Real Mayor. On March 15th, vote John Campagna, Democrat for Mayor.'"

After about fifteen minutes of pounding on the computer keys, Henry wrote the language for the concurring headlines. In the section "Blowing Smoke On The Issues," he wrote about how Prescott had put forward not one substantive issue, and how he had misled voters by claiming he wouldn't raise their taxes. Under "Blowing Smoke On His Record," he claimed that Prescott wasn't a successful businessman, but a child of privilege who managed his family's multi-million-dollar portfolio through investment advisors and lawyers. In the final section, Henry argued that by misleading the voters and distorting the record that Prescott was "Blowing Smoke On You."

"Okay, what are you thinking? I can see that look in your eyes. You've got something," Eddy said. He had worked with Henry long enough to know that mischievous look in his eye.

"Can you make Prescott's picture look like that bloated politician's?"

"It'll take me a few minutes. I gotta do that in Photoshop and then import it into InDesign." Eddy took the image of Jack Prescott, then began distorting the image. He widened the picture to make Prescott appear heavier than he actually was. Then he darkened the background of the photo and put a drop shadow around the image to give it a murky look.

"Perfect, Eddy. Can you give it to me? I need it to look like an actual mailer. So don't give me one of those tape-up jobs. Print it double-sided, so it looks like the real thing."

"It's gonna cost you. You've already got me on overtime."

"Don't worry about it," Henry said as he handed him $300 from his pocket. "I'll take care of this one."

"Wait, so you're not gonna use the smoke piece?" Eddy asked.

"Not a chance. Campagna would never let me do a piece like that. But Prescott doesn't know that."

"I get it. You're gonna make them think you're gonna run this piece. But why?"

"You don't want to know, Eddy-boy. Trust me on this one."

In less than an hour, they had developed a negative direct mail piece that appeared as real as the hundreds of political and other direct mail pieces Eddy had printed over the last ten years. After leaving the office, Henry made the fifteen-minute drive to CampCo, where he planned to sell his piece. He hoped Beako would buy what he was pushing. It was a Sunday night, and the light from Beako's office cast its shadow over City Hall. He called Beako on his cell phone to let him into the building. After about five minutes, a ravaged man emerged, looking like he had been up for the last twenty-four hours. He wasted little time before going right at Henry.

"You better have something good for me, kid, or the next person you talk to is the Attorney General," he said.

"What do you mean, Beako? I gave you the info about Prescott's daughter. Your guy would've been ambushed if it wasn't for me."

"It didn't sound that way to me. I don't think your guy was going to use it at all," Beako replied.

"Trust me. He was gonna hang your guy with it. That's why I gave it to you. I don't want to be any part of a campaign that's going to use those tactics. I mean, look at this piece they're doing. I can't be part of this," Henry said as he handed Beako the piece he had just finished with the graphic designer.

"Wait. Let's go upstairs. I don't want anyone to see us talking," Beako said as he opened the envelope Henry had given him. "What the fuck?" he said, stopping in the middle of the staircase. "That piece of shit is using this? You have to stop this from going out, Henry. I don't care what you have to do. You can't let this fucking thing go out."

"That's why I brought it down here. Campagna did it without me. Used some guy out of Washington. I don't know if I can stop it, but I'll go down to the post office and see if I can pull it. I'll tell Campagna it's too negative, but I don't know if I can stop it. They did it behind my back. I think maybe McNally had something to do with it." Henry dropped these false facts in McNally's name so his lie would sound more real. The piece had the fingerprints of a classic McNally negative mailer. McNally hadn't served five terms in Congress not to realize the dirty little secret in American politics— negative campaigning works.

"It does look like McNally. Can you kill it?" Beako asked him.

"I've probably got enough clout with Campagna, and if it's still at bulk mail, I can probably stop it before it goes out. It's not going to be easy, but I can try."

"Don't try, Henry. Do it like your life depends on it."

"Is that a threat, Beako?"

"It's a fact. If you don't stop that piece from going out, you can kiss our little deal goodbye. I'll personally give your pictures to the attorney general."

"First of all, Beako, you wouldn't do that, because you'd never implicate yourself directly. Second, you won't have to, because I'm going to save your ass and stop this piece from going out. But you have to realize something. These guys aren't what you expected. They're pros at this game. They see that you guys are starting to make gains, so they're going to have to tear your guy down. They've made the decision to go negative. I may be able to kill this piece, convince them it's not the right one to send out first, to hold it till the end, but I have to tell you, I'm not going to be able to stop them from destroying your guy. You have to preempt them. You need to address all the things they plan to hit you with before they release it. You do that, it will totally neutralize the negative shots they take at Prescott."

"You're right. We need to come out swinging. If they want to make this a negative campaign, they've got it. I want you to prepare the negative piece against Campagna."

"No way, Beako. I've done everything you guys asked, but I can't do that. I won't."

"You'll do whatever I fucking say. You got no choice. You see, Henry, I got you by the balls, and now I'm squeezing. I wanna see a Prescott response piece on my desk by tomorrow night. None of your cookie-cutter shit. I want your best work."

"No fucking way. I told you I'd help you, but I'm not going to hurt Campagna, that wasn't part of the deal."

"Henry, you know what the best part about being me is? I've got the power, you don't. So you'll do what I want."

"You can't change the deal in the middle to whatever you want."

"Oh, but I can. That's the best part of this deal."

Henry turned and started to walk out of CampCo. He heard Beako shout back to him, "You've got no choice," but he wore a smile across his face. He sensed his opponent's impending demise.

Beako had totally bought the package. "McNally's" mailer would never go out because it didn't exist, and who better to produce the response pieces for Prescott than Henry himself? Beako had given away the last of his power.

Henry took out his cell and dialed Eddy. "Hey, Eddy. I got another piece to do, and I'll pay you twice as much."

"It's midnight, man. Can't it wait till tomorrow?"

"I'll give you $500 if you come in right now. It'll take an hour."

"Shit. Alright."

28

A wise prince should always rely on himself,
and not upon the will of others.

—Niccolò Machiavelli

Henry found himself in an unusual predicament. To take advantage of the trap he'd set for Beako, he would create an attack piece he believed was so negative it could only backfire for the Prescott campaign, but in doing so, he risked reinforcing a message that was already prevalent, that Campagna was mentally unfit for office. He reasoned that public support was with Campagna and that the voters would see Prescott's negative assault for what it was, an act of desperation from a candidate who would do whatever it took to win.

Eddy didn't know exactly what Henry had up his sleeve, but he didn't question him as he turned Henry's ideas into a flashy piece that would signal the changing mood of the Prescott campaign. What had begun as a discussion about who was best-suited to lead Providence was quickly transforming into a nasty, mud-slinging free-for-all with the victory sullied for either winner.

Henry's latest creation was a ridiculous offense. The cover of the 11x17 mailer had a picture of Frankenstein's monster with electric shock waves emanating from its head. The tag line read, "John Campagna wants to shock you." The not-so-subtle reference to electroshock therapy was blatantly apparent and was only reinforced by the language inside the piece. The headline read, "John Campagna shocked us with his disclosures, now he wants to shock you by raising your taxes. Can we really afford a mayor whose state of mind is more questionable than his policies?" the piece asked. The layout and design was complete, and black-and-white laser copies were produced. Henry didn't want the mock-up he planned to show Beako to resemble the quality of the other fake Campagna piece.

At 2 a.m., he drove back to his apartment to try to catch a few hours of sleep before he unleashed his assault. Lyndsay woke up as Henry tried to slide into bed without disturbing her. She rolled over and gave him a kiss on the cheek and uttered, half asleep, "Hi, honey." Henry didn't answer, but he kissed her forehead.

What was he supposed to say to her? "Hey, babe. I'm about to do something that could destroy my candidate but save my ass?" He figured it was better to lie silently and consider the repercussions of what he was about to do. The time that passed didn't comfort his tangle of guilt, and he doubted he'd receive any relief with the sleep he knew he needed.

He was relieved to wake up to Lyndsay hurrying around the apartment in her frantic effort to get ready.

"What time is it?" Henry grumbled.

"It's almost nine. Shit, I'm going to be late for rounds. Why don't you sleep in, honey? You worked late last night."

"I have to go in. Prescott's supposed to go negative on us, and I gotta be prepared."

"Are you going to be home tonight?"

"Yeah, I'll be home," he told her.

He took a long, hot shower, one of those little pleasures he still enjoyed in life. He figured he would go with the scruffy look today and opted against shaving. He felt as he looked—not fully together. He put on a pair of jeans, a golf shirt, and his black leather jacket. He had no plans to see any clients other than Beako and Campagna, and they didn't care about how he looked. No, they only cared about what Henry could make. Henry called his assistant from the car and told her to schedule a meeting for later in the afternoon with Campagna. He told her he would be in after lunch, that he had some research to do. His next call was to Beako, who agreed to meet him in his office. Henry parked his car next to City Hall so as not to raise any suspicion. He walked the block to CampCo and strode right in through the front door.

"I'm here to see Gordon Beako," he said to the receptionist.

"Sure, Mr. Mercucio. I'll tell him you're here," said the receptionist, a cute blonde who couldn't have been more than twenty-two. She either knew that Henry was working with Beako on Prescott's campaign, or she was totally oblivious to what was going on around her. Henry figured the latter. Beako didn't submit Henry to his usual antics of making him wait a half-hour before seeing him. Instead, he immediately summoned him. "You can go up, Mr. Mercucio. I'm sure you know the way." Perhaps she wasn't as naïve as Henry believed.

"That was fast," Beako said. "Man, you look like shit. Why don't you get some sleep?"

"Well, I'm running two campaigns, so I don't have much time for anything else," Henry said with a feigned grimace.

"So what do you got?"

Henry tossed him the envelope with the negative piece he had designed in the early hours of the morning.

"Shit," Beako said. "You got balls. I like it. I really like it. Holy shit, he's gonna die when he sees this." He set the drafts on his desk. "But I have to clear it with Prescott first. Anything you want me to tell him?"

"Yeah, tell him it's a tough piece, but considering what Campagna plans to do, it's the only way to respond. You guys are down by ten points with less than a month to go. You need to chip away at the lead, and the only way to do that is to go negative. This piece is probably worth five points. You come back with something positive, then you hit him again. Go after him for wanting to raise taxes. The thing with this piece is it's real clever, but it drives home the point. People say when they're polled that if a candidate was being treated for depression that they would vote for him because it's the politically correct thing to say. But when they're in the voting booth, it's a whole different thing, believe me."

"I'll tell him that. I'll get back to you if we've got any changes. I want you to start thinking about the next piece we send out, alright?"

"Fine. You know I was doing this because you left me no choice, but I'm actually starting to believe that Campagna would be a disaster," he lied.

"I'm glad you're with us," Beako said.

Henry left the office and smiled at the receptionist. He had time to return home and freshen up before he met Campagna at their campaign headquarters.

A few hours later, and seconds after he walked through the glass doors, he was hit with a question.

"Henry, we're out of bumper stickers. We need to order more,"

Salaso, the campaign chairman, insisted.

"Fine," Henry said. "Order more. Just remember, they're a buck-fifty a piece, and for the cost of a thousand, I can run TV spots."

Henry politely listened to the eighty-year-old woman who was supposed to be sending "Dear Friend" cards to all her family and friends. The cards had a pre-printed message from Campagna, and the elderly woman was addressing and signing them. After five minutes of listening to whatever she was saying, he patiently waited for his exit and dashed for it when he saw Campagna.

"I thought you should see the campaign headquarters. It's good for you. Kind of reminds you of why we do this."

"It's a colossal waste of time, and if you're in here again instead of out there meeting voters, I'm personally going to come in here and drag your ass out."

"That's my Henry," he said, like a proud father speaking to his precocious son.

"Is there somewhere we can go and talk?" Henry asked, his voice raised over the noise.

"We can go to my office."

"You've even got your own office here? Great. Listen, I've gotten word that Prescott's about to go really negative. The printer called me. There's only one union printer who does really good political work, and we all use him. He let me take a look at the piece before it went to press. We need to respond."

"What does it say?"

"It's got a picture of Frankenstein on the cover, and it says, 'Councilman Campagna wants to shock you.' It's the most negative piece I've ever seen. It makes references to mental illness, says you're now trying to shock people by saying you'd raise taxes. The problem is, even though a lot of people will think it's a low blow, it'll sink in. They'll remember. Negative politics works. It's why we do it."

"I'm not going to lower myself to their level. We'll continue doing things the way we are, staying positive."

"I have to tell you, we can't just sit back and let them whack us around. We've got to show some balls. People will respect that."

"So what do you want me to do? Go against all I believe in? Push the type of cynicism those guys do? No. That's not how I'm getting elected."

"I'm not saying we have to do it like them, but we need to do something. There's a way we can make their shit backfire on them and turn you into the hero. Just hear me out. You hold a press conference the day it hits, you hold up the piece and you publicly chastise Prescott. Say this isn't the kind of politics we need to rebuild our city. That you won't go down to his level. By the time we're done, we'll have turned Prescott into Osama bin Laden."

"You're right, Henry."

29

Convincing Beako he was totally committed to him was no longer a concern, but the line between the reality and the deception was becoming difficult to recognize. Henry now found himself writing copy for a television ad he never planned to air. Like the negative direct mail piece he had developed against Prescott, it too would never run. But Beako didn't know that.

Henry took his deceit to a whole new level, complete with graphics, streamlined dissolves, and grainy photos. His lie would have the look of a $10,000 commercial, but it would never make it past production. It was another bluff in Henry's well-formulated strategy to continue to lure Prescott down the path of negative campaigning. Prescott would be forced to respond to what he perceived as a full-frontal assault by the Campagna camp, unaware that he was being duped.

Henry's disinformation campaign didn't come without costs. There was the risk it would backfire, and it was expensive. Television ads cost money to produce, even if they didn't air, and Henry was personally prepared to shell out $2,500 to develop an ad that would only be seen by him, Beako, and Prescott. But $2,500 was a small price to pay for continuing the dance. There was something about television that made people believe it was real. When clients saw themselves on television, they felt elevated to a higher level. Neither Beako nor Prescott would question an ad's authenticity after they'd watched it on their own television.

Henry had resurrected a friend from his past to help him develop his latest creation. Brad Resnicki was a freelance television consultant Henry had used back in the McNally days. Resnicki had broken away from one of the Providence advertising agencies that had blacklisted the young maverick—not for his work, but for his ambition to open his own shop. Henry had taken a chance on him after Resnicki had called him every day for two weeks, and it had paid off. His concepts were masterful—not enough to put McNally over the top in a hotly contested gubernatorial race, but strong enough to launch a new career.

"So are we doing the same political hack stuff, or you gonna let me get creative?" Resnicki asked.

"New stuff, but you're going to like it. Trust me," Henry said.

"Trust you? You're a political consultant. How could I trust you?"

"Touché. We're somewhere on the food chain between a used car salesman and a divorce lawyer, not to disparage either. But I want to do something really clever."

"What do you have in mind?"

"Can you take this picture of Malcolm Prescott and make him look like this?" Henry asked, referring to a picture of a bloated, cigar-smoking politician.

"Can't make chicken salad out of chicken shit, but let me give it a shot," Resnicki quipped, taking both pictures and scanning them into his computer. "You got copy?"

"I'll do it right now," Henry said, as he took out a piece of paper and began scribbling. In less than fifteen minutes, he had written the commercial.

"What you got?" Resnicki scanned the script and laughed as he read it. He typed Henry's words into the computer, then emailed the script to the two actors he had selected to read the voice-overs. "I got these great voices out of the Midwest. They're not union, so they're cheap. Fifty each for the read."

"Sounds good to me," Henry said.

"Sally? Hi. It's Brad. You got the script? Great, let's hear it."

The voice was piped in via a broadband cable, but it sounded like the woman was right there in the studio. The woman's voice was soft, yet stern. She sounded like a disapproving teacher scolding a student:

> "There's something that Mr. Prescott doesn't want to tell you, something he wants to hide, because he knows that if you learn the truth—how he never really built a business, how he's waffled on the abortion issue, how he's tried to buy your vote —you'll discover that he's just another politician. Tell Malcolm Prescott you're tired of politics as usual, and that you want real leadership for Providence. Help build a better Providence. John Campagna, Democrat for mayor."

"Great job. I love it. Just a couple of things," Henry said through Resnicki's microphone to the woman he would never see. "Really hit the words, 'buy' and 'real.' And it's 'Campagna,' like 'lasagna.' Run it one more time for us?"

***

With the voiceover complete, Resnicki had the task of making the images coincide with the narration. He took Prescott's photo and made five duplicates. He slightly widened each frame by 10 percent, then dissolved each frame into the other. He did the reverse with Prescott's photo. The total commercial ran for thirty seconds and consisted of ten frames, each three seconds long. The final frame was a black screen with the question, "Tired of politics as usual?"

"That's gotta be a record for us. Two hours," Resnicki said. "So where am I gonna see this? You buying 13 and cable?" He was referring to the highly rated Channel 13 that held about a 60 percent market share in Providence.

"You'll never see this one," Henry admitted.

"What do you mean? You gonna leak it or something?"

"Yeah, something like that."

"Hey, I don't really care. I get paid whether it goes on TV or not."

"You got that right," Henry said as he handed him $1,000 in cash.

"Nah, man, that's too much. I give the girl who did the VO fifty bucks and keep the rest. I mean, it only took me like two hours to do."

"Keep it. It'll keep you quiet," Henry said with a smile.

"No problem, Henry. You know when it comes to your skull-duggery, I keep my mouth shut. Can I just ask you what you're gonna do with it?"

"You can ask, but I'm not going to tell. Listen, I'm going to need you again to do some really good stuff for Campagna. Your absolute best. Can you do that?"

"Anytime. You know that."

"When can I get a copy of this?"

"Give me fifteen, and you can leave with it."

"That's what I like to hear."

Henry left Resnicki's office with the video in hand. There were only two other people who would ever see the commercial, and Henry needed to sell it to them. It was one thing to convince them that the commercial was real, but Henry also had to lead them down a path that would ultimately result in their self-destruction. He needed to persuade them to retaliate with such severity that it would unleash a devastating backlash. He had baited them with a fake direct mail piece, and now he was luring them further in with a negative television ad that would be perceived as the beginning of a negative onslaught.

"I need to see you," Henry said into the phone.

"Can't it wait? I'm out with my girl," Beako said. He meant mistress. Otherwise, he would have used the word "wife."

"No, it can't. Why don't you tell her you'll buy her some ice cream later?" Henry said. He couldn't wait for the time when he could tell Beako to go fuck himself. Taking shots at his personal life would suffice for now.

"All right, I'll see you in an hour in my office," he said.

"Will that give you enough time?" Henry asked sarcastically.

"Cute. Real cute. One hour."

One hour in Beako time was really an hour and a half. Henry didn't care. It gave him an extra half an hour to prepare his pitch. He saw Beako pull up to his parking spot and turn off the lights. Henry was waiting outside the front door when the building's lights illuminated his silhouette.

"You been waiting long?" Beako asked.

"About thirty minutes," Henry replied.

"Yeah, sorry about that. You caught me at a bad time."

"I hope I didn't take you away from anything important," Henry chided.

"Ah, that's fine. It'll give her some time with her husband."

"Wait a second. Your mistress is married?"

"Let me tell you something, Henry. You always go with a married girl because they got as much to lose as you. I'll give you that little bit of advice for free. Now, what's so important that you get me out here on a Friday night? Don't you have a life?"

"Don't you remember? You took mine."

"What about that nice girl you were seeing? What happened? She saw the photos and bolted? Hey, that's the price you pay."

"You sent her the pictures?"

"You didn't know? Oh, sorry, I figured she saw them and told you to fuck off."

"She left, but she never told me why," Henry lied, figuring it was important to play along.

"Hey, sorry. I needed to convince you we were serious. You had to pay a price."

"Fuck you, Beako," Henry said, tossing a thumb drive at him. "This is it. The last time. It's over," he said as he tossed over the copy of the negative ad Campagna was supposedly planning to run.

"It's not over until I say so. We fucking own you, so don't forget it. Losing your girlfriend, that's nothing. How about Campagna finding out you were with his niece, or a grand jury? Yeah, keep walking tough guy. You got nowhere to go."

Henry did keep walking, and his shock wasn't totally an act. He had no idea that Beako had sent Lyndsay the pictures. Had she seen the photos and never mentioned it? He needed to know. He needed to see her. As for Beako, the fact that Henry had walked away from him made the video seem even more real. Beako would buy what he was selling. But that didn't matter to Henry now. Lyndsay was the only one on his mind. He went home to see her and was surprised not to find her there. He remembered she had said something about going out with some of her residency friends after her shift. He called her cell phone and told her it was important.

"Well, I'm down here at the Grille with the girls. You want to come down?"

"Yeah, I'm coming down."

***

The Providence Florentine Grille was in a refurbished factory building. Its latest reinvention was an upscale restaurant and martini bar. Earlier, it had been a college bar with cheap beer and lenient carding practices, which had replaced its previous life as a gin joint for factory workers. If Henry had any experience in the Providence nightlife, he would have known that the Grille on a Friday night was a feeding frenzy for young Hipsters. It took him fifteen minutes of shoving his way through the crowd of twenty-somethings, men with skin-tight sweaters and women with low-rise jeans and belly shirts, all dancing their game in a tireless effort to acquire what each of them wanted in the first place. Seeing Lyndsay in the crowded bar reminded him of what a beautiful woman she was, and how truly lucky he was to go home to her. He realized he already had what every drooling Neanderthal in the bar desired. And apparently one of these types was unaware she was engaged. One of the turtle-sweatered patrons, with his black hair slicked back and cologne strong enough to cover his sweating insecurity, seemed to be making a pass at Lyndsay. He had his right arm resting on the back of Lyndsay's chair and was leaning in with his oversized frame. When Henry tapped her on her shoulder, black sweater turned fully around ready to pounce on the predator willing to challenge his pride. Lyndsay noticed her would-be suitor's sudden defensive posture. She turned her head toward the direction of her new friend's sudden obsession and saw that it was her fiancé who had ruffled his ego.

Henry cut down his opponent by sliding right between the two of them at the bar.

"Dude, what's with the cock block?" black sweater asked.

"Dude, she's my fiancée," Henry responded.

"Jarod, this is my fiancé, Henry. Henry, this is Jarod, Laurie's brother," Lyndsay said, trying to de-escalate.

"I didn't know you were engaged, Lyndsay. That's cool. Let me buy you two a round," Jarod offered.

"I'll have a glass of chardonnay," Lyndsay said.

"Thanks, I'll have a Macallan," Henry said. "Can I talk to you?"

"Let me give you guys some space," Jarod said, motioning to Henry to slide in behind him.

"Thanks, man," Henry said, offering him his hand.

"So what is it that brings you out on a Friday night, Henry?" she chided.

"I don't know how to ask you, so I'm just going to come right out with it, okay?"

"Fine," was all she said.

"Did you get pictures of me with Campagna's niece?"

"Pictures? You mean the ones you told me they have of you?"

"Yeah, those. Did you see them and not tell me?"

"No, I haven't. Why?"

"Because I was just with Beako, and he told me he had sent them to you. If neither one of us got them, then where did they go?"

"Maybe he was just messing with you."

"I doubt it. I could tell. He sent you the pictures to show how he could get to me. That's how these guys work. They want me to know that they're not afraid to go nuclear."

"Well, I never saw them. What's so bad about them, anyway? You told me you didn't do anything with the girl. Did you lie to me, Henry?"

"I didn't. I swear to God, Lyndsay. But the pictures sure make it seem like I did."

"Wait a second," she said as she threw up her hands. She had been drinking, and the alcohol was affecting her emotions. "You didn't do anything with her, but the pictures look like you did? Do you know how that sounds?"

"Exactly, Lyndsay. That's why they think they've got me by the balls."

"I don't know if I believe you anymore," she said. "And maybe I never will." She was about to cry.

"Lyndsay..."

"I've always been with you. I came up here for you, stood by you. Through the elections, all the ups and downs, and now this. I just don't know if I can keep going through it, Henry."

"Hey, you knew going in that this is what I do. It's who I am. I'm sorry I can't be like your dad and write a check for everything."

"Don't bring my father into this," she said with sternness in her tone. "I want you to leave."

"What?"

"Leave, Henry. You're always leaving me for something, but this time I'm telling you, just leave."

"Fine," Henry said, storming out. If that was the way she wanted it, then he wouldn't waste his time. Never before had she asked him to leave. For the first time in their relationship, he was uncertain of whether she would return to him. The pang of uncertainty in the pit of his stomach was becoming a full-blown ache. What his friends had joked was his ulcer now cried out in agony. He grabbed his side and ate a handful of Tums from his pocket. Antacids had become a staple in his diet. Through it all, he'd always felt that Lyndsay was his rock. Now, he had no one to turn to and nowhere to run. His rock had possibly weathered her final storm.

30

Terry Silberman didn't enjoy the same type of freedom that Mayor Donovan was experiencing. On the contrary, the iron bars were a constant reminder of the ultimate price he had paid for the racketeering and bribery ring he'd orchestrated through City Hall. His only recourse during the monotonous days was the knowledge that one day, perhaps in as little as five years, he would have access to the $2 million he had swindled away into several bank accounts from Switzerland to the Cayman Islands.

The problem was that Donovan was an extreme extrovert pissing away the money on broads, booze, and bedlam. There was nothing Silberman could do to change the mayor's insatiable appetite, but he could impede his nourishment.

Silberman's "nephew," who dutifully visited his uncle every month, was his link to the world beyond Danbury Penitentiary. Although he wasn't related to Silberman by blood, money was a considerably stronger bond. The "nephew," the name given by Silberman for his fawning loyalty, was his guy on the outside who had uncovered what little the government had on the whereabouts of the elusive mayor. Bribery wasn't as efficient a form of acquiring information as it once had been before the federal indictments. But some police officers were still looking for a steady flow of cash to sustain their vices. Certain secretaries in the FBI office still needed their sugar daddies to whisk them away from their mediocre lives. If there was money available, there was information for sale.

Silberman may have taken the fall for Donovan, but he wouldn't allow him to squander the millions he had earned. He decided to cut off Donovan's supply, leaving him like a rebel insurgent abandoned by his patron state.

"You're a good nephew. Always coming to see your uncle," Silberman said to the young man who sat across from him at a metal folding table.

"You were always good to me, uncle. My mother sends her love. She's in Europe—Prague, to be specific," the young man revealed. In the letters in which they had corresponded, Silberman had made reference to the man's mother, who was actually Donovan. Silberman knew the penitentiary photocopied his letters and forwarded them to the FBI. They were also recording every conversation in hopes that Silberman would reveal the whereabouts of the mayor.

"She's in Prague?"

"Yes, having a wonderful time."

"Does she have enough money?"

"Oh, she's doing fine. Going to the best restaurants. You know, one can still live very well in Prague for cheap."

"I want you to continue to look after her."

"I will, uncle."

"I've been reading the Bible—I've got a lot of free time on my hands—and I want to give you my copy," Silberman said.

"Why are you reading the Bible?" the young man asked.

"I'm reading the Old Testament. I want you to read the Book of Job. Chapter fifteen, verse thirteen."

"What?"

"Satan says to God that Job only follows him because he has rewarded him. To prove Job's faithfulness, he takes away all his possessions and children. Job remains faithful, even after losing everything," Silberman said, sliding the Bible across the table to his nephew. Immediately, this prompted a guard to come over and investigate what the prisoner was passing to the young man. He leafed through the Bible, discovered nothing insidious, and passed it along to the visitor.

"I'll tell my mother you asked about her, uncle. Is there anything else you want me to tell her?"

"Always take care of her."

"I will."

The young man left the penitentiary with Bible in-hand. As soon as he drove off the prison grounds, he pulled over to the side of the road to inspect it. Silberman wasn't one to speak in idle chitchat. Everything he said had meaning, especially since he only had fifteen minutes to speak to visitors. He turned to Job 15:13 and saw a series of numbers written next to the verse. Under the numbers were abbreviations for bank names: "FS" for First Suisse, "GC" for Bank of Grand Cayman, "Z" for Bank of Zurich, and "L" for Bank of Liechtenstein. Some of the banks had several different accounts.

Transferring a little over $2 million was no task to be completed over the phone or the Internet. He needed to travel to Switzerland, Liechtenstein, and the Cayman Islands to move the money. He purchased two first-class airline tickets on Swiss Air from his travel agent and had her reserve four nights at a five-star hotel in Geneva and two nights in Zurich. The next call he made was to his girlfriend, Adriana, who was more than willing to take the vacation time she had coming as an employee of the FBI.

"Pack your bags, baby. We're going to Europe," her boyfriend said to her.

"What are you talking about, Danny?" she asked.

"I'm not kidding. We're going to Switzerland. My firm's got a client there they want me to meet."

"I thought you worked for a small firm," she asked.

"Look, don't ask questions. You gonna bust my balls, or you gonna come?"

"Of course I am. When we leaving?"

"Tomorrow."

***

Perhaps Terry Silberman's small fortune would have been better off in the hands of a Harvard MBA or a Wall Street tax attorney, but neither exhibited the loyalty of Danny Conroy. Silberman had spotted the kid when he was twenty-one and working as a barback at one of his favorite watering holes. He was impressed with how he handled himself, how he was always moving, how he never lost his cool when a patron was belligerent or a bartender attempted to exert his power. Silberman asked the owner of the bar, a Donovan campaign contributor, about Conroy and whether he thought he would be willing to earn some extra money on the side. The owner assured Silberman that he was one of the hardest-working employees he had ever seen.

Conroy had started as an errand boy for Silberman. He didn't only pick up dry cleaning and groceries, but also bribes and pay-offs. It took him a year to win Silberman's trust before he was brought into his inner circle. At first, he was responsible for discreetly bringing the mayor's girlfriends home. Other times, he found himself driving the mayor to those parts of Providence that the police officer assigned to him would never go. Those trips were usually to procure the mayor's white powder. After Conroy had been exposed to the mayor's dependence and remained silent, he was brought further into the fold. Silberman entrusted him to pick up envelopes that were filled with as much as $20,000 in cash. Not once had he taken a little off the top, not even looking inside the envelopes. All he knew was that for babysitting the mayor and picking up packages, he was getting two grand a week. He was able to quit his job at the bar and dress in designer suits instead of the white button-down shirts and clip-on bow ties he'd donned as a barback.

When the FBI had descended on City Hall with their search warrants and indictments, Conroy had disappeared for a month. He'd reappeared in Danbury, Connecticut, had rented a PO box, and had sent a letter to Silberman. He signed it, "Your loving nephew, Tony." Silberman had placed him on his visitor's list, and Danny Conroy—Tony Silberman, according to the Danbury Penitentiary—became Terry Silberman's eyes and ears on the outside.

Silberman had taught Conroy how to acquire information by making friends and greasing the right people. He went back to Providence and stumbled into the FBI's Providence office with a sandwich delivery. He had spent $100 out of his pocket to make the setup seem real. He'd acted like the innocent delivery boy, the victim of a frat prank, and had walked out of the office with his head down in faux shame. But he'd been able to catch a glimpse of a cute secretary in the office, and he had staked out the federal building for a week to see if he could make a chance encounter with the secretary.

The secretary was about thirty years old and anxious to meet someone new. Conroy became the man she longed for, the sum of all her desires. He'd discovered that she lived at home with her parents. He'd seen that she liked dogs since she always stopped at the window of the pet store at the corner of her building. He knew she liked to read John Grisham novels on the bus, so Conroy became a young lawyer, new to Providence, with his own apartment, whose only friend in town was his three-year-old lab, Molly. To begin the charade, he'd worn one of his new suits to the bar across the street from the federal building. While he waited for a beer, he casually bumped into the secretary as she approached the bar to order a glass of white zinfandel.

"I'm sorry," he said. "Excuse me." *Polite—plus one.* "Did I spill anything on you? I'm so sorry. Let me get that drink for you." *Thoughtful—plus two.*

"You didn't spill anything. It's okay. Really," she said.

"Can I still get you a drink? You seem like a really nice person, and I don't know anyone here. I just moved to Providence."

"Where are you from?" she asked.

"New York." *Not from Providence—plus three.* She already seemed to have dated most of the good guys in Providence. She saw the same crowd every weekend, the young women in their tight jeans and the dudes trying to be taken more seriously in their feeble attempts to grow facial hair.

"What do you do?"

"I'm a lawyer. I worked for a big firm, but I wanted a change of lifestyle, so I moved here to work for a small firm." *He's a lawyer —home run.*

"I work in the federal building," she said proudly.

"You work for the government?" he asked.

"I'm a secretary at the Bureau. But I'm getting my degree in criminal justice. I eventually want to go to law school."

"I do criminal law, actually," he lied. "Hey, I know this is going to sound random, but could I take you out or something?"

"Or something?"

"I mean for dinner or a drink. I really don't know anybody. It's just me and my dog, Molly. It would be nice to have dinner with someone besides my TV."

"I'll go to dinner," she offered. She couldn't remember the last time a guy had asked her out. It was always for drinks or lunch at the best, but never dinner. This guy was a gentleman.

Hook, line, and sinker. That was all it took. Of course, he had special intelligence from stalking her for a week. He'd even gone out and bought a dog to make his lie more real. The first date moved into a second. Conroy had done all the right things, not trying to have sex with her that first night, sending flowers to her office the next day, and offering to take her out again over the weekend. It took him only two weeks to begin pumping her for information.

"Hey, you know about the mayor? What's that all about? He took off to Europe?"

"Yeah, with about $2 million bucks. He's never coming back."

"So they have no idea where he is?" he asked.

"Well, I wouldn't say that. They do know he's in Europe. And they do know that large sums of cash were withdrawn from banks all over Europe the day he took off. They've got records of all kinds of transfers, but that's all the Swiss would give us," she offered. "They think he's in some place like Prague or Budapest." She wanted to sound like she was more than a secretary to impress her new lawyer friend. Conroy was careful not to ask about the mayor too often. He wanted it to be an intriguing story they both shared.

Back in prison, Silberman enjoyed hearing the tales of Conroy's romance. He was most proud of Conroy's work and carefully followed the relationship's development over the next month. Conroy wrote to him explaining how he had met the girl of his dreams, how beautiful and intelligent she was. He described her as dark and sultry, not your typical Providence girl. He said he planned to propose to her on their vacation next month in the Cayman Islands. Silberman understood the code and that his money would be secured in the Bank of Grand Cayman. He continued to write about the beautiful sites of Europe and urged his uncle to visit after he was released from prison. Conroy returned to the penitentiary two weeks later to give his uncle the good news, that he was looking forward to a new life with his fiancée.

"That's wonderful," Silberman said. "I'm so happy for you."

"Uncle, I've been reading the Bible like you told me. We're gonna be married in a Catholic Church. Her family's very Catholic, so I've been reading up."

"That's great, Tony. I'm proud of you."

"Uncle, I've got something for you. It's the New Testament. I think you should read Paul's Letter to the Ephesians: *For you were once in darkness, but now you are light in the Lord ... Awake, sleeper, and arise from among the dead and Christ will enlighten you,*" he said as he slid the New Testament across the table to him.

Silberman returned to his cell with the comfort of knowledge that his livelihood was secured. He flipped pages in the New Testament to the verse that Conroy had referenced, and sure enough, new account numbers were written next to it with the abbreviations for the banks in which he had transferred his money. His loyalty to Donovan included sitting in this cell, but it never involved losing the millions he had earned.

31

Ireland, England, France, Germany, and the Czech Republic—Mayor Jack Donovan's European tour was almost complete. He was comfortable in Prague. It wasn't unusual for him to stay in a bistro or pub until 3 a.m., or drink coffee at a café in the middle of the afternoon. No one wondered why he never worked or why he was taking up with a woman half his age. No one asked, and no one cared. They had no idea that despite his faults, Mayor Jack Donovan was considered an extraordinary man. And he had great achievements—relocating the highway that separated the city and erecting a new suspension bridge over the river, creating a vibrant arts district that attracted painters and poets to his so-called crumbling factory town. New hotels and office towers replaced old smokestacks that had previously dominated the skyline. Perhaps the most important thing he had achieved was restoring a sense of pride in his community. But that feeling had been eviscerated the day the mayor had absconded with the city funds.

He was in search of his own personal revival, longing to create his own Renaissance and rehabilitate his tainted image. Where did a man go, disgraced and displaced, a man without a home or a country? He'd turned to the only thing that didn't judge—money. Money cured all woes—erecting glistening skyscrapers in the shadow of crumbling schools, covering dilapidated buildings with shiny new glass and steel—yet all it left was a soulless Oz, a sparkling city devoid of spirit and hope. That was the Providence he'd fled, his great city on the mount. The great man he thought he was had been reduced to a conniving swindler, forced to look over his shoulder for the remainder of his life.

He needed to reacquaint himself with his only true love, so he went to the Deutsche Bank in Prague. He showed his passport to the guard as he entered the bank and went straight to the teller. He gave her the withdrawal slip for $25,000 along with one of the five bank account numbers he had recorded. The teller looked up from her terminal and said in English, "I'm sorry, sir. I show that your account has been closed."

"I must have given you the wrong one. Let me try again," Donovan said, giving her another withdrawal slip, double-checking the numbers.

"I'm sorry, sir. Do you have another account with us?" she asked him.

"Try this one," he said, writing another account number on a withdrawal slip.

Again, the same response. He tried two other account numbers, to no avail.

"What seems to be the problem, sir?" the bank manager asked, seeing the color leave the once vibrant man's face. "Are you okay? Do you want to sit down?"

"No, I don't want to sit down, I want my fucking money. She keeps telling me my accounts have been closed. Could you check into it for me?"

"Certainly, sir. What's that number again?"

Donovan gave him the last account number, and the manager started punching away at the keyboard. He looked up from the computer screen and said, "I'm sorry, sir."

"Where did my money go?"

"It seems that the accounts you have given us have all been closed out. Did you not close them out yourself?"

"Maybe it's a computer error. Can you check again for me?"

"Certainly, sir." He took the two account numbers that Donovan had given the teller. He again started pressing numerous buttons on the computer only to return with the same disappointing answer. "All the accounts have been closed. It appears there has been no error."

"Where the fuck is my money? Listen, I got over a million bucks. Just get me my money," he demanded, lunging at the bank manager, grabbing him by his collar, and ripping his shirt.

"Sir, you need to calm down," he said as he pressed the button below the desk for security. "Did anyone else have access to the accounts?"

"Shit. He cut me off," Donovan said, realizing what had happened. Silberman. He may not have flipped on him, but Silberman had retaliated from beyond the grave.

Donovan walked away without saying another word. His death sentence had just been read, and now he feared the government wouldn't be far behind. They would come down on him with utter severity, retaliating for the embarrassment he had inflicted on them. He couldn't hide his despair as he quickly walked out to Jana, who was waiting nearby in the car.

"What is it?" she asked as she pulled the BMW away from the bank.

"It's gone," he was barely able to utter. "All of it."

"What's gone?"

"The money. It's fucking gone! Every last cent."

"Your money?"

"I've got nothing, Jana. I'm fucked."

"I don't understand. How could this happen? It's your money. There has to be a mistake, no? We'll figure something out. We'll get your money back," she said, realizing for the first time that her sugar daddy was leaving her with an unsavory taste. Without the money, he was just an overweight, middle-aged man with very little to offer. "How could someone take your money?" she asked him.

"My right-hand man. He went to jail, so I was the only one who could get to it, but he must have used someone."

"You'll get it back then, right?"

"Not that easily. The money ain't exactly clean. It's not like I can go to court or anything. There's nothing I can do about it."

"There has to be something. We have to try. You were smart enough to make it once. You just do it again," she said, half-rationalizing to herself as her own reason for sticking with him.

"Yeah, but this ain't exactly Providence. I was somebody there, now I'm just an American schmuck. I've got no money, I've got nothing."

"That's not true. You've got the will. You did it before. It doesn't matter where you are. Maybe you need to go to a place where you have friends?"

"I can't go back to the States. They'll arrest me," he reminded her. "I have nowhere to go. No one to turn to. Except you, Jana. You're the only one I've got. But I can't pay you anymore. You have to decide whether you want to stick with me. I can't guarantee you a future."

"I'll stick with you. We're in this together. We'll lay low. We'll talk to people, and we'll plan our next move. There are always options. We just have to figure it out," Jana said. She really had few options herself. She didn't want to go back to selling her body. That part of her life was over. "I have money, but only about $50,000. I'm in this with you till the end."

***

For the first time in two months, Callahan had his first break in the Donovan case. Even though he was on official sabbatical from the FBI and technically on vacation, he was still in touch with friends at the bureau, including a few close pals who wanted to help him get back on his feet. Interpol had picked up Donovan's face on a bank camera in Prague. The bank had submitted suspicious incidents to the Czech authorities, which in turn were forwarded to Interpol. Interpol shared the footage with the FBI, and the video transaction was transferred over encrypted email to Callahan's laptop. The video feed depicted a middle-aged man, most likely American, based on his clothes and appearance, assaulting a bank manager. There was no audio, but the man appeared visibly upset and highly confrontational. Callahan studied the tape, and he was certain the man who'd accosted the bank manager was Jack Donovan. The mannerisms and the brash behavior were definitely in character. His true self, disguised in the salt-and-pepper hair and straggly gray goatee, had been revealed.

But the video also exposed something about the man analyzing it. While other men his age were taking their sons to Little League practice, Callahan was reviewing video. While other men were out with their wives or girlfriends, he was trying to catch swindlers and scoundrels. Callahan was thirty-five, and his whole life, his very existence, was intertwined with the fate of Jack Donovan. He had no time for anyone in his life, not even himself, except for the one person who was first on his mind when he awoke and last when he slid off to sleep.

Callahan had become obsessed with the mayor. It was why he'd sold his house to finance his own personal investigation. But it was about more than bringing Donovan to justice or exacting his share of revenge. For Callahan, the Donovan case defined him. It was his very reason for being. He had never thought about it that way before, but he had no time to analyze why Donovan meant so much to him. Was Donovan the antithesis of a father who had honestly worked his way up the ranks of the state's labor establishment? Did he signify the ultimate betrayal of the American ideal as a public figure who rose to prominence only to use his influence to cheat his fellow citizens? Or was he simply the focal point that Callahan could turn all his loneliness toward, that could fill the emptiness of his own shallow existence? It was Callahan's calling and a type of symbiotic relationship, where the world produced the Jimmy Callahans to protect against the natural abusers of the law like the Jack Donovans.

If it was Prague where his nemesis was to be found, where he was to find his true meaning, then it was Prague where Callahan would journey. He left Switzerland, where he had attempted to no avail to crack the Swiss banking veil. He wasted no time, did not pack, did not plan, and instead went directly to the international airport in Zurich. He paid three times the usual fare to secure a seat on the next flight to Prague. No distance was too far, no time was too long, no effort was too much, for Jimmy Callahan to bring Donovan to justice.

32

Across the Atlantic, another young man was in search of himself. Henry Mercucio sought the integrity he had lost somewhere along the desolate path of politics. He had traded everything he believed in for an opportunity to spare himself from pain and humiliation, and now he was in a desperate pursuit to hold onto all that was important to him. Like Callahan, Henry was in thrall to his own personal quest for justice. But unlike the man he had once met briefly in McNally's office, Henry had betrayed his own goodness while allowing himself to be caught up in the whirlwind of politics. Not only had he lost his morals; he might lose the one person he loved. Now he was trying to recapture his sense of innocence and restore equilibrium in his life. The moment of reckoning was upon him, and once again, he was forced to bear down on the choices that would determine the final outcome. There was more at stake than Henry Mercucio's personal crusade. There was a city and its people. There was a candidate for mayor who could change minds and perceptions. One man's choices truly made a difference.

Henry decided to confide in his mentor. He stared at his cell phone, knowing he needed to make that first step. He sighed and dialed the number for Ray McNally.

"Congressman, it's Henry. Can I talk to you a minute?" he asked. It was after five, and most of the office staff had already gone home. The only people left in the offices were those lawyers working for the opportunity to be invited to the partners' table. It was already assumed that Henry's seat had been reserved next to McNally's.

"Sure. Come on down," McNally said without hesitation. Henry walked through the office thoroughfare that during the middle of the day was bustling with lawyers, paralegals, and secretaries. The sun was setting over Providence, and McNally's office peered out over the cityscape. The sun eclipsed McNally, who was standing in front of the large panoramic window. Henry saw him in a different light, not as a manipulative politician coveting power, but as a fatherly figure who could guide him through his darkest days.

"What's going on, pal? Come on in and sit down," McNally offered. He always made people feel welcome around him.

Henry prompted McNally to talk about his favorite subject, himself. "How are things going with the port?" Henry asked, referring to McNally's deal to revitalize Providence's old port into marinas and luxury apartments.

"Biggest project in the last twenty years in Providence, and I got these greedy property owners holding out for an extra hundred grand. Don't see the big picture. They're just in it for themselves. They don't care about the city. But it's going to happen. I'm confident. So how's it going with you? You up to your eyeballs in Campagna issues?"

"That's actually what I came to talk about."

"You just have to stick it out for a couple more weeks, then we'll be there. You'll become partner, and that's when the real money comes in, pal."

Henry couldn't hold it back any longer. "I fucked up, Ray. Really bad," he said. There was no easy way to phrase it.

"Whatever it is, Henry, we'll fix it," McNally said quite confidently, even though he had little comprehension of how much trouble his protégé was in.

"Campagna's niece, I was with her the night she died. I went home with her after the campaign event. Didn't do anything, but Beako, he had some guy following me. They've got pictures of me with her."

"If you didn't do anything with her, then who cares about the pictures?" McNally said.

"The pictures make it look like I did. I started to kiss her, but that's it."

"So Beako showed you the pictures, told you he'd go to the press, or even worse, the police, unless you—"

"Worked for them. But I gave them nothing. I convinced them I was on their side, but I've actually been screwing them the whole time."

"So that's why you made Campagna go public about his niece and the taxes. Pretty clever, Henry. So what's the problem?"

"What's the problem? I've been playing two candidates off one another. I've been lying to both of them."

"Hey, have you really done anything wrong here? So you're with some girl you shouldn't have been with, and they caught you with your fly down. You tell them you'll work with them until you figure a way out, and it seems you have."

"You don't have a problem with what I've done?"

"Sure, I do, but my problem is that you didn't come to me sooner. We would've taken care of it, and you wouldn't be killing yourself trying to figure everything out. You never betrayed your client. You did what you had to do. The issue is the end game. How do you play it from here? What's your plan?"

"I win. That's what I do. That's what it's all about in the end— who wins."

"Beako's smart. He knows his guy's got no shot, so he'll want to cut a deal. He thinks he's got you by the balls, so he'll be looking to deal you. I wouldn't be surprised if he tries to sell you out to Campagna. That would be the logical move."

"So what should I do now?"

"Just go out and win the thing. I'll take care of Beako. Let me tell you something. You didn't realize this because you're too close, but if they had something so good on you, they would've already used it. They would've taken you out at the beginning. They played you, pal, but you turned it around on them."

"What do I do about Campagna?" Henry asked.

"You do nothing. Let me tell you something. I know you think he's the second coming of Christ, but he's no different than the rest of us. He cares about winning. You get him elected, and he won't care how you got him there."

"You don't seem that mad about this," Henry said.

"You screwed up. You did. Do I wish maybe I could change some things? Of course. What's really bothering you is Campagna. You feel you betrayed him. But you didn't. The way you handled his depression, it could have been the end of him. You turned him into a hero. Not many people could have done that, Henry."

"I feel like I want to tell him."

"Don't let your guilt guide you. Telling him accomplishes nothing. You'd be doing it to make yourself feel good. It won't. I know you. I know you'd never screw a client. But try explaining to him that you've been moonlighting for Prescott. He'll always question your loyalty. No, this thing's better kept quiet. Real quiet.

You let me deal with Beako. When this thing settles, he'll need some-one close to Campagna."

"That's a relief. It's one thing to be running the campaign, but on top of everything else? Now I can just concentrate on winning and forget about the rest of the shit," Henry said.

"Listen. You do what you were hired for. Win this election, and nothing else matters."

It had been three days since Henry had seen Lyndsay. It was now Tuesday, and she still hadn't returned home, which was unheard of for her. As for Henry, he was preparing for the final stretch of the election. He had two weeks to go, and the polling data had Campagna up by ten to fifteen points. Barring a disaster, Campagna would be elected the next mayor of Providence. Prescott's desperate assault hadn't swayed the electorate; in fact, he had dropped in most polls after his negative barrage. Beako was beside himself, clinging to his belief that Prescott could somehow pull it out. He seemed to be holding some trump card, some bomb he was planning to drop in the final week of the election.

As he attempted to anticipate Beako's next move, Henry was surprised by the receptionist's announcement. "Henry, there's someone here to see you. Says he's Reggie Sinclair, and you'll know who he is."

"I'll be right out," Henry told her as he quickly walked out to greet who he hoped was still his future father-in-law. Henry was unprepared for Lyndsay's father to randomly show up at his office. Lyndsay must have broken down to her parents. It was the only reason he could be there.

"Mr. Sinclair, I had no idea you were in Providence. I hope you weren't waiting long?"

"Call me, Reggie, Henry. You're almost my son-in-law," he said as Henry ushered him into his office and closed the door. "Let's get right to it, Henry. You're a busy guy, and so am I. I wasn't going to do anything about it, but I have to tell you that I wondered what kind of trouble you were in that somebody would send these pictures to my daughter. They arrived on my doorstep addressed to Lyndsay. She doesn't get a lot of mail, so I opened it because I'm the only one who ever gets manila envelopes sent to the house. Usually they're contracts, but this, this was shocking. It made me wonder, what kind of guy is my daughter marrying? I did some further checking into you, but it only confirmed what I already knew. You're a good kid, but you're in way over your head. You know, it was actually Lyndsay who came to me. I never even told her about the pictures. I shredded them. I thought we'd never have this conversation. Look, I was once your age, was a hot shot just like you, and it's not like you two are married yet. Hell, these pictures could be five years old for all I know. But Lyndsay told me you were in some trouble, that these guys had these pictures on you, that they were trying to blackmail you into throwing this election. She asked me to help you. Can you imagine that? She knows there are pictures out there of her future husband with some woman who's dead, and she asks her dad for help. That's the kind of girl she is, and quite frankly, I don't know if you deserve her. But it's hard for a father to say no to his daughter. So here I am. Why don't you tell me what you've gotten yourself into?"

Henry sunk into his chair with the weight of the knowledge that his future father-in-law knew the level of his transgressions. "I don't know what to say, Mr. Sinclair," Henry admitted.

"How about we start with the truth?"

"Well, I had been drinking. I don't usually, but it was the night of the primary. I had fixed it, so we didn't have an actual primary fight, so I was celebrating. Lyndsay was at home, and I got pretty drunk. I was talking to a girl at the bar. It turns out she was Campagna's niece. She says why don't you come back to my apartment? You're not right to drive home. So I go home with her, and the next thing you know, she's all over me. I maybe kissed her, but that's it. She tried to, well, you know. You saw the pictures. But I stopped her, and then I got the hell out of there. The next day, I hear she's found dead, overdosed. Of course, I don't say anything to Campagna. But Gordie Beako, he's the guy running Prescott's campaign, sent a PI to tail people after the primary, and they've got pictures of me with the girl. They tell me they're going to give the pictures to the attorney general unless I work for them. They want me to throw the election."

"Shit, Henry. You're a lawyer. Don't you know they've got nothing on you?"

"Yeah, I know that they couldn't convict me on anything. The girl overdosed, and they were keeping it quiet. But how's it going to look? The campaign manager of a mayoral candidate is involved with his niece the night of her death. It's the type of story the tabloids would love."

"So what did you do to these guys to get them to send the pictures to our home?" Sinclair asked him.

"They did that because I had one of their guys admonished, shall we say, but my guy took it a little too far and beat the crap out of the target, really badly, but he's alright now. That's when Beako sent the pictures to show me he could get to me, and if I didn't play ball, that he could screw me at any time," Henry said, also explaining how he had been doing everything he could to win the election.

"Sounds like you've been playing them the whole time."

"Yeah, you could say that. I outmaneuvered them. This whole time, I've been trying to win the election for Campagna."

"Well, Henry, you've really gotten yourself into a mess, but let's see what we can do about it."

"Mr. Sinclair, I don't know what you can do. It's my problem. It's not Lyndsay's. It's not yours."

"Wrong, Henry. It's Lyndsay's problem because she loves you, and therefore, it's my problem. This is what we're going to do. I want you to arrange for me to meet this guy who's got this stuff on you."

"McNally, the congressman I used to work for, he's already gonna talk to Beako. Really, Mr. Sinclair, I've got this under control."

"Then I want to talk to McNally, and we'll both go see this Beako."

"I don't know what you can do. McNally can offer him access after Campagna's elected."

"Henry, you'd be surprised how persuasive I can be," Sinclair told him.

"I can't let you—"

"She's my daughter, and that's just the way it is. Let me tell you something, Henry. I used to work on Wall Street. These second-rate hoods don't scare me. I was putting together billion-dollar projects when I was your age. I've got more money than probably the entire budget of this city, so for me, taking care of some scumbag who's messing with my family isn't an issue. It's all about bucks, kid. That's all it is. They've got a price you're worth to them. I just have to find out what it is and settle. It's a small price to pay for my daughter's happiness, don't you think?"

"I can't let you pay them off. It's not right. It's my problem,"

Henry said with rising forcefulness.

"The moment you proposed to my daughter, you made it my problem. I'll take care of this. Then it's done. We don't talk about it. You understand?"

"It sounds like I don't have a choice."

"We all have choices, Henry."

"I guess what matters now is what's done from here."

"That's right. There's always a solution. Sometimes you just can't see it, but it's out there. Now, let me talk to McNally."

"I don't know if he's around," Henry said as he dialed McNally's extension. His secretary picked up and told him that McNally was on another call.

"You know, I met McNally once, about ten years ago. We did a legislative reception in Washington back when we were still in tobacco. Seemed like a nice guy. He didn't have a problem taking our money back then."

"Not surprised. He used to be a big smoker, plus he was good friends with a lot of the Southern Democrats, even though his mother died of lung cancer."

"A lot of people died from tobacco. That's why I got my family out of it. That and the lawsuits. We had a pretty good run though—200 years without much regulation. But then came the class action lawsuits. I got us out at the right time."

Henry's phone rang. His caller ID confirmed it was McNally.

"Ray," Henry said as he picked up the line. "I have Reginald Sinclair here, Lyndsay's father. He wants to talk to you. You have a few minutes?"

"What's he want to talk about? Your little problem?"

"Yeah."

"Sure. Come on down," McNally told him.

Henry and Sinclair walked to McNally's office without saying a word. McNally greeted them at his doorway. "Mr. Sinclair. Come in," McNally said as he introduced himself, unaware that they had previously met.

"I appreciate you seeing me on such short notice," Sinclair said.

McNally turned to Henry and said, "Hey, pal, why don't you leave us for a few minutes?"

"No, I think Henry should hear this. It involves him, so it's nothing he can't hear," Sinclair said.

"Okay, then. So what can I do for you, Mr. Sinclair?"

"Well, Henry told me you two discussed his little problem. I have to tell you, I wanted to bury him when I first saw those pictures, but then I thought, what's this kid gotten himself into?" Sinclair said.

"They're bad guys," McNally said, "but Henry's been beating them at their own game. They'll do just about anything to protect their interests. When they find out that Henry's been screwing them, they're gonna come down on him pretty hard. I didn't tell you that, Henry, because I was still trying to figure out a solution. You have to understand something about these guys. They don't play by the rules, but the one thing they understand is money. I was planning to go to Beako and tell him to back off. His guy has no shot, and if he wants any business in the future, then he'd better cut Henry loose. Frankly, I don't know if he'll go for it."

"Why don't you go ahead and set it up? I want to meet this Beako guy. Whatever it takes, I want this whole thing to go away," Sinclair said, speaking to him like one of his subordinates, not a former US Congressman and powerbroker of Providence.

"It's not going to be cheap, Mr. Sinclair. They stand to lose millions without their guy in City Hall. If I can assure them that Campagna's administration will be open to them, I might be able to keep him quiet. But anything you offer him up front would certainly sweeten the offer."

"Wait a second. What makes you think Campagna would do anything to help out CampCo after Beako's been so out in front in this election?" Henry asked.

"Don't worry about Campagna. I'll take care of him," McNally assured him.

"Then set it up—me, you, and Beako," Sinclair said.

***

The meeting for Henry's future took place that evening. McNally phoned Sinclair on his cell phone, and the two agreed to meet at the hotel bar before driving over to the meeting. Sinclair was wearing the same $1,000 suit he'd worn to their earlier meeting. He waved to McNally, who was already sitting at a table in the hotel bar, and joined him for a beer.

"How you doing?" McNally asked him.

"I'm good. Had to make a few calls, move some money around. Not a big deal."

"Let me tell you about this guy Beako. He's a shrewd bastard."

"I'm not worried. Dealt with a hundred guys like him, they're all the same."

"You know what you're going to say?" McNally asked.

"Yeah, I have a few things to tell Mr. Beako."

They drove the few blocks over to CampCo Development in McNally's Lexus. The two men exchanged not a single word on the ride over. A beautiful young woman greeted them at the door and let them into the office building. It was 8 p.m., and the building was all but deserted. The young woman rode with them on the elevator to the top floor, then walked them up the spiral staircase to Beako's lair.

"Gordie Beako," a confident Beako offered as the men entered the room.

"Reggie Sinclair," Sinclair said as he extended his hand.

"What can I do for you, Mr. Sinclair?"

"First of all, you can remove yourself from these premises. I'll give you an hour to get your things. After that, I'll have the police escort you out, Mr. Beako."

"I don't know who the fuck you think you are, but you can't waltz into my office like you own the place and bark orders at me."

"Oh, but I can, Mr. Beako, because you've been relieved of your duties. As the largest single shareholder of CampCo Development, I'm informing you that the Board has decided to dismiss you as president."

"What? You can't buy this company! The Lombardos are the largest shareholders."

"*Were* the largest shareholders. I began buying up large volumes of the stock last month, and when the Lombardos saw their stocks' value go through the roof, they were more than willing to accept my offer."

Beako's phone rang. "Go ahead. Ask them. It's all true," Sinclair told him. It was right as he had planned—8:15 p.m., when the Lombardos' lawyer had been instructed to call. Beako's face betrayed his cool exterior. He realized that this cruel joke was, in fact, reality.

"Mr. Beako, I'm afraid you've been liquidated. I have the votes on the Board, and with the money we'll make, the stockholders will be very pleased. I believe you're a big stockholder, so you should do quite well. Plus, I think you'll find your severance package more than adequate. One thing, though. You get any wild ideas about showing anyone the property you've acquired while working here, any pictures you may have, you blow your golden parachute."

"You knew about this, McNally?" Beako asked him.

"Had no idea, Beako, but I hope Mr. Sinclair considers our firm to assist in the sale," McNally said with a big grin on his face. He and Beako were dwarfed in Sinclair's presence.

"I think my future son-in-law would be real good on this stuff. It's not politics, but maybe it's good for Henry to get his feet wet in some corporate law," Sinclair said. "Those pictures ever turn up, Mr. Beako, I'll hold you personally responsible, you understand me?"

Beako exited the room without another word spoken.

"You could have told me, Mr. Sinclair," McNally said as they walked out of the office.

"Please, call me Reggie."

"Fair enough, Reggie. Are you going to make out alright on this?"

"All said and done, probably a couple of million. Not a real big one for me. I do five or so of these a year. I wouldn't have touched this one if it hadn't been for Henry. I have a network of people I can sell to. I might actually keep the building, nice property, but everything else from the paper clips to their backhoes will be sold off."

"Henry's a good kid, you know?" McNally said.

"Yeah, I know."

"You didn't have to do this. We could have fixed this. The kid was doing a pretty good job on his own."

"Who am I if I can't help out a kid like Henry? What's it all worth if I can't walk into some scumbag's office and stop him from screwing up some kid's life? He really didn't do anything wrong. Sure, maybe it was poor judgment, but nothing probably you or I haven't done. He just needed someone to help him out. It's a small thing to do for my family. Plus, hey, let's not forget, he made me a couple of million."

"It's still good of you."

"It's not about what's good or bad. It's just what you do."

34

McNally called Henry as soon as he had dropped off Sinclair at his hotel. McNally was still a bit awestruck by Sinclair's bold audacity and selfless magnanimity. Few men came into his city and smacked around men like Beako. McNally soon realized that he and Beako weren't in the same league as Sinclair. As a former member of Congress who had dined at the White House and broken bread with heads of state, McNally wasn't easily impressed. There were few men like Sinclair, truly great men, who would utilize their full resources and talents to help another.

"Hey, pal. How's it going?" McNally asked Henry.

"It's going. How'd it go with Beako?"

"Really well. Sinclair's the real deal. He outdid us all."

"What do you mean?"

"He bought the whole thing. CampCo, the building, everything."

"Wait a second. He *bought* CampCo?"

"He bought it all. Old man Lombardo sold him the entire thing. I guess he drove up the price of the stock, then made an offer.

Sinclair owns it now."

"Are you sure about this?"

"Henry, he bought the whole fucking thing. You should have seen Beako's face. It's over."

"I don't get it. How could he?"

"He did it. That's all there is."

"Hold on a second," Henry said, patting his pockets for his phone. "I've got another call."

"That's alright. I'll talk to you tomorrow."

Sinclair was the other call. He asked Henry to meet him at his suite at the Omni. He didn't provide a clue as to why.

***

Henry, still perplexed by the recent course of events, drove over to the Omni. He took the elevator to the top floor, where Sinclair had rented the suite. He knocked on the door and was shocked to see Lyndsay.

He hung his head. "I don't know what to say."

"Don't say anything, Henry," she replied.

"There he is. Come on in," Sinclair said. He rose and embraced Henry. It was the type of hug a father gave to his son.

"Mr. Sinclair, I just spoke with McNally. He told me you bought out CampCo. I'm speechless."

"It's me who should be thanking you, Henry. You made me a couple of million."

"No one's ever done anything like this for me."

"Listen, Henry. I know you're the type of guy who's usually putting all the pieces together. Sometimes that guy needs someone to help him out. That's all I did."

"You didn't need to get involved. I could have gotten myself out of this."

"True. You seemed to be doing a pretty good job of it. But at what cost? Lyndsay? Your sanity? I did what any guy in my situation would have done. I have the money. I have the contacts. Why wouldn't I help out a guy who's gotten too far out over his skis?"

"Not anyone would have done this, Mr. Sinclair."

"What do I have to do to get you to call me Reggie? In fact, how about Dad, when you're married, of course."

"Sorry, Reggie. I don't know what to say."

"Just go out there and win this goddamned election, would you please? So I can get you into some real business."

"It's what I am. It's what I do."

"I know that's what Lyndsay told me. But a kid with your talents? You've got the skills, and you've got the balls to do what I'm doing. You want to affect people's lives? Do the right thing. Create jobs, influence change. Then you come with me. I'll show you how the real business world works. These guys—Beako and McNally—amateurs. Sure, they might be a big deal here in Providence, but I've dealt with a thousand guys like them. You want to make real things happen, do the types of things that really matter? You want to make the kind of money that can fund an endowment at Duke to find a cure for leukemia? Or the kind of money to give to your school to educate another Speaker of the House? My girls, Lyndsay, her sisters, I don't want them in this business. Lyndsay's going to be a doctor. My other girls, they can be whatever they want to be. But you, Henry, you're cut out for what I do. Who's going to manage the money after I retire, to make sure Julie and Jenny can become whatever they want? That's you. So maybe my motives weren't entirely altruistic. Maybe I do get something out of this. But I want you to really consider what I'm offering. No more of this political nonsense."

"Are you offering me a job?"

"Not just a job, Henry. An opportunity to start fresh, to make more money than you ever dreamed of. Real money, the kind of money that allows you to walk into a room and buy a company because the president's screwing with some kid you like. Not millions, but hundreds of millions, the type of money that buys power and respect. Not everyone is cut out to handle that kind of responsibility. Look at all the rich kids who end up dead in alleys with needles in their arms or movie stars and athletes that piss it all away. No, I'm talking about creating jobs, developing products that make people better, promoting science and culture that make mankind better. These opportunities are only open to a select few," Sinclair said.

"I'll think about it. Tell you the truth, I'm sick of the political bullshit."

"That's all I ask. You finish this thing, you and Lyndsay get married, then you come work for me."

"I don't want to be one of those sorry-ass sons-in-law who's given a job because they're so pathetic," Henry admitted.

"It's not like that, Henry. I know plenty of people like that, and you're not one of them. You're the real deal. Let me tell you something. The difference between a successful man and an average man is will—the will to take a chance, the will to seize an opportunity. It's not selling your soul to the almighty dollar; it's doing it honestly, but having the balls to put it all on the line. And you did that, kid. You've got what it takes."

"Daddy, great speech, but I have a year and a half of residency left, so you're going to have to put off your master plan for a bit," Lyndsay said.

"Of course, honey. I know that. We'll just have to work out some deals up here. I think I can do business with his firm. I'm good friends with two of their partners." Bringing in the legal work of

Sinclair's financial empire was a dream client for any partner to land. The landscape of Providence had changed in a fortnight with a new mayor emerging and a local business dynasty crumbling. An era of change was upon the city.

35

The reality of his situation finally gripped Donovan. He was a stranger in a strange land, alone, penniless, and hopeless. The only thing he had was Jana. That was it. The one thing he could count on in his life was a Lithuanian prostitute for whom he'd paid $25,000. For the first time in his life, he was broke. And not the kind of poor experienced by so many young Americans in Europe, who could simply call their parents and have $500 wired over from the States. Without Jana's charity, he didn't know where his next meal would come from.

He couldn't quite comprehend why Jana had stayed with him. They had moved out of the suite at the Marriott and into her one-bedroom apartment in the working-class neighborhood of Prague 3, one of the districts of the city. She had bought their food, had taken him out for beers, but most importantly, she had reassured him. She was the one who'd begged him to contact his cousin in Ireland. It was her suggestion that he open a new email account at one of the cafés in Prague to hide his identity from the authorities. After several emails, his cousin understood it was him and took his own precautionary steps. His cousin advised him to get in contact with Lukas Reid, who could be found in an Irish pub called Flannery's in Old Town. His cousin assured him that if anyone could help in Prague, it was Reid.

Donovan and Jana took the tram from their flat to Old Town. She knew of Flannery's Pub and understood that it was a popular watering hole for expats. She had never heard of Reid but acted as if he was the type of man who could surely solve their predicament. Donovan was in the darkest of his days, and she wanted to act like hope still existed.

"You really think this is going to work?" Donovan asked Jana.

"You know anything better?"

"I don't know how great I feel about meeting this guy."

After calming a nervous Donovan, she made her way to the bar. For a woman who made her living by working closely with bartenders, she knew the drill pretty well.

"Can I have two pints?" she asked as she threw back her hair.

"Sure, love. Anything else?" the bartender said in his thick brogue.

"Actually, there is. I'm looking for someone. A guy."

"Sure you are, love, but looks like you already got one," he said with a bit of flirtation rolling off his tongue.

"We're looking for Lukas Reid."

After a long pause, he asked, "What are you looking for him for?"

"Just tell him Billy Cavanaugh's cousin wants to see him," she said as she handed him a piece of paper with her cell phone number on it.

"Will do if I see him, love."

***

Jana did what she could to provide distractions for Donovan. He was consumed by his despair and had begun talking about turning himself in. She pleaded with him to speak to Reid and assured him they would devise a solution. After double-digit Irish whiskeys between them, they returned to her apartment. Large quantities of alcohol and a few things only she could provide were the only remedies she knew. They were unaware of the stranger waiting for them in her flat.

"Close the door," the stranger said.

"What the fuck? Who are you?"

"You were looking for me."

"Lukas Reid?" Jana asked as she saw his face emerge from the darkness. His hair was black and his eyes were cold slate. He wore a charcoal turtleneck and dark pants and boots. He was brandishing a gun, but soon returned it to its holster after realizing there was little danger.

"It's okay, Jack. It's the guy your cousin set us up with."

"Man, you scared the shit out of me. You could have knocked."

"In my business, you need to be careful. So what can I do for you?" he asked as he pulled up a chair. He wasn't one for pleasantries. A man in his situation couldn't waste time when there was a price on his head.

"I don't even know you. My cousin said you procure things for him. What kind of things?" Donovan asked.

"You could say I'm in the helping business. The Czech Republic makes a lot of things people like your cousin need."

Jana jumped in before Donovan realized he was a gunrunner. "We need your help. Jack's a very prominent man from America. He's in trouble, and I thought you could help us."

"I didn't know we had that sort of relationship," Reid told her. A man in his business needed to be cautious. He was one misstep away from spending the rest of his life in a Czech prison.

"Mr. Cavanaugh told us you could help."

"That depends on the kind of help," Reid replied.

"I'm a mayor from America. I got myself in a little trouble with the law over there. I've been running for months, and my support has run out. We think we have a plan to get my money back. It may sound crazy, but sometimes crazy just works," Donovan told Reid.

"And how does that involve me?" Reid asked, uncertain that he could help this American. Reid knew Cavanaugh and respected him. He would do whatever he could without risking himself and his organization.

Donovan told him what he wanted Reid's organization to do for him, which was met with a quick, "What?" Reid wasn't sure if this so-called mayor was crazy, stupid, or a little bit of both.

"They'll never believe it. It'll never work," Reid told him.

"Why can't it?" Jana pled.

"I told you this was a bad idea," Donovan said.

"Hold on. I may know someone who's crazy enough to do something like this."

"Who?" Donovan asked.

"It just might work," Reid laughed. "It just might."

"Who?"

"Palestinian Jihadis. They're a splinter group of the PLO. They have a cell in London. I've sold them some things. They need the money, and they hate the United States."

"I'm not going to work with terrorists," Donovan said, finding some morality.

"You Americans. You drop bombs on civilians, but they're just, what do you say, collateral damage." Reid was saying what many of his comrades felt about America.

"Can you set it up?" Jana asked him, putting her hand on Donovan's thigh to reassure him.

"I can take care of it. What kind of money we talking?" It always came down to money. But what Donovan was doing was far worse than Jana's selling of her body. He was selling his soul.

"At least a million for them."

"You know someone who'd pay that kind of money?" Reid asked Donovan.

"Yeah, I do," Donovan told him.

"So what do we do next?"

"I'll get you out of Prague to England. That's where they operate," Reid explained.

"Can you do that?"

"I've smuggled bigger packages than you. Don't worry."

Reid's organization had plenty of experience in smuggling weapons out of Eastern Europe. It wasn't as difficult to move contraband across Europe as it once had been. But the illegal weapons trade was a delicate business that required the highest degree of discretion. Cash payments to the right border guards guaranteed a smooth flow of trade. It cost $2,000, which was provided by Jana to Reid since Donovan no longer had a dollar to his name. Reid paid the border guards $500 each and kept a grand for himself.

After a ten-hour drive in the back of a diesel truck through Germany and Belgium, Reid handed off the package to Billy Cavanaugh's friends. IRA operatives took Donovan and delivered them to representatives of the Palestinian Jihad. The Jihadis, who weren't unlike their other revolutionary comrades, took their prized hostage to their safe house in Calais. Donovan and Jana slept the night on a twin mattress on the floor in the cold basement, being woken before dawn for their journey to an undisclosed location somewhere in Britain.

***

There was something Henry wondered, something he had questioned from the very beginning before the election had consumed him. How had Donovan known that the government was planning to arrest him after he returned from Ireland? How many conversations had that deputy US attorney had with other power brokers he wanted to impress? Who had tipped off Donovan and set this madness into motion?

He realized the answer was right around the corner. He walked into McNally's closed office, much to the annoyance of his secretary, who was irritated with his blatant disregard for protocol.

"Henry," McNally said without looking up from the yellow legal pad he was scribbling on. He refused to type into a computer, instead relying on his secretary to translate his hieroglyphics.

"Remember that meeting in your office with that deputy US attorney?"

"Jimmy Callahan," McNally said, still writing.

"That's the one. How do you suppose it got leaked to Donovan that the feds were going to bust him when he came back?"

McNally stopped writing and looked up at his protégé, who had clasped his hands against his desk. He winked at him, then returned to writing his memo. Sometimes in politics, Henry understood, it was about what was left unsaid.

The former congressman who had lost his bid to become governor wanted what most retiring legislators wanted—money and power. He had become accustomed to a certain lifestyle. Now, as a regular citizen, he needed a life that resembled his former one. The only way to achieve his new life was through money. A half a million to start was what he'd earned as a partner at Warner Isikoff. But that was only the salary to lure an influential former congressman into their firm. The real money came from the 30 percent he received for new business that he brought into the firm. With new leadership at City Hall, one that was friendlier to him, he figured he could represent any hotel and office developer, restaurant chain, stadium builder, and casino operator who wanted to do business in town. He planned to make his retirement from politics a lucrative one.

Tipping off Mayor Donovan, no matter how insidious it was, was secondary to his desired goal. Changing the political leadership at City Hall was paramount to his business development plan. A mayor who was friendly to him, someone he helped elect, could mean millions in contracts and legal work. Becoming the king-maker had much more allure than serving at the mercy of a disinterested public. And rather than rely on the judicial system to prosecute Donovan, a branch of government he knew all too well, he hedged his bet on another horse.

He had placed a call to Silberman's lawyer, a man he had battled when he was a prosecutor but had become friendly with over the years and revealed that his client was coming under indictment. McNally expected that Silberman would attempt to distance himself from the mayor, and knowing that his phones were most likely tapped, wouldn't risk tipping him off. So he had his secretary track down the hotel in Ireland where the Providence delegation was staying. He then went out and purchased a burner phone at the local convenience store. Not wanting to risk calling from his office, he called from the alley outside. McNally made the call to Donovan and let the events play themselves out.

As McNally looked back at the firestorm that ensued, he felt little remorse. The city was better off without the public spectacle of their mayor on trial for corruption. He had accomplished his goal of removing his enemy from City Hall and rescuing his city. His bloodless coup had ushered in real change, and so what if he benefited by it? No man understood realpolitik better than McNally, having once played it and having been played by it. Politics was his business and had consumed his entire life, and he had fine-tuned his art over the years. Yet while he was the king-maker of Providence, he was but one little king in a small fiefdom. Often, as in chess, the pawn and king ultimately end up in the same box at the end of the game.

36

It was the final stretch. The election was one week away, and Henry was awaiting the final assault. He was trying to control the things he had power over, knowing all too well there was little he could do against whatever the Prescott people had planned for the waning days of the campaign. For now, plenty of work still existed. He still had to produce the final television spot and place the buy for the last week of the election, the time when most voters made up their minds. Their polling data showed a solid ten-point lead with only 12 percent of the electorate undecided. Henry felt confident in Campagna's victory. But that old adage that the only certainties in life were death and taxes banged in his head.

To shore up support in the final campaign push, Henry had earmarked the largest expenditure for the final week. They poured $100,000 into television ads, and a citywide mailer featuring the Providence cityscape at sunrise with the tagline, "A New Day Is Dawning," was slated to hit the Saturday and Monday prior to the Tuesday election. The last television spot opened with Providence's glistening downtown, then shifted to its major neighborhoods. In the spot, Campagna explained, "Providence's true character is our neighborhoods. We've revived downtown, but now we need to revitalize our neighborhoods." Computerized renderings of parks, community centers, and new, affordable housing developments were superimposed over vacant lots and dilapidated buildings. "Only when we invest in our neighborhoods will Providence live up to its name."

Henry was gearing up for the coordinated Get-Out-The-Vote effort. The campaign office was wallpapered with the names and phone numbers of people who had been identified as likely Campagna voters. The names were supplied to the campaign by the polling company and from volunteers who had been canvassing Providence voters for the past two weeks. Each likely voter was called on Election Day and asked if he or she had voted. If they hadn't, they were politely urged with the phrase, "John Campagna really needs your vote today." Buses were reserved, and pastries and coffee were ordered for the retirement homes. Volunteer drivers were also standing by to chauffer elderly and handicapped Campagna voters to the polls. The entire operation was in place.

Considering that all the plans were set, Henry should have been relaxed. But he wasn't. He preferred the things he could control, like the television commercials, direct mail, and even reporters he could spin. But he couldn't deter whatever desperate ploy the Prescotts resorted to. For that, he was helpless.

The bomb was dropped the Friday before the election. Katrina Paul, the political reporter for the *Providence Journal*, had launched it. She was a veteran state house reporter who had been covering the highly contested mayoral race since statewide politics was tepid during the non-election year for state politicians. She had developed as friendly a relationship with Henry as a reporter could have with a spin-doctor, but she believed the current story surfacing was even too murky for these dirty waters.

"Henry, it's Kat. There's a story going around, and it's not too pretty for you guys," she said.

"Kat, we're coming pretty damned close to the news blackout. What you got better be good."

"It is, but not for you. There's some pictures now floating around Instagram that look a lot like you, Henry. You're with Campagna's niece. We're hearing that you were with her the night she died, and that Campagna knew but kept it quiet anyway."

The news caught Henry totally unprepared. Attempting to keep his composure, he said, "What are you talking about? Pictures of Campagna's niece? What does that have to do with me?"

"Girl's found dead, pictures come out that tie the campaign manager of her uncle to the scene. Sounds like a story to me. You have any comment for me, Henry?"

"I have no comment because I had nothing to do with any of this."

"Can you explain to me why there are pictures of you at her apartment? Have you ever seen her before? Have you ever been with her?"

"Listen, Kat. I'm not going down this road with you." Henry knew if the mainstream media picked up the story it would legitimize the conspiracy theories floating around the Internet.

"Hey, I'm not trying to trip you up. I like you. I'm the one tipping you off. You're lucky you're not getting a microphone shoved in your face when you leave your office. I'll give you an hour before I let this thing out, but then all hell breaks loose, you understand?"

"One hour," Henry said. He opened another line on his phone to make his next call, not even bothering to hang up the receiver. "I need to talk to McNally right now."

"He's in a meeting. He's going to have to call you back," his secretary said in her condescending tone.

"Pull him out now," he told her. "You know what? Forget it. I'm coming down."

Henry ran down to McNally's office and brushed by his secretary. He knocked, then let himself in. "I'm sorry to bother you, Congressman, but I need to talk to you."

"This is my top guy, Henry Mercucio," McNally said to the people gathered around to hear his treatise of the local business climate. "Could you excuse me a minute?" he graciously asked.

McNally pulled Henry into one of the vacant offices. "These guys are in town from New York, they want to open a restaurant here, and they're having a problem getting a liquor license. So what's going on?"

"I've got a problem," Henry said.

"Okay, relax," he said.

"Kat Paul just called me. She's running a story about me, she's got pictures, and she wants a comment."

"You sure she's really got the goods, or is she hearing it at the State House?"

"She said she has pictures and that they look like me."

"You didn't tell her anything, right?"

"I gave her nothing, but you know her. She thinks she's Bob Woodward, and she smells blood. She gave me an hour."

"All right. I'll take care of this. She's a friend, so let me call her," McNally said. He walked back into his office and announced to his guests that he had an emergency he needed to take care of. "Got a client who's gotten himself into a little jam. Have to make a couple of calls," he told them. He looked back at Henry and said, "Go back to your office. Why don't you start writing Campagna's victory speech? Let me worry about this."

Henry returned to his office, closed his door, and began pacing.

He was only comfortable when he was in total control, and the thought of relying on someone else, even if it was McNally, frightened him. Maybe focusing on something entirely different like Campagna's victory speech was what he needed to keep his mind off the possibility that he may have ultimately cost his candidate the race. He cleared his desk of the papers that had accumulated over the course of the last few days and stacked them in a neat pile in the corner. He made the appearance of order, but chaos was all around him. He waited for that phone call and those words from a father figure who could fix whatever problem he had gotten himself into—"Hey, pal. All set. No problem." His computer screen was as blank as his expressionless face. He was worried, terrified of the consequences of his juvenile act. Gordon Beako had the last word. He couldn't leave without launching a firebomb at Henry. *Fucking Beako*, Henry thought. *Why couldn't he just let me be?*

Henry knew that it wasn't personal. It was war, and in war came casualties. Beako had adopted a scorched earth policy, leaving a trail of dead bodies as he'd departed Providence. Henry was the man he wanted to bury in the rubble. He couldn't help but think of Beako as he waited for that call. Would Beako succeed in destroying Henry, or would Henry prevail this day? The call came at exactly three minutes past five.

"It's taken care of," McNally said to him.

"She's not doing the story?"

"Her publisher put the kibosh on it. It seems that your father-in-law plays golf at Augusta with the CEO of the parent company that owns the *Providence Journal*. How's that for contacts?"

"You serious?"

"Yeah. It's over, pal."

"It's over?"

"Henry, it's done. It's Friday night. Get out of here. Go home.

It's over."

And upon that friendly advice, Henry hung up the phone and walked out of the office like the other nine-to-fivers in his building. He called Lyndsay on his cell phone and told her he was coming home. Sure, he would have preferred to have solved his own problem, to be his own man. But some help from some powerful friends was certainly no negative. If he wanted to take a liberal look at it, he *had* done things on his own. He had ingratiated himself to some powerful people who had in turn provided assistance.

McNally, ever so interested in securing his own position with Sinclair, paid heed to his request to inform him if the story they had buried ever made a comeback. As someone who made multi-million-dollar business decisions in minutes, Sinclair knew he needed to be quick and decisive to ensure that Mr. Beako's betrayal didn't derail his plans. He made one phone call. That's all it took.

Sinclair phoned a friend he had played golf with in Augusta last year, one of the four annual trips he made to the famed course. He knew Peter Bellow, CEO of the Bellow Media Group, would honor his friendship and the fact he was one of the media group's largest advertisers. On behalf of his friend, Bellow called the publisher of the *Providence Journal*, a paper his media empire owned. After the editor and Katrina Paul, the reporter who had broken the story, cried foul, screaming that the journalistic integrity of their paper had been compromised, the publisher sided with the man who signed his check. It was over.

Was it all worth it, Henry wondered? Not so much the fateful decision to go home with Campagna's niece—that was obviously a gross misjudgment—but the politics, the race itself? Absolutely. He knew he was helping to elect a person who would restore honor to the mayor's office. At times, he'd thought about running for office, doing his own type of public service. But no, not Henry. His service was in helping those who were too pure to operate in a system that did not want to be reformed. He was who he was—a political consultant. No matter whether he cloaked himself as a lawyer, he would always be a political operative. It was in his veins, the very essence of him. Spin doctor, politico, flak-catcher—call him whatever, but call upon him they did.

37

The moment of reckoning was upon them. All the GOTV calls had been placed, hundreds of volunteers were standing at polling locations, and the final media blitz was underway. It was the one day in the life of a political consultant when he felt most helpless. All Henry's work was reduced to a straight up or down vote. There was something about the competitive nature of politics, the clear winning and losing, that was appealing to men like Henry. Success was easily judged, the winner quickly remembered, and the loser equally forgotten. In few other endeavors was the outcome so simply determined. One person would walk away in victory, the other in defeat.

Henry stood in the campaign office, a place he was rarely seen. The small storefront had been decorated with campaign posters and newspaper advertisements. Long card tables and folding chairs lined the walls, and old touch-tone phones from earlier elections in the 2000s were placed three to a table. During most days, close friends from the neighborhood filtered in and out of the office, and at night, the office was quiet except for a few faithful who came in to make phone calls to their friends to support John Campagna. All the labeling of brochures and stuffing of envelopes was sent to a mail house, and the GOTV campaign was farmed out to a professional phone bank. Professional campaigns, Henry sermonized, couldn't rely on volunteers to label 50,000 pieces of mail or make 10,000 phone calls. Henry was cordial to the older women who used the campaign office as social central and the old political stalwarts who sat around drinking coffee, reminiscing about the political fights of the past.

Partitioned in the back of the room was a makeshift 10x10 space that Henry disappeared into whenever he ventured into the campaign office. He took up camp there with his cell phone and a large TV. From this war room, he could monitor developments in the election. Operatives in the field called in every hour or so from different polling stations to report voter turnout. Henry theorized that a high turnout for this special election would prove advantageous for his candidate. Prescott had been polling in the low 30 percent range and hadn't been able to break over one-third in the polls. In contrast, Campagna showed a steady climb with a majority of the undecided votes breaking his way. The more people that came out, Henry believed, the more likely they would come out to vote for his candidate. According to their polling data, the electorate was tired of what the Campagna campaign labeled as the "politics of personal destruction." Henry predicted that large numbers of motivated voters would cast their vote against the negativity that the Prescott campaign had spewed into the race. But Henry was mentally prepared for whatever decision the voters handed down, ready to move on to the second chance in a life bestowed upon him by a surprising patron.

After an hour in the campaign office and the endless progress of the polls, he decided to abandon the office for the campaign trail.

He started out at the polling station in the elementary school near his apartment. He had already been there at 7 a.m., when the polls had opened. By noon when he returned, there was a steady traffic of voters who used their lunch hour to perform their civic duty. Henry grabbed a Campagna sign and stood among his candidate's supporters, the proper distance away from the polling station allowed by Rhode Island law. He then walked into the school's cafeteria where the ballot booths had replaced the long white lunch tables. The number of people who had voted was displayed on the vote counter machines, recording a thousand votes cast in the seven hours that the polls had been opened in this location. If this location was any indication of voter turnout across the city, Henry figured that about 36,000 voters had already placed their vote. The heaviest number of voters usually came out between 5 and 7 p.m. If the trend continued, Henry figured that about 85,000 voters would come out for the special election. Of Providence's registered voters, it appeared that over 60 percent were likely to vote, marking the highest voter turnout for a special election in the state's history. This was unheard of in a special election. Voters came out in droves during presidential elections. Sixty to 70 percent voter turnout was considered high for presidential elections, but special elections usually performed under 50 percent. Something was compelling the voters of Providence to come out to the polls on a beautiful spring day.

There were two candidates before the electorate, plus the Green Party perennial who usually garnered one or two percentage points. The ads depicted Campagna as a dedicated public servant who had devoted much of his life to Providence. There was the minor scandal over his battle with depression, but for the most part, he was seen as an honest, affable public servant. On the other side, Prescott had paid the top Republican strategists and spin-doctors to portray him as a successful businessman above corruption. A man of his considerable wealth wouldn't be found looting the city coffers.

But who were these men, really, under all the professional spin, clever lines, and poll-tested issues? Few of the voters would ever know the real John Campagna or Malcolm Prescott, just the candidates who had been prepped and prepared for prime time. Few would ever know that after knocking on doors and talking to his neighbors during the campaign, John Campagna had spent Monday through Friday nights caring for his eighty-five-year-old mother, a pledge he had made to his dying father five years ago. Only Prescott's closest family understood the abuse he suffered from his tyrannical father who constantly questioned his son publicly whether he could really continue the family's legacy. The best anyone really knew about the candidates vying for office was what they viewed on television, heard on radio, or read online.

Blame couldn't be cast on the candidates themselves, for they were only playing by the rules of the game. The game itself needed change, and as much as people howled that politics and politicians were corrupt, their apathy as evidenced by their usually low turnout at the polls sustained the corrupt system of governance. Only when their lives were directly affected, when their taxes were raised or their money misappropriated, were their voices heard. Until the people—the teachers, nurses, steel workers, carpenters, businessmen—took an interest in their government, their government would never change.

As much as Henry didn't like playing by the rules, he didn't have any virginal delusions that he was the spark that could ignite a revolution. On the contrary, he relished the idea that he could guide good men like Campagna through the treacherous system. Without professional help, Campagna would never have been able to overcome the depression controversy. Political cronies who still believed that bumper stickers and yard signs won campaigns would have lost him his election. Money would have been spent frivolously rather than on clever direct mail, creative television spots, and targeted digital media. The symbiotic relationship between consultant and candidate was never clearer: each depended on the other. Without candidates like Campagna, the Henrys of the world would be reduced to hawking products like any other advertising and public relations hack. Without consultants like Henry, people like Campagna could expect long careers toiling away on the city council.

The relationship between Henry and Campagna had remained solid throughout the tumultuous turns of the campaign. It had never been tested because Campagna had never discovered that Henry was with his niece the night she overdosed or that he had worked, even as a double agent, for the opponent. Henry felt some tales were best left untold. Campagna was the product of a sausage processing machine that ground the issues and prevailing attitudes into a cohesive winning product. He was an amalgam of a comprehensive strategy and a well-delivered message. Yet there was something that separated Campagna from the rest of the political cogs. Even at the shallowest point of the race, he had maintained his integrity and goodness. It was his inner core values that ultimately made him the leader the city needed.

The victory that Henry had risked his career to secure was delivered at 9:15 p.m. on election night. Henry stood hand-in-hand with Lyndsay in the ballroom of the Providence Biltmore Hotel, a turn-of-the-century building that had witnessed the enlightened transformation of Providence. The Biltmore had been home to Democratic celebrations for the past fifty years. The Republicans were across town in the more modern Marriott hotel, where the costs were cheaper due to the lack of unionized employees. In the middle of the Biltmore's dance floor, a ten-foot placard listed the candidates' names and vote totals from each precinct. Though they could have projected the totals on seventy-two-inch monitors, they opted to go old school. As soon as the polls closed at nine, and the voter machines had calculated the totals, precinct captains called in to the ballroom.

Campaign Chairman Felix Salaso hurriedly wrote the vote totals as they came to him. After a quarter of the votes were in, Henry knew the outcome. Downtown Providence had come in with a slight victory for Prescott, hardly enough to overcome the large disparities in the Campagna strongholds. In the West End of the city, which was considered an open battlefield, the early numbers indicated a Campagna landslide. As each precinct was recorded, the crowd erupted in applause, forcing Salaso to wave his hands so he could hear the precinct captains' calls. Few events were as clear-cut as elections, and while Henry was an avid sports fan, there was nothing quite as satisfying for him as electing someone to office. They savored the taste of victory as the final numbers were recorded: Campagna – 65 percent, Prescott – 35 percent.

The crowd's applause could have been mistaken for a Super Bowl victory. Wives were kissing husbands, friends were high-fiving each other, and tears of joy streamed down cheeks. Henry stood stoically, soaking in the moment. He gave Lyndsay a kiss on the cheek and walked with her out of the room, hand-in-hand. He said nothing and just kept walking with a stunned Lyndsay who wasn't sure what to say.

"Henry," a voice called out. He turned around to see Campagna in the hallway. He walked back to his candidate and embraced him like a player hugging his coach.

"We did it, Henry. We did it," Campagna said into his ear.

"You did it, Mr. Mayor."

Henry said nothing as Campagna continued, "I couldn't have done this without you, buddy. This is your victory. Get in there and celebrate."

"I am celebrating, Mr. Mayor. I'm going home," Henry said, patting him on the shoulder, turning around, and walking out with Lyndsay. His cell phone began vibrating in his suit pocket. He looked at the number, realized it was McNally, and let the call go to voicemail.

"You alright?" Lyndsay asked.

"Yeah, I'm great, Lynds. It's over."

"I thought you'd want to stay and celebrate."

"Not for me. People coming up and telling me what a great job I've done? Don't need it. I'd rather go home with you and have a normal night. I don't need a bunch of screaming people to validate what happened."

"Don't you want to be with Campagna? You worked hard on this," she said.

"I've spent enough time with Campagna, don't you think?"

"Yeah, but this is your night. I hope you're not doing this because of me."

"No, I'm doing this because of us. There's no one I want to be with more than you. It's over. Let's just enjoy it while it lasts."

It was nothing he could share with the people at the party. They were too consumed with who would receive the plush city jobs and board appointments. Only Henry could truly enjoy this moment by himself and with Lyndsay. He could tell by her smile and by the way she gently put her head on his shoulder that she, too, was at that place. Happiness had finally found Henry Mercucio.

Henry's disinterest in the ceremony of victory went unnoticed by the crowd of revelers. It was the reality of the political world. Except for the insiders, everyone else virtually forgot about the political consultant. The victory for Henry was more than just Campagna over Prescott, or Democrat over Republican. It was a personal victory, where honor prevailed over self-preservation. Never before had he been so tested, not only as a political operative, but also as a human being. His very conscience was in play. The conundrum of right versus wrong still ached within Henry. Could he achieve success while maintaining his integrity? Could he become successful without screwing people along the way, or was the screwdriver the essential tool of success? He'd proved that an honest man could achieve victory in the dirtiest of games. The right man had been elected, a man who would serve the people and return Providence back toward righteousness.

38

While the first bombshell fizzled, the second salvo had crippled the entire city. It came just two weeks after the election, prior to the swearing in of John Campagna as mayor of Providence. The Associated Press reported that an Islamic terrorist group, the Palestinian Jihad, had kidnapped an American mayor while on vacation in Europe and were holding him in an undisclosed location. The reporter identified the mayor as Jack Donovan of Providence. The story circulated in Providence like Covid-19, bringing the entire city to a standstill. The much-maligned mayor had once again captured the attention of an entire city. Could this explain Donovan's disappearance? Had he been a victim of terrorists all along, not a deserter like they were led to believe? What did this mean for the case against him? And what of the election? No one was quite sure what to think.

Like scattering rats, rumors ran rampant through Providence. Callers flooded the talk radio stations with wild theories ranging from CIA conspiracies to sinister Islamic plots to destabilize the

American government. The pundits, from legal scholars to terrorism specialists, made the rounds on the media circuit offering their expert opinions. No other story captivated the public like the Jack Donovan saga. He wouldn't fade away quietly. His personality dictated that he leave with an explosion and not a small, measured response, but a devastating nuclear fallout. Even thousands of miles away from Providence, he still ruled his kingdom from exile. Reclaiming his empire had become his personal crusade, especially since his retirement had been reallocated by Terry Silberman.

Silberman received the news from his contact on the outside, Danny Conroy. He shook his head in disbelief. This was too clever for Donovan. Someone had to be behind the scenes. He instructed Conroy to research this Palestinian Jihad through the help of his lady friend in the FBI. "Interesting," he said to himself, "the fucker managed to get himself kidnapped." Silberman had spent half of his professional career running Donovan's political machine, and he was just now realizing the lengths to which the ego-maniacal mayor would go to reclaim his former life. But this one was too smart for Donovan. It was the type of thing that could only have been orchestrated by a professional.

Campagna, like most residents of Providence, had learned about the reemergence of Donovan from the *Providence Journal*. He choked on his morning coffee and clutched at the paper. Before his swearing in as mayor, Donovan had resurfaced to reclaim his crown. Campagna still believed in justice and had faith in government. Even if Donovan was kidnapped and returned, he would still be found guilty of racketeering and bribery and would be removed from office. He had no claim on City Hall—or did he?

Campagna's first call of the morning was to his political consultant. Henry had become accustomed to sleeping in, and the phone call from Campagna was the first he'd heard of the news. He thought he had awakened to a nightmare and asked Campagna to give him fifteen minutes to get himself together and read the story. He went out to the convenience store, read the story before paying for it at the register, then organized his thoughts before he called Campagna back. It was bullshit, he knew. Even if Donovan was legitimately kidnapped, it didn't dismiss the RICO charges against him. He called Campagna from home and argued his case. Donovan was a fugitive with no claim on City Hall.

His cell phone's blaring ring interrupted his explanation to Campagna and offered him a brief reprieve from the new mayor. McNally was enjoying a sailing cruise in the British Virgin Islands and had been contacted by one of his partners with the unsettling news.

"Sounds like all hell is breaking loose up there," he said to Henry. McNally spoke about the legal implications of the Donovan case. The attorneys couldn't cite precedence in arguing their cases, and both agreed that Donovan's claim on City Hall would be seen for what it was—a desperate attempt to regain office. However, they both conceded that if a trial occurred, Donovan's theatrics and charisma could result in a sympathetic jury acquittal. Much to the dismay of his female guest in BVI, who wasn't his wife of twenty-five years, McNally decided to return to Providence to personally head up the legal argument barring Donovan from City Hall.

***

There were two games Mayor Donovan was playing: the highly visible, outside diversion, and the sly, sinister inside extortion. The outside game drove the inside one. The public's outcry that their beloved con-man mayor had been kidnapped by Muslim terrorists only served to drive up the asking price of the ransom. The real negotiation was with Terry Silberman and prying his fingers off the millions he controlled.

Taking a page from their Colombian and Mexican brethren's handbook, the Palestinian Jihad had decided to enter the lucrative business of kidnapping foreigners to fund their operations. But the Donovan case had broken new ground for them. They had never conspired with someone to be kidnapped. To help orchestrate the delicate scheme, the Palestinian Jihad brought in their American-educated attorney and councilor, Hafez Asami. Dressed in a $2,000 suit, he looked less like a terrorist and more like any lawyer in any major American or European city. Well-known to the Israelis as a passionate defender of Palestinian rights on the West Bank, he also freelanced as an advisor to Palestinian freedom fighter groups. While he didn't condone the practice of kidnapping Americans, he under-stood the realities of the Palestinian struggle.

After consultations with Donovan and leaders of the Palestinian Jihad, Asami executed the plan to extort money from the extorter, Terry Silberman. They decided that Jana Strakova would deliver their message and serve as their conduit in the United States. Through the Czech Embassy in London, she obtained a tourist visa and departed for the federal penitentiary in Danbury, Connecticut. Jana gladly pocketed the $2,500 cash they gave her and embarked on her journey to America. She had always dreamed of America but had never envisioned she would visit this way. Then again, she hadn't planned on becoming a prostitute either.

As instructed, she flew to New York, then took a bus to Danbury. She used her own name to sign in at the penitentiary, and under the reason for her visit, she listed "research." Her cover was as an investigative journalist from an English-speaking newspaper in Prague. She was investigating public corruption in America and its similarities and differences from that in Eastern Europe.

Silberman agreed to meet the visitor, who had written to him from Prague, for the mere reason that it broke up the otherwise monotonous days.

"It's good to see you, Mr. Silberman. I've heard, I mean, I've read so much about you," she said to him.

"Sounds like you know a lot about me and my former boss, Mayor Donovan," he replied, indicating he understood her true reason for their visit.

"He's an interesting man."

"Indeed he is."

"What do you think of his kidnapping?"

"You tell me. What should I think?" he said, pressing her.

"I think that if you could, you would help him."

"Look where I am. How can I help him?" Silberman clearly felt he was doing his part by serving out his time. That was the deal. He would fall on his sword to protect their interests, but now that the mayor had spent money throughout Europe like a sailor on shore leave, he hardly felt the responsibility to help him.

"So are you saying you won't help him?"

"I'm saying I'm the one serving time. He's going to have to solve this one on his own."

"I understand, Mr. Silberman."

"No, I don't think you do. I'm the one in jail. This well's all dried up. You tell them to find another well."

***

Special Agent Michael Carbonerri had been staking out Danbury Penitentiary for the last few weeks when he received word from the prison that a young man claiming lineage to Silberman had been visiting on what they believed was beyond-family regularity.

Although stakeouts had been glamorized by detective shows and movies, they were hardly exciting. According to Carbonerri, it was more a lesson in patience than anything else and far more monotonous than eventful. But it didn't take the fifteen-year veteran of the FBI much to perk up when a leggy brunette walked to the penitentiary gate. Jana apparently didn't take seriously the insistence by Donovan's people that she dress less provocatively.

After verifying Danbury sign-in records that "the fox" in fact had been in to see Silberman, he tailed her back to the bus station. He took a dozen digital photos and called the FBI field office to put a tail on her after she stepped off the bus in New York. He also called the Providence field office and asked how to get a hold of Jimmy Callahan. He had worked with Callahan for the past several years building the case against Silberman and Donovan. Carbonerri had heard that he'd gone off to chase Donovan, and he needed someone to tail "the fox" if she landed in Europe. One of the young women in the office who had kept in touch via email with Callahan told Carbonerri he was in Ireland following up on Donovan leads. She gave him his email address, and he headed for the FBI field office in Stamford, Connecticut. The agent tailing the woman in New York City watched her board a Virgin Atlantic flight to London. She was able to review the flight records with just a flash of her badge due to the heightened security measures. The woman's name, which the agent reported back to Carbonerri, was "Jana Strakova," a Czech national. Carbonerri emailed Jimmy Callahan her name, flight number, and description in hopes he was still in the game.

***

Jimmy Callahan had run into more pints of Pilsner Urquell than leads in Prague until the news broke that Jihadist terrorists had kidnapped Donovan. He immediately took a flight to London and interviewed the Associated Press reporter who had broken the story. Like any journalist, she refused to give up her sources, but Callahan had a strong suspicion Donovan was in England. He was pleased to receive an email from Carbonerri, but he never expected the email to reveal a lead in the Donovan case. He printed the flight number and picture of Jana Strakova and looked at his watch. He had four hours before the flight landed at Heathrow. He sent an email back to Carbonerri: "Understood."

If he'd had a girlfriend, Callahan imagined that this would be what it was like to wait for her return at the airport. He had a dozen roses, like he was just another man longing for his true love. He saw the woman who fit the description walk from the plane and swagger past baggage claim toward the parking garage. As she stepped into a black Jaguar, he quickly scribbled down the plate number. He ran back to his car and drove toward the exit of the long-term parking garage. Turning off his lights, he waited for the car he hoped would lead him to his prize. The black jaguar sped out of the parking garage and headed toward London. As a US Attorney, Callahan didn't have any official surveillance training, so he practiced what he'd picked up from his FBI friends. He followed the Jaguar from a distance of three cars back and refrained from making similar directional signals.

The car continued past London and headed north. Callahan kept his distance and was careful to compensate as the traffic thinned by expanding the distance at which he followed her. Was he following the right car? Was he doing the right thing? Was he over his head? These questions pounded in his head as he made the lonely journey to Scotland, which wasn't made any easier by the dense fog blanketing the road. While it made his travel difficult, it concealed his tracking of his prey. But at the same time, the long road led him to question his life. He was thirty-five, not even close to married, but was chasing robbers across the continent.

Alone in the car for seven hours, the drive was punctuated with his self-doubt. Having heard from his FBI buddies from stakeouts, he used a water bottle to relieve himself. This wasn't supposed to be how his life turned out. Like the other lawyers in his office, he was supposed to be married with children. Here he was in some far-away place, chasing what exactly? Was he searching to fill his own emptiness? He wanted it so badly, and everything else was secondary. He was now forced to come to terms with the choices he'd made in his life as he took his lonely drive through the fog. He'd made a pact with himself. When this was over, no matter what happened, he was going back home. And what the hell? He was finally going to ask out that nice secretary in the FBI field office. He heard she liked lawyers.

His focus returned to him when the jaguar turned onto a dirt road. There weren't any lights on the dusty road, which had been designed more for horses than automobiles. Callahan turned off the lights from his car, figuring that his headlights would give away his shadowing. He was guided by a haloed moon and the flashlight he had purchased for his stealth mission. He wanted to hear the car off in the distance, so he opened his window as the misty fog enveloped him and the car. He used the beam of light from his flashlight to guide his way, and after about a mile, he saw the lights of civilization. He noticed the black jaguar next to a crumbled stone wall. He got out of the car and followed a cobbled path to a small cottage that was illuminated by the moon. He crept up to the windows like a burglar or peeping Tom. For a burglar, the mark would be the large-screen television on rollers; for the peeping Tom, it would be the woman changing into her negligee; but for Jimmy Callahan, it was Mayor Jack Donovan embracing the young woman he had followed from London. Percival had found his holy grail.

His methodical thinking and trained discipline prevented him from charging into the cottage and arresting the mayor. First, he was an attorney, not a policeman, and second, he was in a foreign country. He ran toward his car, stumbled over a rock, and skinned his knee. He climbed back up and ran the rest of the way. He took his cell phone out and called Michael Carbonerri at the number he had emailed him, knowing full well that Carbonerri would be camped out even with the six-hour time difference.

"Mikey," he said in a short breath, still recovering from his five-minute mile.

"Callahan?" Carbonerri asked.

"Yeah, it's me. I found our guy."

"Slow down, Jimmy. Catch your breath. Who do you have?"

"Donovan. The girl led me right to him," Callahan said.

"Shit."

"What do I do?" he asked Carbonerri.

"Take him down," Carbonerri said at first, but then he quickly retreated. "Hold up. I'll have to call Washington. State will have to get involved. You stay put. Don't go anywhere. Can you give me your location?"

"I've got GPS in the car, so I can give you my exact coordinates."

"That's great, Jimmy."

Callahan gave Carbonerri the exact location and explained that the cottage was about a half mile north. "Can you tell me if there are any other cars, any other people around?"

"No, it looks like just him and the girl," he told the agent.

"All right. I need you to sit tight. It's gonna take some time. The Brits will have to take him down."

"Fine with me, as long as we nail the bastard."

***

Callahan didn't quite comprehend what getting the Brits involved meant. After three hours, a swarm of special operatives descended from the sky. Eight black-cloaked soldiers fast-roped down from the hovering helicopter. They carried tactical loadouts with weapons at the ready. They dispersed quickly, within what seemed like seconds. Before Callahan could comprehend what was happening, one of the shrouded soldiers grabbed him from behind, covering his mouth.

"You Jim Callahan?" the man demanded. "Nod if you are."

Callahan nodded.

"How far to the target?" the operator asked, removing his hand so Callahan could speak. He looked at the operator's face, which was covered by a black mask. He was dressed in full black body armor, topped with a ballistic helmet and night vision. Callahan figured he was SAS, the British Special Airborne Services. They were among the elite of the world's special forces and were infamous for taking down Iranian terrorists in London in 1981. The prospect of Palestinian terrorists had prompted the British government to take the severest precautions and call in the SAS counter terrorism team.

"It's about a half mile that way," Callahan told the soldier, pointing with his hand in the direction. Without wasting another breath, the soldiers disappeared into the mist. Their only traces were the dirt their boots kicked up from the field. The two four-man teams ran with a steady sprint to the house and quickly executed their mission. Two men stayed in the front, two men went around the back, and two men climbed onto the roof. Like a well-choreographed dance, two men simultaneously stormed through the front of the cottage, two from the rear, and two through the side windows. Each team threw a flash-bang that emanated a blaring sound and blinding light. There were no terrorists. There was no opposition. There was only a man and a woman in bed.

They were zip tied, gagged, hooded, and hurried away, likely traumatized. As quickly as it had arrived over Callahan, the Black Hawk swooped in on the cottage. It hovered five feet above the ground, and the SAS soldiers tossed in their package—Donovan and Jana—and boarded their helicopter. The Black Hawk ascended into the night, fifteen minutes after it had arrived.

***

"The rumors of my demise have been greatly exaggerated," Mayor Jack Donovan exclaimed outside his arraignment in Providence. "There are no blemishes on this record," he continued. "I look forward to proving my innocence. In the meantime, I will continue the people's business and will serve as your mayor. I wasn't afforded the right to defend myself. I was held captive against my will for six months, my rights stripped from me, only to come home to find out that my rights had been trampled on by the federal government. My attorney, William Eagleton, will discuss our legal motions. We have petitioned the Rhode Island Supreme Court to have the results of the special election overturned. Until a decision is handed down, we are filing a motion barring Councilman Campagna from the mayor's office."

This was a brazen statement from a man who forty-eight hours ago had been held in a US military prison, awaiting trial. Upon his abduction from Scotland, he had been released into American custody and had flown to a US airbase in England. He was extradited back to the States, shackled like any fugitive, then delivered to Providence, where he appeared in front of a federal magistrate. The US Attorney had argued that the mayor was a flight risk, as evidenced by his six-month absence, and should be incarcerated while they decided what to do with him. The judge ordered Donovan to turn over his passport and wear an electronic anklet.

"Mayor, are you saying that the special election for mayor was illegal and that Mayor Campagna should step aside?" asked Katrina Paul from the *Providence Journal.*

"Not only should he step aside. He will be legally forced to," Attorney Eagleton responded.

"What legal standing do you have? I mean, the mayor was gone, whether he was kidnapped or not. There had to be a mayor to serve," Paul insisted.

"The special election came too soon. The city charter reads that if the mayor is incapacitated, then the council president will assume the role of mayor until a special election is held ninety days after," Eagleton argued. "They had the special election too soon after the mayor was kidnapped."

Steve Rose, a radio reporter from WBSL, said, "Government sources say that the mayor wasn't kidnapped, and that when British forces found him, he was in bed, asleep, with a woman."

"That's the same government that trumped up these charges against the mayor. Do you believe everything your government tells you?" the lawyer said.

"Have there been any discussions about a plea bargain?" Rose asked.

"I'll let the mayor answer that."

"Absolutely not," Donovan said. "I'm innocent of these charges."

"What's the next step?" asked Casey Giuliano, a television reporter from the NBC affiliate.

"We're hoping that considering the importance of this development, the Supreme Court will immediately convene to hear our case."

"How do you respond to the government's case against you?"

she asked.

"Absolutely innocent!" the mayor exclaimed. "I look forward to my day in court to prove it."

***

The next day, a political maelstrom hit Providence. Donovan showed up for work at City Hall. The Providence police were forced to call in the state police to block Donovan's entrance into the mayor's office. This prompted Donovan to hold an impromptu press conference on the steps.

"I am the legitimately elected mayor of Providence. They are denying me entrance into City Hall. They are denying you your mayor," Donovan said to the assembled press corps camping outside City Hall and the 150 supporters who'd come down to rally for him. "They have resorted to using police to bar my entrance. Is this the United States of America or some fascist state? For six months, I was held by terrorists only to come home to be denied my rights."

Mayor-elect Campagna watched the live coverage from McNally's law office with Henry. They could see from the office the television news trucks surrounding City Hall.

"What do I do?" Campagna asked.

"You do absolutely nothing," McNally said.

"I agree," Henry added. "If you engage him, you give credence to his claims. Ignore him—he's got no claim."

"Does he have anything with this legitimacy stuff?" Campagna asked.

"He's got shit. The Supreme Court won't hear his case."

"Yeah, but he's getting the public all fired up," Henry acknowledged.

"Not for long. The feds have a guy who'd been tracking Donovan across Europe. They're going to leak it to the *Journal*. They wanted to hold it for the trial, but because he's stirring up all this shit, they want to slam him. Guess who? Jimmy Callahan," McNally said.

"I thought he took off after the botched Donovan arrest," Henry asked.

"He did. Took a leave from the US Attorney's office, sold the house his parents left him, and went looking for Donovan. He's got bank pictures from Prague and hotel receipts. Of course he wasn't kidnapped. They're going to bring a lieutenant from British SAS to testify that they stormed the cottage where he was allegedly kidnapped and that there were no terrorists. The FBI has pictures of this woman meeting with Silberman and a recording of the conversation she had with him."

"How do you know all this?" Campagna asked McNally.

"It's my business to know what's going on, Mr. Mayor."

***

McNally was right. The day after Donovan's spectacle at City Hall, the *Providence Journal* ran a front-page story with a picture showing Donovan in a bank in Prague. The caption read, "Photos taken from a surveillance camera in a Prague bank." It was the equivalent of the smoking gun, the actual evidence clearly demonstrating that Donovan had not been kidnapped and held for the last six months as he had argued, and that he had enjoyed considerable freedom in Europe. The story included a receipt from the Marriott in Prague that detailed the thousands of dollars in room charges, including bottles of Dom Perignon and advances for the casino. All the expenses were charged off to a man named Sean Murphy who had threatened a Czech bank manager when he was told that his account had been closed. The story was lethal.

The legions of supporters who had rallied at Donovan's return now abandoned him. He had been forsaken, his indiscretions no longer accepted. The Donovan era was officially over. Recognizing defeat, he instructed his lawyer to make the deal with the government. It would be no less than ten years in a federal penitentiary, twice the time of the highest convicted criminal in the RICO indictments. The man who had vehemently pleaded his innocence was swayed by the real possibility of spending the rest of his life in prison.

Reality overwhelmed his claim of innocence. He wouldn't receive his pension, and he wouldn't be transferred to a minimum-security facility. But the charges against Jana were dropped, and she was scheduled for deportation back to the Czech Republic. In a cruel twist of fate, the US Attorney's office lobbied the Federal Bureau of Prisons for a special handling of Donovan. He was incarcerated at Danbury Federal Penitentiary beside his former chief-of-staff. The two would share the same address for the next five years.

In prison, Silberman was the first to break the silence. While in the dinner line, he took a pendant from around his neck and tossed it at the former mayor.

"What's this?" Donovan asked him.

"I see you've got half of Jana's pendant," Silberman told him, throwing the gold trinket to his former boss. Donovan removed the pendant from around his neck and realized that the two pieces matched perfectly together.

"How did you—"

"You didn't think I'd leave you alone in Europe with my money?"

"She worked for you?"

"She was working for me the whole time."

"How did she—"

"You think you just happened to meet a girl like that in a bar? I met her at the Irish cultural exchange in Providence, the night before the feds got me. The Irish delegation brought her. That's what girls like her do. I hired her for the evening, then I offered her $30,000 to follow you and do whatever. I knew you'd go to the bank, so I told her to stake you out at First Suisse in Frankfurt. Remember, I gave you the accounts and the bank names. I knew where you'd go. After she marked you, she followed you to Prague."

"The whole fucking time," Donovan muttered.

"You really didn't think she was in love with you."

His silence betrayed his answer.

"You did. You fell in love with a whore. Idiot," Silberman laughed. "Serves you right. You've been a whore your whole life."

"I made you, you fucking bastard. I deserve respect," Donovan countered.

"You're nothing. Not the mayor, and not a man. You're federal inmate number 202194. Get used to it."

"And what does that make you, my friend?"

"The guy who gets out five years before you," Silberman told him, leaning over and whispering in his ear. "Remember, I know where it's all buried."

39

Henry sat on the white sandy beach and stared at the ocean. He was in a state of tranquility, a place where little else mattered in his life—not the election, not McNally, not Campagna. He was at peace, his own Nirvana, which was only achievable in his life after he had stared down defeat and persevered with his grit and determination. Winning the good fight, playing by his own rules, and using his full arsenal of skills and contacts, had brought him to this place. There was no outside interference. No politicians pulling him apart, no operatives exploiting his life. Now he could just live. There was only the simple crash of the waves and the humming of the tropical birds. And there was Lyndsay too.

Lyndsay and Henry's wedding was no spectacle of ceremony, but a simple sacrament on a beach in Grand Cayman. Only twenty people were in attendance, including Lyndsay's parents and sisters, along with Henry's mother, brother, sister-in-law, nephews, niece, and maternal uncle. No McNally. No Campagna. No senators or governors or corporate types. Not even friends or cousins. Only the most important people in their lives boarded Reggie Sinclair's Citation-700 for the five-hour flight to paradise. After a Jesuit priest gave his blessing to the couple, the jet whisked them away to a private island off the Caymans. While the Mercucios and Sinclairs stayed four nights on Grand Cayman, the newlyweds enjoyed their privacy at an exclusive resort.

"Honey, you're not going to believe this," Lyndsay said to Henry as she handed him a mojito. Henry looked up from his sunglasses and turned his head toward Lyndsay.

"What am I not going to believe?"

"I just met a couple from Providence. They're here on their honeymoon. I think she's European. Has a real thick accent."

"Really."

"And he's this big guy, said he was in development or something. He knows you."

"Really," Henry said again, showing little interest.

"They asked us to join them for dinner. Do you wanna go?"

"Not really."

"Yeah, I figured you'd say that, so I told them maybe we'd meet them for a drink."

"That's fine, honey," Henry said, returning back to his book. "What are you reading?" she asked.

"*The Art of War.*"

Henry flipped from his book to the encrypted email on his iPad. Vincent, his connection to the Providence underworld, proved useful once again. Henry enlisted him on a special project, and Vincent reported back. Henry knew that while the Lombardo family controlled CampCo Development, they still ran drugs in New England with the Port of Providence as their gateway into the region. Vincent was in tune with the dealers who sold oxycodone in the neighborhoods.

Vincent had brought his cousin, Joey, for some muscle to confront the local dealer where Campagna's niece had lived. As his cousin had the dealer pinned to the ground, Vincent had given him a choice. "Listen, kid, you either tell me who gave you the drugs you sold Campagna's niece, or I let Joey use your face as a punching bag."

"I never saw his face. He had slicked-back black hair, wore a suit."

"Not enough. Give it to him again, Joey."

"Wait, he drove a BMW, one of those big ones. He told me to move the stuff we had gotten in, even though we knew it was laced with Fentanyl. I told him it was bad for business, that I can't have people in the neighborhood dying."

"What did he say?" Vincent asked.

"He said don't talk to me about business. I run this town."

Classic Beako, Henry knew, as he read the recount of the conversation that Vincent must have had someone write up for him. At the bottom of the email, he left Henry with a place to ponder: Ritz Carlton, Key Biscayne. Henry had him.

***

Jana Strakova and Danny Conroy were enjoying a different kind of honeymoon. After stashing $2 million in banks in the Caymans and Europe, Jana and Danny decided to take their own holiday. And why not? For the first time, these two working people wanted to know what it felt like to be doted upon for a change.

In one of life's little ironies, the two had been propelled toward each other by some mysterious force. Neither of them had experienced it before, and for two people who were cynical about life's outrageous fortunes, it had to be real. What else could explain how two hardened souls could end up together? Of course, there was also that matter of $2 million of Terry Silberman's money.

Neither of them had set out to defraud Silberman. When Jana had agreed to watch Donovan for Silberman, she'd looked at it only as a means to make some quick cash. She had no loyalty to Silberman, and especially none for Donovan, but the young, ambitious man in the tight suit that she met in the ballroom in Providence, he was the one. Even though he'd arranged the sale of her body, there was something kind in his eyes. He was better than those finely clad politicians and businessmen in the room. His fancy designer threads didn't suit the man he was. He was better than all of them, and so was she. She may have sold her body, but she had never given herself away. To Danny, however, she gave of herself freely.

Fortune favored those who challenged the existing order. And that was exactly what they'd done; they'd turned the screws on the ones who had screwed countless other people over the years. While the disaster that was Donovan wallowed in the self-pity of his mercurial rise and defeat, Jana had found someone watching over her. At first, Danny was tracking the sultry brunette across the continent, keeping tabs on Silberman's $2 million investment. But when she'd walked through the crowd of expats who enjoyed the excess of their counter-culture lifestyles, he was struck and became fully enthralled by her. The tumultuous confrontation that followed caught him off guard.

"Why are you following me?" she'd demanded, making an attempt to get right up into his face, which was considerably difficult, since he was half of a foot taller than her.

"I don't know what you're talking about, Miss."

"You're the boy from Providence. I know you," she had said, stumbling through her broken English.

"You don't know me."

"You had no problem pimping me to your friend."

"You went quite freely. I'm sorry, wrong word. It wasn't exactly free, now was it?" She slapped his face, but Danny didn't even blink. He had taken worse. "Fucking whore." She attempted to slap him again, but this time, he put his arm up and blocked the swing. "I don't like being hit. Now, sit down before you draw attention, and someone starts asking questions." She sat down at the table, which was conveniently located in a dark corner not far from the door. But, she would never forget that he had treated her like the person she was, not the woman she planned to become.

"I'm sorry. I didn't mean to call you a whore. As far as I'm concerned, we're all whores at different times in our lives. You're only using what you've got to get ahead. I respect that."

After a full night of Prague debauchery, they had begun to formulate a plan. The mayor was immaterial, a mere nuisance who was fully expendable. She would hatch an insane plan for a fake kidnapping to conceal her true motives. The key to her happiness was in Silberman's bank accounts, and Danny had his number. Actually, it wasn't one number—more like seven accounts in five different countries.

It wasn't a difficult decision for Danny. It was between a father figure who had entrusted him with his livelihood or a runway model with a body that did not quit and a mind that could rival her boss. Add two million into the mix, and the choice was quite simple. As for Jana, this was her big score, the one she had waited for her entire life, the way to fuck all those guys who had done it to her. She had been with so many blow-hard politicians and businessmen who always needed to tell her how important they were. They bragged about their power and influence and treated her as a means to an end. In the end, it wasn't a difficult decision for Jana. It was always about the money.

Even on vacation, Danny rose at 5 a.m., just as he could see the sun beginning to emerge over the Caribbean. Loving how Jana slept naked, he went to caress her back. But his hand fell upon a cold bed. Silberman's voice was running through his head reminding him to never trust her. It's why Silberman had him tail her throughout Europe. Danny quickly gained his composure and grabbed for his computer. He logged on to their Grand Cayman account. Closed. Then he went to the First Suisse Account. Closed. Then the Lichtenstein account. Closed. He didn't need to look at the other accounts. He knew. He threw his laptop across the room and jumped out of bed, heading for the room's safe where they had stashed $10,000. Gone. Jana had taken them all.